THE
LEGAL KILLER

THE LEGAL KILLER

ELLIOT MASON

Printed in the United States of America
ISBN 978-1-64133-994-0 (sc)
ISBN 978-1-64133-995-7 (e)
ISBN 978-1-64133-993-3 (hc)

2025.04.15

This book is printed on acid-free paper.

Because of the dynamic nature of the Internet, any web addresses or links contained in this book may have changed since publication and may no longer be valid. The views expressed in this work are solely those of the author and do not necessarily reflect the views of the publisher, and the publisher hereby disclaims any responsibility for them.

Blue Ink Media Solutions
1111B S Governors Ave
STE 7582 Dover,
DE 19904

www.blueinkmediasolutions.com

For Mom, your strength gave me confidence in my words. You boosted me when I was down. Pushed me when I was reluctant, and sometimes dragged me, kicking, and screaming, but always nurturing, to explore my capabilities. Though I may not have verbalized it, I know how blessed I am to have you as my beacon… and my work forevermore will serve as a testament to the love you have given me, and the unwavering appreciation, admiration, and love I have for you.

*The greatest trick the devil ever pulled was
convincing the world he didn't exist.*

—Christopher McQuarrie,
The Usual Suspects

Fact

American founding father John Adams was often asked which of his accomplishments he was most proud. To the surprise of many, he did not mention his contributions to the American Revolution, his service as a delegate and ambassador to France, or even his term as the second president of the United States. Instead, he stated it was his involvement in the trial of the British soldiers charged with murder after the infamous Boston Massacre… He acted as defense counsel.

PROLOGUE

Arlington, Virginia

THE ONLY NOISE breaking through was the screaming of the siren. Although she could see their mouths moving, she could make out nothing. The young woman turned to look out the rectangular window at the back of the ambulance. All that met her eyes was the mass of humanity crisscrossing the street, most with dazed or anguished expressions on their faces.

"Here, keep pressure on it," the emergency medical technician said as he pressed a piece of gauze to the side of her head. "It's a small gash… you'll be fine."

Madison Callum hadn't noticed that she had been injured by the explosion. She was still in a semi-state of shock from the terrifying event that had just transpired. She looked down at Des, who was lying unconscious on the gurney. His torn and tattered shirt was drenched in blood. His complexion was that of talcum powder.

"He's going to be okay?" she asked, looking for reassurance.

"He's lost a lot of blood. The hospital has prepared a triage… we'll do all we can."

Madison closed her eyes. It hardly seemed possible that this could be the final result. It was less than a week ago that she and Des had stumbled upon the clues they thought could lead them to one of the greatest finds in American history.

They were naive, blinded by the fantasy of finding the lost treasure of the Confederacy, letting their excitement obscure the facts. They were negligent, failing to recognize there would be others whose drive for the artifact would not be so altruistic. But most of all, they were ignorant of the very nature of what they were seeking.

In the end, only one had recognized it. It was not her, the college professor, or Des, the graduate student. Neither was it the clever and deviously resourceful Judge who had surmised what lay underneath Arlington National Cemetery. Instead, it was the disheveled, misguided, and unstable young man William Hatton, who identified the treasure's power, its true nature.

Where his ancestors had failed to ignite the massive bomb, which would have annihilated the Union headquarters, killed President Abraham Lincoln, and possibly ended the Civil War, he had succeeded more than a century and a half later.

For William, though the years had changed, the cause had not. He was completing his life's mission, a destiny delegated to him by his family's ancestry. By lighting the spark that ignited the nineteenth-century technology into a fireball, in his mind, he was not committing an act of terror but the culminating of a war. Its initial combatants were long gone, but the grievances were every bit as prevalent in these modern times. He was striking back at what he saw as the Goliath, the entity that had overstepped its bounds and only increased its level of injustice since the the Civil War. His goal was to alter the nation's direction. Whether it would was yet to be seen.

For Madison, though, none of that mattered. She could not change the horror surrounding her. All she could do was hope... hope that the bomb had not taken innocent lives... hope that the president was safe, and hope that the nation would mend. But most of all, she hoped the man on the gurney in front of her, the one who had taken a bullet in her defense, would survive.

CHAPTER 1

Washington, DC

IT HAD BEEN a little over two weeks since the attack at Arlington National Cemetery, and the nightmares had only increased in power. This night would be no different. Desmond Cook shot up in his bed and immediately felt the gut-wrenching pain in his shoulder and chest. The wound was still going to take several more months to heal.

It was just shy of four in the morning, and his sterile room at Washington Memorial Hospital in the nation's capital was only slightly illuminated by the green lights of the computer monitors tracking his vital signs. The space was silent with the exception of the occasional sound of the blood pressure machine inflating at timed intervals.

He reached over with his right hand and touched the bandages encasing his left shoulder, moving his fingers softly to the edges before they were interrupted by the rigid sling holding his arm in place. Taking his thumb and index finger to massage the bridge of his nose, he tried to relax. He closed his eyes, but it was of no use. Every time he shut them, he saw the face of William Hatton. His expression was one of cocky satisfaction when he knew there was no way Des would be able to halt his efforts to ignite the bomb under the sacred ground. That expression would then morph into the crazed individual with the wild eyes as he readied himself to fire. Then finally, there was the sound of the gunshot, which still rung in his ears, and the agonizing pain that followed.

Des was able to keep the president out of harm's way, but thirty-seven innocent bystanders who had come to hear him speak had lost their lives. Scores more were injured. Images now appeared before him of the screaming chaos of the aftermath and the torn-up, cratered-out fields of that national landmark.

He was not going to be able to fall back asleep. He felt a sensation of warm wetness on his chest and soon realized his earlier sudden motion had ripped his stitches, causing the wound to leak anew.

Breathing in deeply, Des looked out his window. There was almost a full moon backlighting the banks of clouds, which, when combined with the streetlamps, allowed him to make out the outlines of the majestic oak trees on the other side of the hospital parking lot.

He gazed toward the glow of the lamps and could see tiny raindrops reflect their illumination as they descended to the earth. It was one of those late storms of spring that always seemed to be pushing in vain against the arrival of the impending summer.

He fumbled in the darkness for the button to alert the nurse, being careful not to agitate his injury any further. Des was still in a great deal of pain, but he was going to keep that information to himself. He wanted out of this place and refused to provide them with any excuse to detain him another day. The misery of being confined was nearly as painful as the injury. The only release from this discomfort was his daily visits from Madison.

He had fallen for her, but his shyness and absence from the dating world for the last several years had left him tentative and unsure. She would touch his hand and kiss him on the cheek whenever she greeted or departed. Yet he was unpracticed and did not know whether these were signs of friendship or flirtation.

Des had come back for her. He had not only emerged from this whole experience as a friend, but a loyal protector. However, he did not wish to use those attributes as a method in which to garner her affections. That would not be love but obligation, and nothing could be worse.

Approximately five hours later, his room was flooded with light, the dim green being replaced by a dazzlingly white. He had turned on the TV, surfing the channels to find the latest takes on the catastrophe at Arlington. *If they only knew... no one would believe it anyway,* he thought.

"Good morning," the smiling brown face said, peeking into the room from the doorway.

"Hey, good morning," Des answered, achingly trying to sit up.

"I stopped by Starbucks on the way and picked you up a latte. I even added some sugar for you," she said with a grin.

"Madison, you're a godsend. I don't think I could stomach another one of those terrible hospital coffees. If they brought me one more, I was going to ask them to put me out of my misery."

"How are you feeling?"

"Good, I feel a lot better. I can't wait to get out of here."

"You're not a very good liar."

Madison touched his hand. She looked more beautiful than ever. Her dark skin, curly locks of hair that fell gently onto her shoulders, and tiny creases next to her eyes when she smiled gave her an irresistible allure.

"Hello, Mr. Desmond," the mature woman said, entering the room.

"Hello, Lydia, how's my favorite nurse?"

Lydia Naranjo had been wonderful to Des since the moment he arrived. She was short with a pleasantly plump figure, salt-and-pepper hair, and a round face. Her broken English, Spanish accent, and mannerisms offered a nurturing quality.

"I'm very tired. How you feeling after last night?"

"What happened last night?" Madison interjected with a look of concern.

"Oh... Mr. Desmond ripped open his stitches early this morning."

"It's nothing," he said. "I had a bad dream and sat up quickly. It pulled some of them out. I'm fine. Don't worry about it."

"Mr. Desmond, you must be careful. It's big day for you. You go home."

"I will, Lydia. I promise."

"I'll take good care of him," added Madison.

A few hours later, Des was helped into a wheelchair. "Do I really need this thing?" he protested. "I can walk."

"Des, it's hospital policy. You can stand up when we're out the doors," Madison responded.

"Yeah, I know. But it makes me feel like I'm helpless."

"Now you just be a good boy." Then she leaned over, placing her lips just an inch from his ear, and whispered, "Besides, I have a surprise for you."

Her breath against his skin was intoxicating, and the sound of her voice sent a warm rush through his body. But did she feel the same way? Was this genuine affection or gratitude? He hated that he could not tell the difference.

Lydia wheeled him down the corridor into the elevator and through the lobby. She then pushed Des through the sliding glass doors. The damp air and scent of the previous night's rain was refreshing beyond words. For over two weeks, he had smelled nothing but disinfectant and hospital food. It immediately comforted him.

Helping him out of his wheelchair, Madison eased him into the front passenger seat of the car. Unlike the last time she performed this maneuver, this was a joyous occasion. It was just a short time ago that she struggled getting a bullet-ridden Des into a vehicle just before he demanded that she take him to Arlington to prevent a disaster.

"Thanks for everything, Lydia. You're wonderful," he said.

"You take good care of him," she responded, looking at Madison.

"I will. I promise." Madison got into the driver's seat. The smile she had earlier had only grown in its brightness. "I think Ms. Lydia has a crush on you."

"Yeah, something about the way she changed my bed pan gave me that idea as well."

Both of them laughed as she put the car in drive and pulled out of the parking lot.

CHAPTER 2

Traveling south through Virginia

THE RIDE BACK home could only be described as pure emotion. Although they had their share of small talk, there was an underlying sense that there was more to be said of their shared experience.

For Des, it was a mixed bag. His actions did save the president. But it was not in time to save so many innocents from injury and death. Sometimes he would try to sleep. However, closing his eyes would only reveal those horrifying images of his re-encounter with William Hatton.

On the other hand, Madison felt nothing but bliss. The one who had risked everything to protect her and nearly died in the attempt, the man she had grown to love, was safe and with her.

When the silence became noticeable, she would glance over at Des, only to find him gazing at the greenery of Virginia outside his window.

"Hey," she said, placing her hand on his knee. "Are you going to be okay? I'm worried about you."

He looked at her beautiful face; it was warm and inviting. Her cocoa-brown skin had been turned into a rich mahogany from spending hours in the sun walking back and forth to the hospital.

"I'll be okay. I'm just a little tired. I guess I need to unwind."

"Well, that brings me to my surprise. I took the liberty of making us reservations at one of the nicest resorts in Virginia. It's my treat."

"Isn't that kind of expensive?" he asked, a little shocked.

"Sweetheart, with what we've been through, we deserve it."

"I was kind of wondering why we were taking this route back to Georgia."

The resort was located in a rural area about two hours from Richmond, bordering the Shenandoah Valley. Small communities that if you blinked you would miss them sailed by his window as they got closer to their destination. Finally, they reached the out-of-the-way road heading directly into the complex. As they crested the hill, it came into view like a jewel in a sandbox.

After stopping by the resort's main office to pick up the key, they drove along a small road that stretched quite a distance. The complex was huge but managed to hide its enormity among the rich foliage surrounding it.

As they turned up another hill, Des spied deer filling up on supper as they munched on the lush greens in which they were encamped. About a minute later, they reached a small parking lot adjacent to very modern-looking condos.

Des exited the car and breathed in the crisp air. The ground was wet from a light sprinkle that had fallen about thirty minutes prior to their arrival. He then reached back into the car to retrieve his bag, struggling mightily with his injury.

"What are you doing?" Madison said, painting him with a disapproving look. "I'll take care of that. The condo is up those stairs. Here's the key, it's 9B."

He was not used to feeling helpless. Yet now, he was no longer the protector but the protected. Making his way up the stairs, he didn't know what to expect. His uncertainty about their relationship did nothing to ease his mind.

Once he turned the key, he was impressed with what he saw. The condo was beautiful. There was a spacious living and family room with a connecting sliding glass door leading out to a deck. Next to a large dining room table was a fully furnished kitchen with all the amenities. On a glass coffee table in the family room, brochures were neatly displayed, giving detailed information on the various luxuries and activities the resort provided.

Des walked through the family room, opened the sliding glass door, and stepped onto the brown wood-stained deck. The view was spectacular. It overlooked the southern side of the valley and included the picturesque Shenandoah River bordered by a sea of trees. He took in the magnificent sunset as it inched further beneath the valley walls, its radiance exploding into pinks and violets reflected by the cloud formations.

Peering to his left, he watched as fireflies orchestrated a dance of light in a small grove running parallel to the parking lot. Although he had seen them a million times in his home state of Georgia, for some reason, they seemed miraculous now. He was so transfixed that he failed to hear Madison walk onto the deck behind him, not noticing her until she placed her chin on his right shoulder.

"What do you think?" she asked, pressing her face close to his.

"It's incredible."

"I'm glad you like it. Now I want you to relax. The doctor said we have to keep those bandages dry, so a shower is out. I'll draw you a bath. It will only take a moment."

She disappeared down the hallway. The scent of her hair still hung in the air. The feelings he had for her had only grown and were increasing with every additional moment they spent together.

Those emotions had been dormant in him for so long he was having difficulty grappling with them. It had been years since he had been in anything resembling a relationship. His time in Afghanistan did not lend to that part of his life. When he returned to college after his service, his age difference with his fellow female students negated anything of substance. They were just kids and had not been exposed to the horrors he had experienced.

Des was becoming nervous and fidgety. For the first time, he had feelings for a woman who shared his intellect and passions. He began to second-guess himself. Were her feelings identical? Was she affectionate out of love, or was she simply nursing him back to health out of thankfulness?

"Des," he heard her sweet voice calling. "Your bath is ready."

He moved down the hallway, grasping for ways to tell her how he felt. *She'll think I'm an idiot. God, I'm such a fool!*

He peered around the corner of the bathroom door, like a kid who was up past his bedtime. Madison was standing in front of a large luxurious spa-styled bath, wearing a white satin robe decorated with patterns of roses and violets. The steam emanating off the water smelled of lilacs.

"Come in… Why are you hiding?" she said with a playful smile.

He entered and stood in front of her. There was a momentary pause as they silently looked at each other. She then slowly undid her robe and let it fall to her feet. Her nude form was something not even a Renaissance painter could do justice.

Her skin glowed. Her slender frame, the shape of her breast, the curvature of her hips could only be described as elegant.

Des remained silent as she moved toward him. Placing her hand on his cheek, she let her index finger move gradually downward to his chin.

"I thought I would help you relax," she said. Then she leaned in and pressed her soft lips against his, delicately darting her tongue to the corner of his mouth.

Without a word, she cautiously began to undress him, being ever so careful not to cause him pain. As she unbuttoned his shirt, she kissed his neck and chest, moving further south with the release of each clasp. She undid his belt while nestling her lips on his abdomen.

As each piece of his clothing descended to the ground, he stood in wonderment. She continued to take in his body until she reached the area just above his evidence of excitement.

Standing up, she kissed him once more. His arm wrapped around her waist as their forms connected. Then taking his hand, she led him into the bath and gently rested him against its wall. As he inhaled, all the stress, all the tension dissipated into the steam. There was no bomb or William Hatton or tragedy. There was just them.

She hovered over him, her breasts resting on his torso, and placed her lips hard onto his. He had never felt emotions like this.

"I want you to let me take care of you," she whispered.

Reaching for a sponge, she immersed it in the water, never once letting her eyes leave his. Then holding it just slightly above him, she squeezed, allowing the hot liquid to drape his body in warmth. It was soothing beyond description. There could not exist an elixir to equal this moment.

He placed his hand on her cheek as she moved in to kiss him once more, and then resumed her pampering.

They did not make love, as Des was in no condition for that kind of exertion. However, it was the most sensual experience of his life.

That night, as they lay in bed together with Madison's nude body touching every conceivable part of his available to her, he never felt such contentment. The terror of two weeks ago seemed like an eternity away. This is where he belonged.

CHAPTER 3

Santa Ana, California
One year later...

THE RONALD REAGAN Federal Courthouse is located in Orange County, in the city of Santa Ana, California. It is one of the oldest incorporated areas in the region with its origins tracing back to the Mexican rancho system. The small town was founded in the late 1800s, and many of its sections continue to hail to earlier days. Some of the finest examples of nineteenth and early twentieth-century California homes still dot the landscape, and several of its more historic parts remain among favorite locations for Hollywood movie and television production shoots.

However, the modern federal courthouse does not fit into this charm. Its tall dark glass siding brings a cold if not ominous presence to the charming Spanish-ranch-style structures surrounding it.

Inside the building, little was done to create any feeling of warmth. Desolate tile floors bring the visitor past unadorned marble walls to the x-ray machines at the security checkpoint. Voices echo in its interior, making one feel self-conscious that they are disturbing this place of justice, much like a person speaking too loudly during a church service. Nothing about its design puts one at ease, purposely being created to bring on the opposite effect. The experience upon entering the building could be likened to that of walking into a crypt, void of any humanity.

On the ninth floor, Assistant US Attorney Patricia Owens was sitting in Judge Sheldon's courtroom, a place every bit as vacant of a human touch as was the rest of the building. She sat past the almost completely empty pews at a table to the right of the podium where attorneys addressed the judge. Directly in front of her was the court reporter, diligently typing every syllable uttered from those in attendance. Also, in an imposing wood enclosure sat the Honorable Judge Sheldon, his white hair offering a terrific contrast to his black robe. The symbolism of those two colors could not be more apropos, as the grays of the world were kept at bay in what was supposed to be this microcosm of society.

His chair and desk were elevated above the rest of the floor in a manner to covey authority and even wisdom. Yet Patricia knew this was symbolic of years long since passed. Like the British monarchy, he reigned but did not rule. It was more traditional than substantive.

"Counselor, it's now your opportunity to address the court," said Judge Sheldon.

Patricia stood up, pulling slightly on her gray suit and touching the back of her chestnut-brown hair, which came together in a tight small bun at the base of her neck. Grabbing her papers, she strode confidently to the podium. Like most government attorneys, her statements were prepared from a template that the Department of Justice had approved for each type of case. Originality was not something such an entity endorsed.

Clearing her throat, she began. "Your Honor, I realize this is the first offense the defendant has committed. However, we have community standards… guidelines that have been set forth to prevent the proliferation of this terrible problem. Therefore, it's the government's position on the two counts that he should receive a two-hundred-and-forty-month sentence."

The judge fidgeted in frustration. Ever since the 1980s, their power in making determinations had been greatly diminished.

The defendant had no criminal history, and the total monies he had accumulated in his drug activities amounted to a little over seven thousand dollars. It was a paltry sum.

The young attorney kept a good poker face, trying not to let on to the fact that she was already recalculating her conviction rate in her head. *This will look good on a résumé.* The system allowed her that luxury.

Patricia had no illusions that she would get what she was asking for, but it didn't matter. The judge's hands were tied. He couldn't go below the mandatory minimum. Yet knowing his ego, he would want some say in the matter.

As his gavel came down with a definitive whack on its wood tablet, Patricia smiled with the twelve-year sentence. She could report to her superiors that she had upheld their mandate.

Gathering her papers, she turned in time to see the marshals handcuff the defendant. To his right she saw his mother, wife, and young son in tears as they watched their loved one removed from the courtroom. It was a familiar scene and at one time it affected her. Yet after three years of reminding herself that the defendants had committed crimes, she had become hardened, immune to the wreckage left in its wake.

The young prosecutor turned away, not wanting to endure the hatred in the family's glare. She knew this man was not a hardened criminal. He was simply a person who made a poor choice. *I don't make the rules, I just enforce them*, Patricia told herself as she pushed through the small flapping dividers, bypassing the pews and exiting the courtroom into the hallway.

The floors of the featureless passage glistened as she proceeded toward the elevators. The only thing accompanying her was the sound of her shoes tapping on the tile and her rolling briefcase being pulled in tow.

She removed her phone from her pocket, eager to let her boss know the outcome of the sentencing. She was beginning to make a name for herself. Although she had little trial experience, she had proven her ability to obtain the desired results.

After exiting the elevator, she made her way through the lobby and then exited the building through its tinted glass doors. Her pace quickened as she headed in the direction of the parking structure, bolstered by the words of praise from her superior. Patricia was going to celebrate tonight, dinner with friends, perhaps a nice bottle of wine.

Opening up her car door, she threw her briefcase onto the front passenger seat. It was a chilly spring night, and she adjusted the heat accordingly. She was glad daylight savings time had kicked in. The shorter days always made her feel like she was working longer hours.

Patricia was just about to put the car in reverse, never seeing the hands until the knife was pressed against her throat. She froze instinctively.

"Take whatever you want," she gasped.

The breathing of her abductor was deep and rhythmic. She could smell the leather gloves, one on her forehead, and the other below her chin. The glimmer of the knife reflected the dim yellow garage lights into her eyes.

"Here… my purse is in the front seat. You can have it," she pleaded.

"You only have one thing that I want," a voice whispered in a raspy tone.

She trembled. Her face was moist with perspiration as she could feel her captor's hot breath against the back of her neck.

"Do you know what I want?" the abductor asked.

She closed her eyes, trying to ascertain what the answer would be. That kind of violation was unimaginable.

"Please do you have to…?"

"You still don't know?" her captor answered with an anger resembling that of someone on the receiving end of a personal insult.

"I don't understand. I don't know what you mean."

"I want your penance."

"I don't understand," she panted, the knife starting to break the skin near her jugular. Her eyes watered as she felt the slow trickle of blood dribbling down her neck and then staining her blouse. "I will give you my penance. Please I will…"

"You don't even know what it's for," the kidnapper growled. "It's for the label you carry. Accept responsibility."

"Label? What label?"

"Felon…" the voice said in a long drawn-out hiss.

The knife sunk deeply into her neck, and that sharp sensation was followed by the air exiting her body. She wanted to scream, but no sound was forthcoming. The life quickly drained from her as blood gushed from the fatal wound. Her last thoughts were of the courtroom and the career that would never be realized. Her body went limp as it fell forward, and all was silent and dark.

CHAPTER 4

Athens, Georgia

IT WAS ALWAYS more difficult in the morning as the stiffness from the previous night's sleep seemed to try to hold on for the first few hours of the day. The scar was prominent, and even though it looked healed, it was still not 100 percent.

Glancing over at the clock, he let out a deep sigh knowing he should begin his day. Throwing off the covers, he moved over to the bed's edge and sat up. He rubbed his eyes and then moved his left arm in a circular motion to loosen it. Another deep breath in an effort to shake the sleep from his system set him a little more balanced.

Groggily, he stood up and walked down the hallway of his small apartment. When he entered the kitchen, he squinted at the sunlight pouring in through the window. Opening the refrigerator, he saw nothing that looked appetizing. *All I need is some coffee.*

Des Cook had hardly slept last week. He had just finished his final exams and turned in his term paper. With those last tasks he had completed his obligations in order to earn his master's degree in history from the University of Georgia.

The sound of the coffeemaker dripping into the pot was like music to his ears. The aroma of the brew was perfectly relaxing as the scent wafted around him. This, combined with the knowledge that he had accomplished another goal, made this morning especially satisfying.

It was the relief that accompanies having a huge burden lifted from your shoulders. In a few weeks, he would leave for Savannah where he would spend the remainder of the summer with Madison.

Since his departure from the hospital, their relationship had flourished. Most nights were spent talking with her over the phone, his connection to her only deepening. Being apart was difficult. He missed her terribly and often times had to check himself while studying as thoughts of her entered his mind on a frequent basis. However, now his obligations were completed. The time to hold, kiss, and make love to her could not get here fast enough.

Though he knew how he felt about her, he had refrained from uttering the words. His leanings toward caution always took over. Des also knew that Madison wanted to hear them, but she was patient and never pressured him.

Des broke out of his short daydream and grabbed his favorite mug from the cupboard. He had just begun to fill his cup when a stern knock at the door put an abrupt end to those joyous thoughts. *Who the hell could that be this early?* As he was grabbing his robe that was draped over the kitchen chair, the knock came again.

"Coming!" he called out as he tied his garment.

When he opened the door, there standing in front of him were two solidly built men, both wearing charcoal-colored suits and sunglasses. Their dark hair was parted on the same side. It looked as if they came off an assembly line.

"Hello, are you Mr. Desmond Cook?" asked the man to his right.

"Yes, what can I do for you?"

"I'm Special Agent John Arnett. This is Special Agent Paul McDonald," he said, gesturing to his partner. "We're with the FBI. I was wondering if we could speak with you for a moment."

Des's heart was racing. *Does this have something to do with Arlington?* He fumbled around with the knot on his robe and uttered, "Uh… yeah… sure… come in."

The two agents entered the small apartment. Their heads turned 180 degrees as they took in the surroundings. There wasn't much to see. Sparse furniture, a few pictures on the walls, some dirty laundry on a chair were all that seemed to comprise the dwelling.

"You can have a seat over there," Des said, pointing to the couch in the family room. "I was just about to have some coffee. Would you like some?"

"No, thank you, we won't take up much of your time," responded Agent Arnett.

"Okay, I'll be right back."

He walked into the kitchen, his hand already trembling. *What the hell did I do?* He was so nervous he could barely keep from spilling when he added cream to his brew. Once he finished, he gingerly came back into the family room and sat in the large brown leather recliner across from the couch where the two agents were now seated.

"Agent Arnett, if this has anything to do with Arlington, I have nothing more to add. I told the FBI and the Secret Service everything."

"Mr. Cook, this has nothing to do with Arlington. This is dealing with a completely separate issue."

"Uh… okay," he responded confusedly. "What can I help you with?"

"When was the last time you've been to California?"

"California? Wow, I've only been there once, and that was over twenty years ago. My family took a trip to Disneyland. Why?"

"You were not in California last week?"

"No, I just finished my last semester at the university. I had final exams. You can check with the school if you don't believe me," Des said defensively.

"No, that won't be necessary."

"What's this about?"

"Mr. Cook, do you know a Patricia Owens?"

"No, I don't believe so. Who is she?"

"She was an assistant US attorney who worked out of their Los Angeles office."

"She *was* a US attorney?" Des responded, wondering why the past tense was being used.

"Yes, Ms. Owens was found murdered. Her throat was slit. Her body was dumped on a small farm about an hour north of LA."

Agent McDonald reached into his coat pocket and pulled out a manila envelope. Carefully opening it, he removed a small bundle of pictures and silently dealt them out onto the coffee table like a deck of cards. They were of the most gruesome of natures.

There in a neat row were photographs showing the corpse of a young woman who appeared to be in her late twenties or early thirties. She was stripped naked from the waist up, her hands were bound above her head with the palms pressed together, and she was blindfolded. The slit across her throat was a gaping one. Des was sickened by the images.

"I don't understand. What does this have to do with me?"

"You're sure you don't recognize this woman?" Agent Arnett said, pointing to the photos.

"Yes, I'm quite sure. Like I said, the last time I was in California I was ten years old. Could you please tell me what this is about?"

"Mr. Cook, the reason we're here is that something was left at the crime scene."

"Something was left?"

"Yes, a note," he answered, reaching out across the table with a folded piece of white paper in his hand.

Des, with great caution, took the offering. Delicately unfolding it, his breath felt like it was forcibly removed from his body. In darkred ink it stated,

> Find Des Cook
> University of Georgia
> He has the answers.

Bewildered, Des looked up. His eyes widened, his brow tensed with shock. "I have no idea what this is about. I've never seen this woman before. Why would someone want to kill her?"

"We were hoping you could tell us."

"I haven't the first clue. I have no idea who she is. When did this happen?"

"Her body was found yesterday. The last time she was seen alive was exiting the courthouse in Santa Ana after a sentencing hearing Wednesday evening."

"Sentencing hearing? Was it some big case?"

"Hardly… garden-variety drug case. It certainly wasn't high-profile. The defendant had no organized crime or gang connections, just a small-time dealer. We believe she was murdered shortly after leaving the courthouse. We don't think it had anything to do with the defendant. If this were some type of drug hit, it would be unusual to see a knife as the murder weapon, too messy."

"Was she, um… sexually assaulted?" Des asked, looking for the politically correct term to describe that most distasteful crime.

"No, there was no indication of that. This appears to be a straight murder. Unfortunately, we have no other leads other than that note."

"What's this?" Des asked, pointing to what looked to be charred material sitting on two brass plates laid out next to the body.

"It's just soot. We believe the perpetrator tried to burn evidence, but we found nothing that could help us. It could have been some ritual, but it's too early to tell."

"How will you be able to tell?"

"If another body turns up."

Des took a deep breath. His head was swirling as he struggled to take all this in. "What do you think the likelihood of that is?"

"Well, Mr. Cook, I've been doing this for a long time, and in my opinion, it's an absolute certainty."

The sound of Agent Arnett uttering those words sent needlelike pricks up Des's spine. Although he didn't want to believe it, he felt the agent's assessment was probably correct. Yet how he was involved and why this individual identified him was the most disconcerting part of the situation. Something also told him that his own involvement was far from over.

CHAPTER 5

BY THE TIME the agents had left, Des was shaken to the core. He was sweating profusely, and every time he exhaled, he sounded like someone who had just emerged from holding their breath underwater for an extended amount of time.

He walked back into the kitchen to top off his coffee, but his hand was so unsteady he spilled all over the counter-top. His mind couldn't hold a thought long enough for him to use any power of deductive reasoning. It just jumped from possibility to possibility. The more he searched for answers, the deeper the void became. There were no logical conclusions to how he held the interest of a murderer in California.

He sat down at his kitchen table completely bewildered and horrified. The fact he was mentioned by name by the individual who performed this brutality was both fascinating and terrifying. Having no apparent connections to this circumstance only exacerbated those feelings. He tried once again to repeat the name of the murdered woman, but still, there was not even a hint of recognition.

Des got up and walked back toward his room, having to place his hands on the hallway walls to steady himself. Upon entering, he sat down on his bed, put his hands on his knees, leaned forward, and bowed his head. The weight of the situation had settled on his shoulders and chest like a giant albatross hanging around his neck. He then reversed course and lay on his back while trying to slow his breathing. He needed to think, but unless he calmed himself, it would be a fruitless effort. Closing his eyes, he allowed the darkness of the room to swallow him.

Colors swirled and rotated from black to red to blinding white. They bled into each other than seemed chiseled and separated as they ventured into the primary hues of a prism. The colors converged, sending him into the rich greenness of a peaceful field.

"You know the answers," a genderless voice whispered. Des walked toward it. "You know the answers."

He could feel the cool grass under his bare feet, the blades edging between his toes.

"You have the answers."

He continued to move in the direction he believed was the voice's epicenter.

"You have the answers."

Though he felt he had ascertained its location, the volume did not increase as he continued his path. But what had begun as a statement of calm affirmation had now turned into a taunt.

"You have the answers."

He quickened his pace until he was in a full sprint. The volume of the voice began to increase. Yet he still could not locate its source.

"You have the answers."

He halted his pursuit and scanned the landscape for additional clues. However, nothing but empty space presented itself. He took one step forward, but his foot was suddenly blocked.

He looked down to investigate the impediment stopping his momentum. The pale skin of a woman's torso invaded his vision. Startled, he jerked back, yet this time grass did not greet his feet. Rather it was something that felt like powder. Lifting his foot, he saw it was covered in soot.

"You have the answers."

"What is this!" he screamed.

"Accept responsibility."

"For what?"

He felt a sensation of warmth engulf his hand. Examining it, he was stunned to see, clutched tightly in his fingers, a large blade dripping with blood, which cascaded down his palm, wrist, and arm. He instantly let go, repulsed by the realization.

Des sprung up, panting and covered in sweat. It had been the most horrific of dreams. He rubbed his eyes vigorously, trying to wipe away the images swarming his mind. Catching a glimpse of the clock, he was stunned at how much time had passed. It was mid-afternoon, just before 2:00 p.m.

He had to get out of his apartment, maybe get something to eat. He threw on a pair of jeans, grabbed the nearest T-shirt and moved quickly out the front door.

Rapidly heading down the stairs, he nearly flew by the mailroom before stopping in as much an effort to regroup as it was to retrieve his mail. Taking out his key, he inserted it into the brass-plated cover of his mailbox, opened it, and removed the clumps of paper. Sorting through the items, he mainly came across advertisements for department stores, local eateries, and of course the ever-present preapproved credit card application. *I have enough debt already... thank you very much.*

As he sifted through each piece, it came from nowhere and felt like he had been hit by a sledgehammer. The last envelope he inspected had red lettering and looked to be in the same hand as the note discovered at the murder scene. It was addressed simply:

Mr. Desmond Cook "He has the answers."

The mail fell from his clutch as his body went numb. The killer knew where he lived.

CHAPTER 6

DES STARED AT the envelope. He was conflicted, desperately wanting to see what was inside and at the same time mortified at what might be its contents.

His palms were moist, and once again, the tremors returned. His stomach churned with a mixture of hunger and nausea.

Turning the letter over, he inspected it for any other marks or warnings. He then took a long last look into the open mailbox, checking for any other items the individual might have left. Its hollow space seemed to suck him in like a black hole.

Sticking his finger beneath the envelope's edge, he quickly ran its full length. The tearing sound made him even more uneasy as he reflected upon the knife running across the victim's neck. He parted its sides and then removed the paper, wondering what dilemma awaited him.

As he unfolded it, his breathing quickened and eyes widened. When it had been opened, he scanned the writing but without reading it. The same red ink was used in what was an obvious ploy to grab his attention. *Come on, Des… slow down. Read it and then make a judgment.*

He moved his eyes to the top line:

To Mr. Desmond Cook, Leader of the Enemy

Enemy? Enemy of who?

I trust that you have already been visited by the FBI. Of course, that was my intention.

I am sure you are unaware, but you must be made to understand. You are a criminal of the worst kind.

There have been victims and there will be more. And this is why you must be made to comprehend the nature of my deeds, for they are necessary to combat the calamity that now befalls us.

I am not unreasonable. I will allow you a chance to redeem yourself. You can prevent more carnage if you accept responsibility. If you choose not to receive my gift, the next horror will be on your shoulders.

Your destination is New Amsterdam, where you will be given further instructions. You must leave tonight as my gift is time sensitive. You will be contacted again once you arrive.

If you refuse to participate or if you contact the authorities, another will pay the heftiest of prices for your actions or lack thereof.

Remember, this task you must take alone. Good luck, I will be watching.

CHAPTER 7

THE KILLER'S KNOWLEDGE of Des was obvious given the historical reference he used. New Amsterdam was the settlement name for what would become the most famous location in America, New York City. Only someone with detailed information of his background would make such a reference.

He wanted to contact the authorities. He itched to get on his phone and call Agent Arnett, going as far as to remove his business card from his pocket. However, that feeling quickly abated when he noticed a number, a letter, and two words printed at the bottom of the paper. They read "6146K" and "no contact."

He recognized it immediately. It was the address of Madison's apartment building and the letter signifying her space. It was a dire warning spelled out in the most definitive of terms.

There was no way he would let that happen. Under no circumstances would he risk losing her. He had been put in that situation before; he swore it would be the last time.

He arrived at the airport three hours later. The flight ran up his credit card to uncomfortable amounts, but that was something he would deal with later.

On the way he had purchased a prepaid cell phone, nervous from previous experience that any calls he made from his other phone had the possibility of being tracked. He only needed it for one reason.

"Hello," her sweet voice was unmistakable.

"Madison, it's me."

"Des, what phone are you using? I don't recognize this number."

"That's not important. I need you to listen to me carefully. You need to leave your apartment immediately."

"What are you talking about?"

"I'll explain everything soon. You need to do this. Go to Kelly's house."

"Des, you sound crazy right now. What's going on?"

"I don't have time to explain, please, just do what I say."

"Sweetheart, what's happening? You're scaring me."

"I'm at the airport. I'll explain everything later."

"Where are you going?"

"Madison, please, just do what I ask. I have to go now. Don't answer your phone unless it's this number."

"Des, you have—" There was no response as the only thing greeting her ear was silence. The last time she heard him sound like that was in the tunnel under Arlington. She trusted him then; she would trust him now. She grabbed a few items, threw them in a bag, and headed to her friend's house.

CHAPTER 8

New York, New York

IT'S A LITTLE over a two-hour flight to New York from Georgia. Yet by its appearance from the sky, as the plane descended toward JFK airport, it might as well have been on another planet.

When flying over southern states, expansive fields and farms dominate the landscape with the occasional small town or midsized metropolis to break the pattern. New York City, especially at night, seemed to be a country unto itself. Thousands of colored lights pierced through a black canopy like Christmas decorations; it looked like a civilization that had no end.

The activity appeared as endless as the lights. Movement was constant, and even though he was several thousand feet in the air, Des could feel the momentum of its inhabitants. It was an energy only New York could provide.

As the plane continued its pathway down toward the earth, the illumination of the lights began to bring some of the city's iconic landmarks into view. The flickering billboards of Times Square; the Empire State Building with its red, white, and blue light display painting its facade; and the Chrysler Building showcasing its radiant art-deco silver cap announced the city's greatness. When the plane touched ground and brought its passengers to the gate, there was a bustle, an excitement that while difficult to describe could not be mistaken.

Des was not sure what his next set of instructions would entail or where the most opportune place to receive them would be. But judging from the killer's previous use of a historical reference, he guessed it would be advantageous for him to stay in Manhattan.

The area had been one of the first settled by Europeans. Called Man-a-hata by the Lenape tribe who were indigenous to the area, the name translates to "Island of the Hills." It would later become a major Dutch settlement and trading area renamed New Amsterdam.

From the 1650s to the 1670s, the English and Dutch fought a series of naval wars over the settlement. It was eventually given to England as part of a peace agreement and renamed New York by its new landlords.

The city has five boroughs, all of which have gained fame and recognition due to their rich histories. Yet Manhattan holds a special place in the city's lore. It's one that is central to its identity. While boroughs such as Brooklyn, Staten Island, and Queens represent New York's body and strength, Manhattan is its soul.

Situated between the Hudson and East Rivers, it is separated from its brethren, developing a culture so distinctive it has become the definition of this part of the country. It's a state within a state.

After exiting the terminal, he hailed a cab. Des decided to stay in a hotel on the Upper West Side. He chose the spot for two reasons. One, it was located fairly close to the most historic parts of the city, and two, it was the only area that had rooms in a price range he could afford.

Once he checked in, there was little more he could do. He didn't even know what form the communication would come in. All he did know was that it was coming.

He hated being in this position. War was chaotic and terrifying, but there was usually some objective. Even in the smallest of actions, there was a goal. Here, there was nothing to claim, no objective other than to wait for further orders. It wasn't a battle. There were no actions or ideology he had slighted in the least, let alone cause someone to see him as an adversary.

Yet here he found himself. Far away from the calm campus life at the University of Georgia. Now he was in the organized chaos of Manhattan.

He had to do it. Once he saw those photos of that butchered woman, he couldn't sit idle and ever expect to sleep again. Whether he was successful or not, putting forth no effort would only rail against his conscience for the rest of his life.

For now, though, he would try to get some rest. Tomorrow would most likely be frantic. The motivation that drove this individual now stalking him was a mystery. Des was only positive about one thing. This would not be easy.

CHAPTER 9

Location unknown

CHECKING THE CLOCK on the wall, the self-proclaimed leader of the revolt paced anxiously. However, this nervousness was not from anger, frustration, or worry, but excitement. It was the feeling a child might have before entering their first amusement park.

The plan, thus far, was perfection. Des Cook was a puppet on their string and at the mercy of the plot.

This was his punishment. He alone would carry the burden of saving the next potential victim. The killer had no accountability in whether the crime occurred or not. Cook's success or failure would be the determining factor. *I am relinquishing the wheel. He carries the responsibility. He will be held accountable.*

Walking into the back room, the killer's keen eyes took in the sight of the metallic dishes and chain. It was exhilaration to use the very tools that had been implemented against the innocent in the so-called name of their cause. *Such poetry.*

There was time. The examination could begin. Moving into the bedroom, the killer checked to see if everything was pristine. The hatred was saved for the back room and the back room alone. Standing in front of the full-length mirror, the towel was dropped. The reflected image was near perfection. The torso was flawless, only lean muscle mass. The shoulders were balanced. The sinewy legs displayed power. The arms were contoured, their bulk only offset by the slender hands.

Slowly turning around, the inspection continued. The back was chiseled and matched buttocks equally as taut. There was no impediment, no flaw to slow down any activity.

While rubbing the smooth skin on the chest, a smile began to form. The mark would be there soon enough. The hole that had penetrated their life would be emblazoned on the silky canvas, just above the nipple.

Then it would be complete. The turn would be 180 degrees, restoring order, resetting the boundaries to where they were meant to be. No more victims, no more pain. The scales would be balanced.

CHAPTER 10

Washington, DC

IT HAD BEEN a brutal week for the middle-aged man as he looked at the image staring back at him in his office men's room mirror. The usually handsome individual barely recognized his face.

The eyes were red and puffy with heavy bags of fatigue lilting beneath them. The gray hair on the side of his head, once distinguished, now made him appear old and tired. The pressures of upcoming events were no doubt, taking their toll. He could influence, but not control.

US Attorney General Robert Cantwell spent a lifetime to get where he was today. He began as the top graduate at his high school in Dearborn, Michigan. Strikingly good-looking, his six-foot two-inch frame housed a powerful body highlighted by a face featuring deep-set brown eyes and a square jawline. His thick black hair with its graceful dangling locks hanging just above his brow softened his features. Yet it also allowed him to look intimidatingly intense as well as kindly and gentle, depending on need.

His academics combined with his athletic prowess led to his acceptance to Harvard University. As a star wide receiver on the football team and a student of keen wit, he was on a missile ride to success. Chased by women, he chose the pathway of perpetual bachelorhood, leaving many young females in a state of frustration at their failed attempts to gain his complete devotion.

Upon his graduation from law school, his looks combined with his pedigree made him candy to the most prestigious law firms across the nation. They wined and dined him from coast to coast, hoping to obtain his favor.

In the end, he chose the famous New York law firm of Neil and Sachs. It was arguably the most successful and well-known on the East Coast. Many of their clients were on the "who's who" lists of the entertainment and political world.

Placed on partnership track, he attained it while still in his early thirties, almost unheard of in the legal realm. His performances in the courtroom became the stuff of legend as his ability to woo juries led to one of the highest success rates in the nation.

His notoriety, combined with his good looks and celebrity clientele, made Robert Cantwell as well-known as any of the entertainers or professional athletes in New York. He frequented the city's hotspots, usually accompanied by some of its most beautiful women. His picture and name not only appeared in newspapers like the *New York Times* and the *Wall Street Journal* but could also be found in supermarket tabloids.

When he entered his early forties, local political parties started courting him to run for office. After serving on several high-profile councils, his popularity made him the ideal candidate for state attorney general, which he won in a landslide.

Ten years later, the national stage was all that was left to conquer. When the new president was elected, there was only one name on his list for US attorney general, Robert Cantwell.

He attacked the job with an intense fervor, leading some of the most notable criminal prosecutions of the past half century. Organized crime leaders, dirty politicians, and corrupt corporations were all fodder for him. His successes only boosted his popularity.

He became a favorite on the lecture circuit. His baritone voice, self-effacing humor, and straightforward talk added to his legend, giving him an almost mythological stature.

In poll after poll, Americans rated him among their most admired leaders, far out-popularizing his boss, whose numbers had dipped significantly in the waning days of his second term. For that simple reason, he was the natural choice to be the successor to the highest office in the land. It was the worst-kept secret on the political scene, and even though he had not made the announcement, most knew it was a mere formality.

However, the closer he came to making it official, the more he was beginning to unravel. He knew once he made that leap, there would be a vetting. These were not the circumstances under which he wished to run for the presidency.

For now, it was safe and nothing would give any indication of his involvement. He needed them. It was actually the perfect arrangement. They had bankrolled everything while he provided access to the most powerful man in the world.

He wanted the office, but on his terms. Unfortunately, that was fantasy. The reality of politics was much more distasteful and did not allow for such principles. As much as they needed him, he was inextricably tied to and dependent on them. It was more out of necessity than of trust. If they were successful, everyone would win. If they failed, it was suicide.

CHAPTER 11

New York, New York

IT CAME PRECISELY at 9:00 a.m. The sound of his ringing cell phone made him jerk as if he had been struck by lightning. He looked at the display; it was a number he did not recognize. *This has to be him.*

"Hello."

"Hello, Desmond Cook." It was a cold computerized voice meant to leave no clue to who might be on the other end of the line. "I trust your flight went well."

"Why are you doing this? I'm not the leader of anything. I haven't been to California in twenty years!"

"You have the answers, it's all in the presentation. Your knowledge of history should be your guide… and unless you want another to pay such a price, you will go on foot to Times Square now."

"What do I do when I get there?"

"You better leave now. I warn that it would not be wise to wait."

"But what—"

Des did not hear a click, but for some reason he knew the killer had disconnected. Not wasting any time, he left his hotel room and headed to the exit of the building.

The air outside had a small dose of humidity, a warning of the long hot summer, which would be arriving shortly. It was overcast, providing a gray backdrop to the city streets.

His first instinct was to run, but the instructions did not contain a time constraint, only that he would be on foot. In addition, if he did go into a full gallop, by the time he arrived, he would be out of breath, limiting his ability to concentrate. Not to mention the fact that a man sprinting through streets of New York like a wild animal would probably draw unwanted attention.

Des walked east until he hit the perimeter of Central Park and then went southwest toward Times Square. He took solace in the fact that the city's grid-like formation made locations relatively easy to find.

As he walked briskly, he reached down to tighten his belt. His clothes were still bagging up on him, having not completely regained the weight he had lost after his injury.

Looking to his left, he kept the rich green island of the park in view as a guide. The two-and-a-half-mile long and half-mile-wide expanse is one of New York's true treasures. It is such a landmark that Manhattan's regions are often defined by where they lie on its borders. It offers tranquility among the chaos.

The sidewalk and streets of the sprawling metropolis was a sea of humanity. People heading toward their offices, cafés with outdoor seating, and customers eagerly awaiting stores to open made the city burgeon with life. Even though the situation was far from ideal, it was difficult not to be mesmerized by the sheer grandeur of the place.

The blocks passed quickly. Although it sounded far, the numbered streets running from north to south only measured about thirty to forty yards in length. When he initiated his journey at 102nd and Central Park West, he thought he was embarking on a long trek, his destination being nearly sixty blocks away. Yet before Des knew it, he found himself nearly past the edge of Central Park at Fifty-Ninth Street.

As he passed the park's western boundary, he could see the tip of Cleopatra's Needle, the Egyptian obelisk, reaching skyward. Many who travel to New York and even a large portion of its residents frequently pass this significant piece of history brought to the city in the 1800s. They oftentimes also miss the uniqueness of having one of ancient history's treasures sitting in the heart of the New World.

While contemplating his surroundings, Des recognized that even with its historical importance, New York was not static. "The city that never sleeps" also never seems to stop shape-shifting. As Des traversed the sidewalks, he was constantly met with mazes of steel piping, catwalks, and wood planking tunnels covering the walkways, their presence indicating the construction going on above his head. The metropolis was always adding to its personality, constantly mixing modern with the traditional architecture already resting there.

His gait quickened as he began to near Times Square. The pressure of his ordeal was increasing with each step. Finally, New York's most famous gathering point came into view. The dazzling lights and colors were impossible to ignore. The area seemed like a city within itself.

High-end shops and stores with windows full of eye-catching displays surrounded the visitor who entered its confines. Electronic advertisements, including video screens, animated billboards, and stock market tracking hovered above the streets, flooding the senses with brilliant hues and vibrant sounds.

Des gazed at the vast expanse, which actually looked more like a triangle than a square. Many of the structures lining its borders were oddly shaped to match the form of the odd corners and the configurations of the walkways. Most notably representative of the unusual architecture near this area is the famous Flat Iron Building. The triangular structure was the first building ever to use an iron skeletal frame. Its construction in 1903 set off a building boom, transforming New York into a skyward city. It would also transform Andrew Carnegie's pocketbook, making him the richest man in the world.

Des continued moving forward, trying to explore the space while anxiously awaiting his next set of orders. He traveled in the direction of the large billboards, examining the latest in twenty-first-century marketing ploys, which were offset by the art-deco structures adjacent to Broadway.

His trancelike state was finally interrupted when his phone rang. Recognizing the number the killer had used earlier, he inhaled deeply and then answered.

"I'm here in Times Square," said Des.

"I know you are," said the unnerving electronic voice. It was void of expressiveness yet seemed to contain a sinister quality.

"What do you want me to do?"

There was a brief pause. Des pressed his hand against his left ear in an attempt to filter out the all-consuming noise emanating from the streets. Then came the response.

"In the triumvirate of sacred ground lies where the problem first began. A relic of our birth and the beginning of our misguidedness. Find it. Call at this number by 10:30 a.m. An incorrect answer or failing to call before or by the indicated time will result in another victim. Good luck."

Des did not attempt to ask any questions. He knew there would be no point. Looking at his phone, it read 9:43. He had less than an hour.

Triumvirate of sacred ground, triumvirate of sacred ground. Des tried to compartmentalize the clue. Recognizing he had to concentrate on a general location first, he focused on the initial part of the instruction. Attempting to take the clue in its entirety would only distract him from reaching where he needed to be. *What's sacred ground? Come on, Des, think!*

It's not uncommon for an area of a significant event to be referred to as "sacred ground." Battlefields, birthplaces, and locations of famous happenings are often spoken of in such terms. Unfortunately, that in itself was not very helpful as New York has literally dozens of such places if not more. He didn't have that kind of time.

He ran his hand through his sandy-brown hair, attempting to come up with some kind of formula to eliminate possibilities. He was always taught that on a multiple-choice exam, the first task is to eliminate what are obviously wrong answers.

First, he eliminated items or locations of distance, that is, things that were so far away from his current location to make it impossible to reach in the given time. The killer wanted him in Times Square, which meant it had to be in Manhattan. *What would be considered sacred ground around here?*

From where he currently stood, close to Forty-Second Street, the nearest historical area was the Theater District. However, as famous as Broadway is, it's hardly sacred ground. In addition, it's a collection of places, not a single point, thus disqualifying it.

In fact, he realized much of New York City's famed landscape fell under that category. They were well-known, historic, and even iconic, but not sacred. *This is impossible. He didn't give me enough info!* Des turned a full 360 degrees. The overwhelming stimulus his senses took in, combined with the strain, caused him to become dizzy. Waves of humanity passed by him from all directions, making him feel like a drowning man who couldn't alert a passersby to throw him a life preserver.

The faces of the individuals surrounding him represented the diversity of the city itself. They were black and brown, white, and yellow and everything in between. Some were long and thin, while others were round and full. Dialects from everywhere entered his ears. Spanish, Chinese, Russian, Yiddish, Hindi, and many other foreign languages added to the beautiful but complex tapestry. It was all impressive, but not helpful.

Rely on your training. When he was in the military, he used to assess his situation by separating his senses. Sight, smell, and sound were meted out to gain clarity by not allowing one sense to override the other. He would determine what sense to trust the most given the situation. For instance, using one's hearing, you could often determine an enemy's location even if you could not see them.

Yet in this predicament, listening did not seem to make much sense. Smell would be of no use either. It was going to have to be visual.

He turned around once more and then looked at his watch. Already, four minutes had been lost and he still had not moved in any definitive direction.

He wanted to ask someone for help, but what would he ask? He would be incomprehensible. He placed his palm on his forehead as confusion was beginning to edge toward despair. Removing his hand from his face, he looked down to see it dripping with perspiration. He stared at the patterns the lines of his palm created. They seemed to zigzag in every direction. When he was younger, they were clearly defined. However, age had created something that resembled a highway map, with lines turning and crossing over one another. *Crossing… crossing.*

His eyes arched upward just in time to see an elderly woman in a black dress approaching. Her cheeks were puffy, and the wrinkles in her skin confirmed what she must have endured over her lifetime. *Crossing… crossing.*

Between her fingers she held an item that was impossible to make out but was obviously of great importance to her. Des could see her mumble to it as if in private meditation. As she moved closer, the item's features could be seen. It was a small crucifix. *Could it be the same as before?*

He immediately flashed back to the set of clues he had come across a year earlier that sent him and Madison traipsing up the East Coast in search of the lost treasure of the Confederacy. It too referred to a sacred place. Though he did not believe in divine intervention, this inspiration seemed to come from heaven. Like before, he would be heading for a church.

CHAPTER 12

Savannah, Georgia

MADISON PACED THE backyard lawn of her friend's house on a clear and comfortable morning. They had met while working as hostesses at a local seafood restaurant. Though Kelly and Madison were quite different, they hit it off immediately. Kelly proved to be the one person outside of Des that she felt she could confide in.

"Maddy, why don't you sit down with me," Kelly said, gesturing toward a chair on the back porch. "Struttin' back and forth ain't going to help things."

"I know, but I haven't heard from him since he told me to come over here… and that's not like him not to call."

"And he didn't give you any hint of where he was going?"

"No, but he sounded very concerned."

"Are you sure this isn't just some elaborate plan?"

Madison stopped in her tracks and stared intently at her friend. "What the hell do you mean by that?"

"Oh, come on, Maddy! You know what I mean."

"Kelly, I really don't need this shit right now," she retorted as she walked angrily toward her. "I'm sorry, I'm not some pretty blond white girl like you, but I don't think that's the case."

"You know damn well what it could be, and don't give me that 'white girl' bullshit. You've been seeing each other for how long now? He hasn't even said the words!"

"I know he feels it."

"But has he said it?"

Madison just looked at her with no reply. Her bottom lip started to quiver, making Kelly realize she had pushed too far. She got up and walked over to her emotionally injured friend.

"Hey," she said, brushing the curly locks off Madison's face. Her eyes were red and beginning to well up with tears. "I'm sorry, I had no right to suggest that."

"This can't be happening again," Madison sobbed. "He's the one. I know it. Do you really think there's somebody else… some girl with a prettier face and bigger tits?" she said mockingly.

"Come on, Maddy, how's that even possible? You're gorgeous… the most beautiful girl I know. But in all honesty, honey," she said, holding Madison's arms apart and staring at her chest, "it wouldn't take much to have bigger tits."

At first Madison tried to maintain a stern look but started to giggle at her friend's good-natured ribbing. Yet the laugh was soon replaced by a frown as those disparaging thoughts crept in. "I don't… I can't lose him."

Kelly reached over and embraced her. "Come on now, let's not fall into my bad habits. We can't assume anything. Why don't you come inside and I'll fix us something to eat."

CHAPTER 13

New York, New York

DES WHIPPED OUT his phone and launched his search using the keywords "famous churches, New York City." One immediately appeared at the top of the list. It was Saint Patrick's Cathedral, the seat of the Roman Catholic Archdiocese in New York.

He touched the link and up popped pictures of the beautiful Gothic-style structure. As he peered in closer, it looked like a piece of Medieval Europe had been dropped into the heart of modernity. Yet it wasn't its sharp edges and geometric shapes that caught his eye; it was the three entrances at its base and the three stained-glass windows above them. *In the triumvirate of sacred ground... Catholic Church... Trinity... God, Son, Holy Spirit... Trinity... triumvirate... tri... three! That has to be it.* It was located only ten short blocks away at the corner of Fifth Avenue and Fiftieth Street, just across from Rockefeller Plaza.

Des darted east on Fortieth Street, not caring anymore about the strange looks he was receiving from pedestrians. He looked to his right and could see the towering Empire State Building dwarfing its surroundings. As he made a left onto Fifth Avenue, the Empire State Building's cousin, the Chrysler Building, gleamed its silver rays across the skyline. It almost seemed that its luminosity had single-handedly burned through the cloud cover blanketing the city.

The blocks were passing quickly. He glanced down at his phone still gripped in his hand and saw 9:53. There remained a good amount of time.

Just before he reached Fiftieth, the famous Rockefeller Plaza and Radio City Music Hall came into view. Crowds were already beginning to line up for the *Late Night Show*, which was taped on its famous stages. Tourists barely noticed him now as he flew past the cafés crammed with families taking snapshots. Finally, he arrived at the plaza in front of the famous house of worship.

A large gray paved area surrounded the only slightly less gray building. Its edges were angular and sharp, meant to display the power and stableness of the institution. Its spires reached toward the heavens, and even though it was considerably smaller than many of the towering twentieth-century edifices around it, it somehow gave an impression of immensity, outdoing its more recent rivals.

As he approached the church, he slowed his movements, realizing he could not just go sprinting into New York's most famous house of worship. Entering through the massive front doors, the beauty of the landmark greeted his eyes. It was illuminated by light, which penetrated the windows just below its magnificently high ceiling. It poured in with a striking array of colors, the result of being filtered through the intricate stained glass lining both the front and sides of the building. Beautiful marble floors echoed with the steps of its occupants, causing one to stride lightly for fear of disturbing the sanctity of this holy place.

In the triumvirate of sacred ground lies where the problem first began.

Looking around for any significant markings or signs, Des was at a loss. The word *lies* suggested something on the ground. Yet it could also mean that whatever he was searching for could also just reside there. He felt he was in the right place, but in reality, he had no idea what he was looking for.

He ran over the clue once more. *In the triumvirate of sacred ground lies where the problem first began. A relic of our birth and the beginning of our misguidedness.* Des shook his head. *I don't understand. There are three windows and three doors, and I'm in a place that reveres the Trinity. Okay, Des, collect your thoughts. There must be more.*

He continued to stare at the floor, still looking for what "lies" on the ground. However, only cold marble greeted his eyes. He moved up and down the aisles with enough irregular motion to garner the attention of worshipers who painted him with disapproving stares. *A relic of our birth and the beginning of our misguidedness.*

"Our birth… our birth," he muttered to himself. "Oh, you idiot!" he said loud enough for an elderly woman to respond with an emphatic "Sshh!"

Noticing a priest exiting the confessional booth, Des walked as quickly as he could to intercept him before he disappeared into his office. "Father… Father," he spoke in a voice slightly louder than a whisper.

The priest turned around, looking every bit the part. His black garb accentuated his silver hair and steel-blue eyes. A kind and welcoming smile accompanied his handsome face.

"Yes, my son, what can I do for you?" Seeing Des's expression, his face went from warmth to concern.

"Father, I was wondering… when was this church established?"

"It was erected in 1879 by the New York Archdiocese," he answered.

Des looked down disappointedly.

"Is everything okay, son? You look troubled."

"Father, I wish I could tell you."

"I've been told that I'm a good listener," he said with a reassuring smile.

"Thanks, but I can't."

"Are you sure you don't want to talk about it?"

"I really want to, but there's no time… What other historic churches are in New York?"

"My goodness, there are quite a few. Not too far from here is the Little Church Around the Corner… and of course there's Trinity Church near Wall Street, a few blocks from the World Trade Center."

Des's face lit up. "Trinity Church?" *Triumvirate.* "When was it established?"

"Oh, I don't know the exact date, but it was during colonial times. Son, are you sure you're all right?"

"I don't know, but thank you."

Des darted down the corridor and out the door. He had to get to the subway. *Trinity Church, it makes sense.*

CHAPTER 14

SPRINTING DOWN FIFTH Avenue, Des saw the sign for the subway station. The killer had instructed him to go to Times Square on foot but made no mention on how he must travel once he reached that destination. Besides, there was no way he could get to the area by foot in time to meet the deadline. He would have to chance it.

He bounded down the stairwell to the station below. Subway performers sat on various levels of the spiral, playing instruments in hopes of receiving a few extra dollars from passengers who appreciated their contribution to city culture.

In the background, he could hear the roar of the trains as their power echoed through the deep tunnels. He arrived at the platform, staring anxiously into the darkness, trying to will the train to move faster. He was hoping to soon see its lights dancing on the tunnel walls.

The roar became louder and the floors vibrated as he finally saw the iron car heading toward him. People crowded to the edge of the platform as they readied themselves in what appeared to be a choreographed movement to board the subway car.

Its airbrakes squealed as the train gradually came to a stop. A flood of people exited onto the platform while the mad rush to enter once they passed was about to commence. They packed into the narrow compartment. Some dashed to seats, while others resigned themselves to hold on to rails and bars while standing.

People from all walks of life made up its occupants. It was an eclectic mix. There was a middle-aged man in a dark suit, his face etched with stress as he read the *Wall Street Journal*. There was a black teen bobbing his head up and down to the music pumping through his ridiculously large headphones. Sitting next to him was an elderly Hispanic woman, her gnarled hands clinging tightly to a bag of groceries.

The motion of the subway car bounced its occupants as their bodies moved back and forth in a synchronized rhythm. Des peered at the advertisements lining the train's walls where it met the ceiling. As his eyes continued to venture left, he came upon a map of its various stops. He tried to ascertain the closest one to Wall Street.

While attempting not to, he habitually checked the time, hoping if he concentrated, he could somehow slow down the progression of the passing seconds. Already, he was dangerously close to the deadline.

Snapping himself out of it, he contemplated on what he might find at Trinity Church. He tried to open the internet browser on his phone, but the tons of earth above his head blocked any signal. He wouldn't have time to look at his phone once he reached ground level.

Valuable minutes continued to hemorrhage away as they made each stop. Des was nearing a frantic state as the train seemed to be moving slower than molasses.

Finally, the brakes began to screech once more as the train slowed to a halt at his designated spot. He edged toward the doors, getting into a position that would have as little impediment as possible.

They slid open, and he shot out like a race horse from a starting gate. Although he was moving as quickly as he could, the crowds still converged on him. He pushed and shoved his way through the mass.

"Asshole!" an angry man yelled as Des fought his way up the stairs.

He soon emptied into the maze of buildings that made up the Financial District. Quickly, he looked up to find his marker. There it was, the tallest building in the Western Hemisphere, the new World

Trade Center, its onyx glass now reflecting the bright sunshine, which had finally broken through the banks of gloomy clouds.

He sprinted in the direction of the beacon, dodging any road block in his path, human or otherwise. Cutting left, there before him was the symbol of the financial might of the industrialized world, Wall Street.

Crowds of men and women entered and exited out of its cold Greek colonnaded exterior. Each of them had their heads down, checking the stock tickers on their phones as it scrolled across their tiny screens. In a way, they looked more like lambs headed to the slaughter than confident business professionals. It was hard to believe this area, which was named for a small, ill-constructed protective wall that once stood there during early colonial times, had the eyes of the financial world on it every day.

Des moved down the street as rapidly as he could. He hardly noticed the statue of George Washington on the steps of Founders Hall, marking the exact place where he took the oath of office to become the nation's first president. The distinctive face of the "Father of the Nation" looked in the direction of the financial icon. The expression was one of pride bordering on wonderment of what his country had become.

Time was running out as he took another panicked look his phone. *Jesus, only twelve minutes left!* Asking a pedestrian where Trinity Church was located, he was directed to go left once more at the northern base of the World Trade Center. As he turned, he saw a sign advertising the famous Fraunces Tavern, the place where many of the founding fathers discussed the issues of their new country over pints of ale.

Suddenly, he came upon the quaint house of worship. It was the polar opposite of Saint Patrick's Cathedral. Rather than rising Gothic towers, immense stained-glass windows, and an intimidating presence, Trinity Church displayed the personality of the country's humble origins. Its white wooden facade and modest outer décor harkened to the simpler life most colonist led. It looked more like an eloquent home than it did a church.

Entering its front doors, Des was greeted by the small congregational hall. Its oak benches and cherrywood fixtures gave it a much warmer feel than the cold marble and stone of Saint Patrick's Cathedral. As he moved delicately through the pews, he looked for any markers indicating points of significance.

After passing through the area, he entered a foyer. No massive works of art or items of religious importance adorned its plain white walls. In fact, the only decorations at all were a collection of photographs that recorded the aftermath of the tragedy of September 11, 2001.

Pictures showing thousands of pieces of paper along with a thick layer of dust covering the church's walkways were displayed. Others featured the remnants of computer monitors that had been hurled nearly half a mile when the towers collapsed on that fateful day, lying in heaps in the church cemetery. It was a haunting exhibit.

In the triumvirate of sacred ground lies where the problem began. A relic of our birth and the beginning of our misguidedness... lies... lies... cemetery!

He quickly exited the church into its back courtyard. Gray stone tablets marking burial plots were spread across a small carpet of green grass in nondescript patterns. He walked up and down the pathways, staring down at the headstones. Their dates definitely coincided with the correct time frame of the nation's birth.

He looked once more at the time. *Oh my god! Only two minutes left!* He began to jog up and down the brick pathways, hoping any of the names would ring a bell. Yet he saw nothing. His opportunity was melting away, a little over one minute remained.

In a panic, he turned full circle but was convinced he was near. Perspiration beaded on his forehead, his shirt now plastered to his chest with moisture. His hand began to tremble as images of the young slain attorney flashed in his mind. He darted back and forth, desperately searching for something... anything that would aid him.

Then seemingly out of nowhere, an obelisk grave marker caught his eye. He stopped at once, nearly falling over from the momentum of his sudden halt. At first, he thought he was seeing things, yet it was no apparition. There in front of him was the tombstone of Alexander Hamilton.

Time was up; there was nothing left to do but make the call and pray.

"Hello, Desmond," the eerie computerized voice answered.

"It's Alexander Hamilton! That's what you wanted," he said, panting with nervous exhaustion.

"Correct."

Des closed his eyes as some of the adrenaline began to seep out of his system.

"However, Desmond, you are too late. Another will pay for your failure."

"No! I found it! You don't have to do this!"

"You need to accept responsibility. But there will be other opportunities, I promise."

With that final comment, the line went dead. Despondent, he fell to his knees at the foot of the grave of the Revolutionary hero. Another would be sacrificed.

CHAPTER 15

Savannah, Georgia

MADISON SAT ON the bed in the guestroom with her knees pulled to her chest. She stared at her phone, desperately wanting to pick it up and call him. The only thing stopping her was the realization of what that meant, which was terrifying.

If she did call, she might put herself at risk, but even more frightening and disheartening, she would be admitting her trust was no longer there. She couldn't bring herself to do it.

She kept thinking of her earlier conversation with Kelly about her relationship with Des. It seemed to be going wonderfully, but they hadn't seen each other in over five months as he was finishing school. *Long distance relationships never work.*

Could he have found someone else? Is he with her now? Maybe their closeness, the intensity of their relationship, was beginning to scare him away. *He hasn't said the words.*

She ached for him to say it. On several occasions, she thought he was going to, only to finish the evening with the disappointment that the wait was not over.

Madison began to flashback to her failed marriage. Her husband's infidelity had torn her apart. *God, I was such a fool!* She remembered her feeble attempts to forgive and move on, only to see him do it again. It made her feel pathetic and helpless.

She closed her eyes, praying this was not again the case. At the same time, she cursed herself for being so fragile.

She loved him. She did not want to believe it was true. She wanted him there with her. She wanted to feel his arms wrapped around her and her lips pressed against his. She longed for him to be inside her, their bodies moving in unison and to feel the ecstasy that came with that union.

The more she thought, the angrier she became—angry that she was not with him, angry that he might be with someone else, but most of all, angry at her own insecurities.

She pushed the thoughts out of her head. Yet it brought little relief. They were soon replaced by the terrible alternative. He was in trouble.

The anger she was holding now transformed to worry. She needed him to be safe but found herself helpless to aid him. Not knowing where he was, was the most difficult part. She needed him to come home.

CHAPTER 16

New York, New York

DES WALKED INTO his hotel and dejectedly headed to the elevator. By the time he made it to his room, agony had been substituted for depression. The guilt was overwhelming, and he had already entered a stage of grief over the next victim who would pay the price for his failure. *Why is this happening to me?*

He began to ponder the reasons he was led to the grave of Alexander Hamilton. It made no sense. He knew the killer had more on his mind than just a glorified treasure hunt. However, he could not decipher why someone who was considered to be a true patriot be portrayed as a "problem" and the "beginning of our misguidedness."

Hamilton was one of the true geniuses of that era, only matched in intellect by Thomas Jefferson. Both men were instrumental in the factors shaping the American national identity. Even though, however, they shared little else. While each had tremendous influence, their philosophies on what the new republic should be greatly diverged.

Jefferson was raised in Virginia, where he identified with the aristocratic planter class. He came from a family with its roots in the agrarian slave owner culture. This would later shape his views on how the young country should develop.

In Jefferson's opinion, most power should reside with local governments and not with a federal entity. He believed this was the only path that would lead the United States into a sort of utopian farmer society.

Although Jefferson, being the author of the Declaration of Independence, may be seen as Western democracy's greatest spokesman, Hamilton's upbringing was far more representative of the American dream. He was born on the island of Nevis in the West Indies. Abandoned by his father at age ten, he was thrust into the role of provider before he was a teenager.

Before his thirteenth birthday, he began working for a trading company in St. Croix, which is presently part of the American Virgin Islands. By the time he reached his early teens, he was one of its most important staff members. His distinct talents and impressive mind motivated his employers to send him to the colonies to be educated. The young Hamilton's dynamic thought process made a mark on his professors and fellow students alike.

When war broke out with the British, he was eager to serve. As captain of a New York artillery regiment, his value became obvious. He wowed his superiors enough to later be made an assistant to General George Washington.

At the end of the war, he was admitted to the bar and then elected as a delegate. Recognizing the document that the former colonies were using to govern themselves, the Articles of Confederation, was weak, he led a push for a constitutional convention to replace it.

Yet the agreement resulting from the convention, to him, was unsatisfactory, because in his view, it made the federal government feeble. In the ensuing years, he would attempt to strengthen it and, in many ways, succeeded in doing so.

As secretary of the treasury under President Washington, he established a national bank. He was also a strong advocate for providing government monetary support to aid the nation's burgeoning manufacturing base. America's modern financial system, in large part, is a result of his genius.

Though his intent was to create a more stable nation, Hamilton's consistent leanings toward a stronger national government created political enemies. One in particular was Thomas Jefferson. The acrimony between the two camps led to the formation of opposing political parties, a tradition that continues to this day.

This battle between the supporters of Hamilton and the backers of Jefferson represented the constant struggle the United States would have in defining itself. It is a struggle that is still ongoing between the rights of local governments and the powers of a federal entity.

Yet with all of Hamilton's monumental contributions to the formation of what is now the most powerful nation on earth, he is more famous for how he died. The man who was one of the true architects of the New World died in the old-world tradition of dueling with political rival Aaron Burr.

Even with all his knowledge of Hamilton's past, Des could not fathom how the killer had labeled him. *How could anybody in their right mind consider this loyal servant of the nation a problem?*

Everything about this situation was nonsensical, and he was out of answers. He could not continue dealing with this monster without some kind of aid. The only result of that would be a higher body count.

He paced the room trying to assess his options. However, as much as he tried to expand upon scenarios, his choices boiled down to two. Either he could await the killer to contact him again and send him on another wild goose chase, or he could alert the FBI. He knew the latter would only infuriate this maniac.

Neither seemed to be a solid course of action. Yet one thing was certain: both choices had the potential to result in more dead bodies. When hit with such a reality, the decision was made. He grabbed the letter sitting on top of the dresser and headed out the door.

CHAPTER 17

DES ENTERED THE FBI offices located at 26 Federal Plaza. He did so hesitantly yet knew he really had no choice. If either decision could result in more victims, it was better to leave it to the professionals. In addition, he had an obligation to let them know that they could have another corpse on their hands.

He had called Agent Arnett to inform him of what had transpired. Arnett told him he would notify the New York office and referred him to Agent Zachary Keller, the individual in charge of that department.

He moved slowly down the hallway, his footsteps clomping down its lengthy corridor. Feelings of guilt consumed him—guilt for the next victim and guilt for the potential more that might come from his current action. As much as it weighed on him, there was no way he could allow this emotion to keep him from sharing what he knew.

Spotting office 453, he opened the door to a carpeted enclosure. "Hello, I'm Desmond Cook. I'm here to see Agent Keller," he said to the heavy-set secretary sitting behind the desk.

"He's expecting you. I'll let him know you're here," she replied.

As she left to notify her boss, Des scanned the walls. The first thing garnering his attention was a large picture of the president proudly displayed in the center of the west wall. Surrounding that were various framed articles of FBI successes. There was one about the capture of the Hudson River Killer, who was finally apprehended after murdering nine teenage boys. He had attained his name due to his practice of leaving their bodies at various points along its banks. Another glowing tale of FBI heroism was displayed in a *Time* magazine piece. It detailed the case and capture of the Night Snatcher, an individual who pulled young women from their beds before brutally raping and murdering them.

However, the most prominently displayed article was a story from *Newsweek* magazine. It covered the most famous case, the Central Park Strangler. He killed eleven people over a six-year period, leaving their bodies around the park's borders. He was caught in the most sensational of manners by Agent Keller, who ran him down and tackled the culprit after using himself as bait.

"Agent Keller will see you now," she said, pointing to the office door.

Des walked into the small and chaotic room. Stacks of papers were everywhere—on his desk, his chair, and even the floor. Behind the desk were two small bookcases in which there was no discernable pattern of organization. On the walls was a very impressive collection of commendations and awards, which would have probably looked more impressive if they were actually hung with any symmetry whatsoever. Directly behind the desk, just a few feet above the chair, was a framed degree from California State University of Fullerton's School of Criminal Justice.

"I'll be right there," a strong voice called from an adjoining room.

A moment later, Agent Zachary Keller emerged. He was not at all what Des was expecting. Unlike the agents who had appeared at his door in dark suits and looking every bit like Dick Tracy and Joe Friday, the man standing before him looked like your friendly neighborhood accountant.

He wore an out-of-date cardigan sweater that his short and slightly pudgy body barely squeezed into. With his dark curly hair and oval spectacles, it was hard to envision this man running through Central Park, taking down murderers. He would look more at home behind a library counter, stamping books.

However, his physical stature was not representative of the esteem that he was held. He was a man the other agents revered as a sort of department messiah. After a series of botched cases that allowed some of New York's most violent thugs to slip through the cracks, Keller's successes and heroics had brought honor back to the department. Within three years, the New York office had one of the highest capture rates in the nation.

"Yeah, I get teased about that a lot… a Southern California boy from Orange County in the Big Apple," Keller said, noticing Des examining his diploma.

"They have a great baseball program."

"One of the best. I'm Zack Keller," he said in a friendly tone while extending his hand. His grip was surprisingly strong… like being caught in a vice. "I talked to Agent Arnett in Georgia. He filled me in on the murder of the assistant US attorney in LA. Kind of weird they would put your name on a note so prominently… and you have no idea why?"

"No, I don't, but it's obvious this individual wants to taunt me," Des replied.

"Why do you say that?"

"I got this letter in the mail the day your agents visited me," he said, pulling out the envelope and handing it almost ashamedly to him.

Keller took it and began reading its contents.

"It's in the same…"

"Red ink that was on the note left at the crime scene," Keller interjected, finishing Des's sentence. "So obviously this brought you to New York. Then what happened?"

"He called me this morning."

"You talked to him?"

"Just for a few moments. The voice was computerized."

"What did he tell you?"

"He told me to go on foot to Times Square. Once I got there, he called me again to give me further instructions."

"What were they?"

"In the triumvirate of sacred ground lies where the problem first began, a relic of our birth and the beginning of our misguidedness... he gave me less than an hour."

"What the hell does that mean?"

Des felt uncomfortable. He did not want to relive his failure but knew he needed to provide him with any useful information. "It was Alexander Hamilton's grave at Trinity Church."

"And that was the correct answer?"

"Yes... but I got there too late. He told me that another would pay the price for not getting the answer in time."

"I don't understand. How did he know you were capable of figuring this out? It's not like somebody with only a rudimentary knowledge of history would know where to go. Your average Joe would be clueless."

"He seems to know about me. I just finished my master's degree in history at the University of Georgia."

"What are these about?" Keller asked, pointing to the numbers at the bottom of the page.

"That's my girlfriend's address."

Keller looked up, recognizing the dire threat at once. "I would ask you why you didn't come to us immediately, but that's obvious. Whoever he is, he's smart... doesn't leave us much to go on. I'll run this letter through our lab, but I don't expect we'll find anything. He has obviously thought this well through."

"He told me I would have another opportunity."

Keller looked down. "Yeah, I was afraid of that. All that means is there's going to be a higher body count." Keller walked a few feet and sat behind his desk, staring at the letter intently. "Why does he refer to you as the 'Leader of the Enemy'?"

"I have no idea," Des said, stressfully running his fingers through his hair.

"Well, for some reason, he wants to keep you on the end of a string. Which basically means without you, we don't have shit."

"You've got his phone number."

"That's fucking worthless," he said, waving his hand in a brush-away motion. "It's most likely a prepaid cell phone he has already gotten rid of."

A light tap on the door shook Des from the discomfort of the situation.

"Come on in," said Keller.

The door slowly opened, and in walked an extremely attractive woman in a dark business suit that, although was formal, highlighted a beautiful figure. She looked to be in her early thirties. Her long dark auburn hair accentuated the soft features of her face.

"Hi, Zack, you called for me? What's up?"

"Yes, this is Mr. Cook. Mr. Cook, this is Dr. Amanda Hertzel. She's our chief profiler for this type of crime."

"So, we finally meet," she said, extending her hand.

Des just gave her a curious look as he accepted her introduction.

"I see you're a little confused. I was one of the profilers who worked the Arlington Case… so I know quite a bit about you. I'm sure you're wondering how you're involved in all this."

"You read my mind."

Amanda Hertzel was the wonder kid of the FBI's psychological profiler department. Born in Boise, Idaho, her mother was killed in a violent car crash when she was only four years old. Amanda was in the back seat at the time but suffered only minor injuries.

With only a father who felt overwhelmed at the prospect of raising Amanda and her younger brother Cal alone, the family struggled. Distraught over the loss of their loved one and left without a second income, the emotional and financial damage was severe. But no matter the horrible circumstances, their father did his best to hold the family together.

As Amanda grew older, she became more involved in the raising of Cal while at the same time becoming her father's most reliable emotional support. Though she tried to not allow herself to be consumed with how deeply her father had been hurt by the loss of his wife, the reminders were all around her. This was especially true at night when she would sometimes catch him sobbing at the kitchen table after he thought the kids were asleep.

Misfortune continued to stalk the Hertzels. After losing his job at a tractor-manufacturing plant, they were forced to uproot and move to Arkansas. There he found a low-paying job at a paint factory.

Leaving her friends and school was difficult enough, but after salary cuts and layoffs, her father's meager income was not enough to get by. Desperate and scared, he turned to brewing moonshine and growing marijuana to make sure they could survive. Things gradually started to improve until Amanda's fifteenth birthday, when her father was arrested. With no parents, Amanda was sent to live with her aunt in Tempe, Arizona, while Cal moved in with his cousins in Alabama.

At first, Amanda felt isolated, displaying all the signs of a recluse. Yet gradually, she worked her way out of her shell. She made new friends, became involved in school activities, and excelled in her classes, obtaining the highest marks in her school.

Her prowess in the classroom earned her an academic scholarship to Yale. Choosing the major of psychology, she quickly became the department's most prominent student, as well as the favorite protégé of the dean, Dr. Samuel Tabbot.

After graduating at the top of her class with her doctorate, the offers came pouring in. Think tanks desired her services in determining the psychological makeup of politicians and big-corporation CEOs. They saw an advantage to finding out how they might lean in relation to important decisions and how it would affect the nation.

Top medical schools such as John Hopkins University and Harvard wanted to utilize her talents in determining the psychological effects of certain cancer treatments. Of course, there was also the never-ending stream of teaching opportunities that flooded her mailbox from prestigious universities such as Stanford, Michigan, Northwestern, and USC.

The government also got in on the action. The CIA, always looking to psychoanalyze the nation's enemies, went as far as to fly her to Washington, DC, to interview her almost as soon as she took off her cap and gown.

However, while pondering her options in the summer after her graduation, a series of bizarre murders took place in New Haven, Connecticut, that horrified and at the same time captivated her. The murders were of women between the ages of thirty to forty-five. In each case, the victims had their left arm amputated and their mouths sewn shut with gold thread. They had also been stripped of their original clothing and then dressed in all white. Other than the similarities of the mutilations and the sex of the victims, the police and FBI seemed to have no leads or ideas of where to look for the perpetrator.

Going on a hunch after following the lack of progress by the authorities, Amanda contacted the FBI with a theory. She suggested that the investigators look into recent nasty divorces in the area, where the husband claimed the wife's infidelity as one of the causes of their marriage's failure.

Her deductions had led her to believe that the removal of the left arm was due to the fact it held the hand that carried the wedding ring. The white clothing represented the day they took their vows, and the gold thread used to bind the mouth closed symbolized the gold ring. Closing the mouth was a way of signifying the wife had broken her vows.

At first, her suggestions were ignored, scoffed at like the ramblings of an inexperienced kid trying to play into their TV show fantasies. Yet as more victims were found across a half dozen states, the authorities decided to give her theory a second look.

Three weeks later, a suspect was identified and arrested based on Amanda's suggestions. At the suspect's residence were found boxes of white clothing, cutting tools consistent with the amputations, and over two hundred spools of gold thread.

A month after the successful capture, Amanda received a call from the FBI office in New York, asking her if she would be interested in interviewing for a job in their criminal profiling department. She had found her calling.

In America's most famous city, Amanda became the rising star, helping to crack over twenty high-priority, extremely difficult cases. Some of which had been unsolved for years. She worked closely with famous profiler and the second-highest ranking person in the department, Dr. Gregory Feller. Within five years, she was leading the department and was one of the most sought-after lecturers on criminal behavior in the country.

"Well, I think Dr. Hertzel will help us figure out how you're involved. She's the best profiler in the country, and I've assigned her to this case," Keller said.

"I really hope you can find out how I'm mixed up in this whole thing, Dr. Hertzel."

"Well, I hope so too… and please, call me Amanda. It makes me feel old when I'm called doctor," she said smiling.

Des immediately noticed the aura of confidence surrounding this young woman. He could tell there was nothing that would disturb her eternal calm or dissuade her belief in herself.

"I assume you've already seen the photos of the first victim in Los Angeles… a Miss Patricia Owens," said Keller.

"Yes, she was an attorney," answered Des.

"An assistant US attorney," Amanda said, correcting him. "She was found stripped naked from the waist up. Her hands were bound above her head. She was blindfolded and dumped on a small farm outside of Bakersfield. I also find it interesting they found two metal dishes filled with soot at the crime scene."

"What do you think that means?" Des asked, hoping for clarification.

"It's too early to tell. He could have been destroying evidence, or it could have been some type of purification ritual."

"You mean like cleansing his sins?" questioned Keller.

"Yes, possibly… But in most cases where there are purification rituals, we tend to find sexual abuse. There's no evidence of that."

"Mr. Cook just had contact with the killer," said Keller while handing her the letter.

"Same red ink," she said, examining the envelope.

"That's not the only communication Mr. Cook has had with him," Keller added.

"You spoke to him? What did he sound like?"

"The voice was electronically altered," Keller interjected. "He told him to go to Times Square and then contacted him again with a riddle." Keller had Des repeat the riddle.

Amanda had a perplexed expression. "What does that mean?"

"He wanted me to go to Trinity Church and find the grave of Alexander Hamilton."

"I don't understand. He said in the clue that it's where 'the problem first began' and it was 'the beginning of our misguidedness.' Hamilton was one of the founders of the nation. Was there something else you may have missed?" she asked.

"No, he told me I was correct. But unfortunately, I didn't meet his time deadline… It doesn't make much sense to me either."

"I take it you'll run that letter through the lab. What's the chance we'll find anything?" Amanda asked, handing the letter back to Keller.

"A snowball's chance in hell," he responded.

"Did he say anything else to you?" she asked, looking at Des.

"He told me that I would have to accept responsibility… and that another would have to pay."

"Accept responsibility for what?"

"The next victim, I guess." Des then paused for a moment. "He's not going to stop, is he?" he said rhetorically.

"I'm sorry, but no. He's obviously obsessed with you. He'll definitely contact you again."

"What do you think he wants?"

"Judging from what I've seen thus far… to torment and then kill you."

CHAPTER 18

Location unknown

IT WAS A release. All the wrongs had dissipated, if only for a moment. The commandments were understood; killing is against God's law. Yet in this case, the Almighty would understand. The list of grievances was too long, the justification too clear cut.

Gazing at the implement that was the main tool of the craft, the killer admired the blade. It was always important to examine it for any imperfection that its most recent use might have caused.

People will understand there existed no personal animosity toward these victims. They were necessary casualties of the war. The results were quick and methodical, wishing to cause as little distress as possible.

Unfortunately, there were more battles to be fought, and that meant more carnage. If that was the cost, so be it.

However, there was one individual who had committed acts so egregious to the cause they could not be ignored. He must be dealt with in the harshest of terms. He had become the symbol that allowed the skewed belief system to perpetuate the calamity and made the situation more dire with each passing day. The more the thoughts continued, the greater the hatred swelled inside the killer.

Staring at the pictures pasted to the wall of the back room, the plan was further refined. The focus of this rage would eventually meet the same fate. But before that time, they must be made to feel the suffering that they had caused. He would be made to know the responsibility of carrying the burden. The others were simply fodder. They were part of the problem of course, but merely pawns. They were useful only in statement.

He was different. His sins could not be overlooked. He was not the final part of the process, but his transgression had to be addressed. *He will be forced into the chase. His success or failure will be the determining factor in the level of devastation. He will pay the price for aiding The Enemy.*

CHAPTER 19

Washington, DC

THE VIBRATION OF the phone in his shirt pocket woke US Attorney General Robert Cantwell from a peaceful nap. It was 9:20 p.m., and after an exhausting day, he was attempting to get some rest on his office couch on this Wednesday night. His days were always relentless, and he ceased trying to get a full night's sleep a long time ago. Instead, he resorted to short respites wherever he could find them.

Looking down at his phone, it took a moment for his eyes to gain focus. It was coming from his old college buddy Adam Slayborne, CEO of General Correction Services. Cantwell sighed, knowing exactly what it was about. Since the beginning of the year, there had been a stream of congressmen proposing a plethora of bills for reform. This included one in particular that had not yet reached Capitol Hill, which if passed would alter everything.

"Yeah, Adam, what can I do for you?" Cantwell said, rubbing his eyes.

"I hate to bother you so late, but we have a lot of worried people here who are breathing down my neck. I can't stress enough how important it is that this bill gets to the president before he leaves office."

"Adam, I've told you a dozen times that I'm on it. The president has informed me personally that he was against those reforms," Cantwell said, his voice filling with frustration.

"Damn it, Robert! You know that's not the concern. There's a lot of talk that Senator Wayman is planning to delay its release until your man is out. Which basically leaves us depending on you to win the election, and you know that's not a sure thing."

Cantwell stood up, walked over to his desk, and pulled out a thirty-year-old bottle of single-malt scotch from the top side drawer. He then took out a small glass and filled it.

"What the hell do you want me to do about that? I can't force Wayman to send the bill out. He has no interest in helping me. I mean, for God's sake, I'll most likely be running against the son of a bitch."

"Well, you need to do something, or it's going to be all our asses in a sling," Slayborne retorted.

He knew he was right. There was so much on the line now, so much more than just the presidency. If they did not tread carefully, it would all be exposed. That would leave winning the election as their only safety net, an unsure backup plan at that.

"Now, Adam, haven't I always pushed and gotten everything you've asked for? Name one time I haven't delivered."

"I know, Robert, but this is not like the others. I just want you to understand the gravity of the situation. We need to make sure that bill lands in the right hands one way or another, or the whole goddamn thing blows up… and that means the well dries up for you, me… everyone."

The call ended, and Cantwell gulped down the shot of the strong drink and then immediately refilled his glass. Resting both hands on top of his desk, he inhaled deeply and then let his shoulders droop as he released his breath.

He stared at the photos lining the opposite side of his workstation. There were pictures of him smiling with dignitaries and foreign leaders. There was one with his "friend" Carrie on his yacht in the

Florida Keys and another with the president. They now only served to remind him of all he had to lose.

And of course, there was the file. It was one of those old-fashioned brown accordion files that allowed for the storing of a great amount of information. He hated having it in the office, usually refraining from bringing it in. However, he needed to keep it updated, and there was only one other who had access to its contents. It was the life blood for him and so many others.

There were no solutions tonight, but a resolution needed to be achieved. He took another sip of the scotch, and as the golden liquid passed his throat, he let its warmth fill his chest. He gazed out the window. The lights of the city sparkled against their black canvas. To his right, he could see the Capitol Building awash in brightness. Its cupola, once serving as a beacon of inspiration, was now only a reminder of the perilous days that lay ahead.

CHAPTER 20

New York, New York

IT CAME AT 6:00 a.m., a loud chime from his phone, jolting Des awake like he had been shocked by a cattle prod.

"Good morning, Desmond," the computer voice said in a chilling monotone. "I'm sorry to have woken you so early."

Des jumped out of his bed with such force that he pulled the sheets completely off the mattress. "What do you want from me?" he yelled. "Why are you doing this? I want answers!"

"Everything you need is in the presentation."

He started to pace as fear and anger take hold. The phone trembled in his hand as his nerves became frayed at this electronic menace now taunting him. "I don't understand what you mean."

"You will when you meet the end."

"What are you after?" he asked. Des's chest felt like something heavy had been dropped upon it. Rage flowed through him as the grip on his phone became so intense it could have only been loosened by the jaws of life.

"It's all in the presentation. Your knowledge of history should be your guide. You need to go where the bird protects and feeds its brood. The number is one, eight, five, six and honors the one who was a hero and then became a tyrant of tears."

"I don't understand what you mean. You're not giving me enough to go on."

"Don't worry, Desmond. I'm sure you'll succeed, and I'm certain you will find her in the proper condition."

"But I—"

The line went silent, creating an environment more terrifying than the expressionless voice. The phone dropped from his hand, landing with a definitive thud on the carpet of his hotel room.

Sitting down on the bed, he rubbed his hand across his mouth and chin in an action resembling someone trying to brush away a sin. Pondering the killer's remarks, he immediately recognized some differences. There was no time limit, which suggested more distance or difficulty. However, this was just a theory; there was no way to tell. And even though there were no constraints from a time standpoint, the sense of urgency, if not implied, was ever present. The other change was there were no restrictions placed on enlisting aid from others.

Yet his main inquiry still remained unanswered: Why was he the target of such a scheme? Nothing made sense. But the disdain, the pure hatred this individual had for him, was obvious.

His phone chimed again, causing him to jerk once more. Looking at the screen, he was relieved to see it was Amanda Hertzel.

"Hello."

"Des, it's Amanda. We were able to record the call."

"Were you able to trace it?"

"We only know that it came from the southern part of Manhattan. He hung up before we could get a more accurate trace."

"Damn!"

"Are you okay?"

"Yeah, I'm all right, just frustrated, that's all."

"Can you be at my office by seven?"

"Yes, I can make it."

"Good, because I could use your expertise. I'm great at profiling, but historical riddles are not my strong suit."

"I'll try and help."

"Thanks, see you in a little bit."

Des tossed his phone back onto the bed with the adrenaline still pumping through his veins. Looking around the room like a lost child, he decided to shower and get some quick nourishment. He did not know what to expect this time, but at least he would not be alone.

CHAPTER 21

IT WAS ABOUT 6:45 a.m. when Des was finally able to hail a cab after picking up a doughnut and coffee at the mom-and-pop pastry place located about a hundred yards from his hotel.

Since the call from the killer a little less than an hour earlier, his head had been swirling around the clues. There was nothing surfacing or even coming remotely close to matching any historical reference he knew of.

He believed the killer was in Manhattan, but there was no marker or location he was aware of in the city, which was made famous by a bird "protecting and feeding its brood." Like before, he tried to compartmentalize the clue. The first part was probably a general gathering place as the second was more specific in that it gave a number, possibly an address. But no matter how hard he tried to extract any new information, he came up empty.

He sat anxiously as the driver weaved in and out of traffic. He eyed the endless sea of buildings that enclosed every road they traversed. The movement of people was constant. He became lost in the hypnotic rhythm of the bouncing heads as they treaded across the sidewalks. Becoming engrossed in the trance, he allowed his mind to float over the killer's verbal conundrum.

Des loved puzzles. While he was in the military, his attraction to crosswords and mind benders became a source of good-natured teasing among his fellow soldiers. While his comrades hit local town bars, he was perfectly content remaining in the barracks with pencil and paper in hand. When he returned to college, his break times from studying were filled with reading books on historical mysteries and legends. It was this talent and interest in solving puzzles he was now hoping would aid his efforts. However, it also confused and worried him. The killer must know his life in great detail; otherwise, he wouldn't try to exploit those attributes.

As the cab continued its journey, he spied the large billboards with their various advertisements. They seemed to be plastered all over the city. An ad for a clothing retailer was prominently displayed on a sign hovering above an office building. Another peeked out from behind an old hotel, notifying the viewer of the latest Beyonce album release. A prominent one fell in line with the numerous ads from various realms of the fashion industry. It showed a porcelain-looking male model displaying an expression of abundant confidence and determination. He was wearing an expensive sweater and slacks with the simple tagline "Barney's, New York."

Name and location… location and name… location and marker… region and marker. Could he be referring to a large region and a specific marker?

He pondered the idea, at first thinking of a bordered region with a vast expanse, such as a park. Unfortunately, he did not know New York well enough to deal with the first part of the clue.

Maybe Amanda will have an idea. He pulled out his phone to call her. He did not wish to waste a second.

"Yes, Des."

"I think it may be a large tract of land, maybe a park, but I don't have any idea where. Is there a place where birds gather at… some historical place in New York?"

"The only place I know of is Central Park. But other than being the most famous park in the state, I don't know of any historical significance it holds. The only feeding of the birds there is when people feed the pigeons."

"That doesn't match. The clue talks about a bird feeding its young, not people feeding birds. I'll keep working on it. I should be there in a few minutes."

Only moments passed before the cab pulled up in front of the FBI building. Still bewildered, Des handed his money over to the driver and exited the car.

He was now having doubts about his original assumption, not to mention his ability to figure this one out. *Maybe it's something else within the city.* That was possible. But Amanda, whose job was to pay attention to details, was equally as lost, and she had lived in New York for several years.

As he walked up the stairs, he looked at the flagpole just to the right of the entrance. A gentle breeze from the west sent Old Glory swaying. Right below the red, white, and blue icon was the state flag of New York.

As he crested the top of the flight, he stopped in his tracks. Quickly, he moved back to where he had just passed. Staring at the waving symbols once more, a smile grew across his weary face. He had his answer.

CHAPTER 22

Savannah, Georgia

TWO DAYS HAD passed and not a word. Agonizing over what message was being sent, her incessant habit of pacing began anew. It was not like him. Even though many times she felt he withheld his feelings, to cut off all communication was out of the ordinary, to say the least.

Madison had been trying to keep her mind away from distressing assumptions, filling the hours with work or activities with Kelly. But as more time went by, the horrible thoughts mixed with the terrible memories of her failed marriage would not allow her to keep her worry at bay.

She could no longer sit idly by. No matter how she broke it down, the news would most likely be bleak. Either Des was in trouble or he had moved away emotionally.

Questions started to rise in her mind. She reflected on their past conversations. She rehashed situations where she had hinted at a deeper commitment. He would be evasive, and the reasons for that were never clear.

Did I push too hard? Have I been driving him away? Even though Kelly had rescinded her comments, the sting of them was still felt. Maybe Kelly's response was correct. Maybe she could see things more clearly through glasses not so tainted by emotion.

It tore into her and begged so many questions. Was knowing worse than not knowing? Was giving into her own insecurities of betrayal inevitable given the deep hurt of her past? Did it make her a hypocrite of the worst kind? Was she now becoming the antithesis of the very values she held most dear?

She had to make a decision. Yet now she realized it was a decision that would not only define their future but herself as well.

CHAPTER 23

New York, New York

HUSTLING DOWN THE hallway to the elevator, Des was anxious to present his revelation to Amanda. It would explain quite a bit, including the lack of a time demand, though the killer hinted that time was still a luxury they could not afford.

Arriving at the waiting room of her office, it was hard not to be impressed. What she had accomplished in such a short amount of time could only be described as astounding. Like the entrance of Keller's office, articles and accolades adorned the walls. Case after case that she had been instrumental in solving highlighted the young profiler's extraordinary talent. Along with the articles were photographs of perpetrators being taken into custody, victims being saved, and one that accompanied a *People* magazine article featuring Amanda and her mentor, Dr. Gregory Feller.

Drawing one's eye to the center of the wall was a display about the case that brought her to national prominence. It led to the recovery of several teenage girls who had been kidnapped and were almost certainly slated for death.

Her deft perceptions made her a celebrity in the criminal justice world. Her successes found her receiving awards from prominent businessmen and politicians and even the mayor of New York.

"You must be Mr. Cook," said her assistant. "Dr. Hertzel said to go into her office and have a seat. She'll be here shortly."

The fact she hadn't arrived made him feel increased pressure. He knew how critical time was in this scenario.

Upon entering, he immediately recognized the meticulousness of the individual whom he was now partnered. Unlike Agent Keller, where it appeared like someone had gone through his workspace with a leaf blower, Amanda's office was flawless. There was a small cherrywood end table in the corner, decorated with photographs of her graduation from high school and Yale. Next to the table was a quaint but tasteful bookshelf that held approximately a dozen texts on criminal behavior, one that she had coauthored with her mentor.

Her oak desk was large, but not ostentatious. Its front was a rich brown with corners inlaid with intricate carvings of vines that wound their way to the desk surface. On top of the desk sat a single stack of manila folders with case names fixed to the top right corner of each one. At the very top was a folder labeled "Legal Killer."

Behind her desk were her framed bachelor's, master's, and doctorate degrees she had received from Yale. To the right side of her accreditations was a small photograph of a gentlemen who appeared to be in his late forties.

"I see you noticed my files," a female voice said, entering the room.

"Is the 'Legal Killer' what you're calling this guy?" asked Des.

"Well, it's as good a name as any, considering the victim we found was an assistant US attorney."

"I guess that makes sense," he responded, shrugging his shoulders. "I think I know what we need to be looking for."

"You do?"

"The clue where the bird protects and feeds its brood is not a place, but a symbol of one. Really, it's an insignia."

"I'm not following you."

"The clue is segmented into two parts, one that gives an area or region and one giving the location of that region, like Albany, New York."

"So, you think we're looking for a city within a state?"

"Maybe, but I think it may be even more specific. Can I show you?" he asked, pointing to her computer.

"Of course."

Des sat behind the monitor and within moments brought up a website displaying state flags. He started scanning the site. "Animals have a long history of being used for state and national emblems. The most obvious would be the American bald eagle. But there are many states who identify with an animal to such an extent that they put them on their flag. For instance, California has the bear and… Louisiana has this."

Des stopped and clicked on the icon to enlarge the photo of the Louisiana state flag. Appearing boldly was the artwork showcasing a pelican hovering over its young to protect and feed them.

"I guess we're going to Louisiana," she said excitedly.

"We still have to figure out where in Louisiana," he responded, trying to rein in the attempt to become overconfident.

"We'll have time to figure that out on the plane ride there."

CHAPTER 24

AMANDA MADE A call to alert the necessary individuals that she would require a flight to Louisiana as soon as possible. From there, she hustled Des down the corridor to the elevator; they needed to get to JFK airport quickly.

As they exited the building through its main lobby, they were immediately greeted by the noise and commotion of a busy New York City morning. Crowds of people were walking in every conceivable direction. Yellow taxis swarmed the streets like bees hovering around a hive. The endless sound of honking horns blared and mixed with the harsh noise of jackhammers as work crews continued their never-ending street construction projects.

As the two turned toward the busy boulevard to hail a cab, Amanda suddenly froze and fell silent. Des, at first unaware of her change in demeanor, continued his futile efforts until he noticed her standing motionless. She was staring into the mass of humanity endlessly flowing past them.

"What is it? What's wrong?" he asked, looking in the same direction she was facing.

In a voice barely audible over the ceaseless noise, she responded, "It's Dr. Feller."

Dr. Gregory Feller had spent over twenty-five years as one of the nation's leading criminal profilers, with his last sixteen working for the FBI. Educated at the University of Michigan, he graduated near the top of his class. With the prestigious degree, it looked as if all avenues were open to him.

He first started working in partnership with other psychologists but eventually went into private practice. While it was very lucrative, the long hours of listening to people gripe about their lives wore thin on him.

Garden-variety manic-depressives and those suffering from mild anxiety disorders did nothing to stimulate or challenge his intellect. Thus, only five years into his practice, he reassigned all his patients, closed shop, and moved to Illinois to work exclusively for the Chicago Police Department.

His initial duties began with treating officers who were suffering from post-traumatic stress disorder. It was a common problem with cops who encountered Chicago's violent gang and drug culture. Yet his focus began to lean toward other fields of interest.

While in their employ, he soon became captivated by the practice and theories of Dr. Simon Bollier, a brilliant expert of the criminal mind and the Chicago PD's most exceptional profiler. Feller quickly became his protégé, grasping on to this burgeoning field of psychology. The timing was perfect, as police departments were becoming more and more interested in understanding the motivations of violent criminals and how it could possibly lead to their capture. Working alongside his idol and mentor, Feller became an expert on tracking clues and identifying the patterns of behavior and compulsions among some of the city's worst offenders. Together, the team cracked many of Chicago's toughest cases, including a string of murders on the borders of Lake Erie and a rapist who terrorized the South Side.

When Bollier retired, Feller became the head of the department, solving many more cases while increasing the brightness of the star he had become. After solving the case of the Lingerie Killer, a horrific individual who would dress his victims in expensive get-ups from Victoria's Secret before decapitating them, the FBI came calling.

Brought to Washington, DC, he served admirably before being transferred to New York as the heir apparent to the legendary Dr.

James Katney. Feller worked on a plethora of New York's most important cases as well as being called in for his expertise on other violent crimes throughout the nation. This included the recent bombing attack at Arlington National Cemetery.

At fifty-four years old, he was one of the most sought-after profilers in the country and was a mentor to several up-and-comers who were under his tutelage. One was a young woman by the name of Amanda Hertzel, whom he took under his wing and showcased her talents, successfully partnering with her on many cases.

When Dr. Katney announced he would retire at the end of the year, Feller seemed to be the obvious choice to take the helm of the prestigious department. It was the opportunity he had been waiting for.

All that would change with the terrifying kidnappings beginning in June of the previous year. Six teenage girls had been abducted in Queens and Stanton Island during the early days of summer. More of the same occurred in New Jersey as four more girls were taken. When the first kidnapping victim was found dead in a park in the Bronx, murdered after she had been sexually assaulted, the city was in upheaval. Not since the Son of Sam killings in the 1970s had such panic engulfed New York.

With Katney winding down his career, Feller took the lead. Yet his theories did not appear to be pointing in the right direction. After two more bodies were discovered, enormous pressure had begun to mount on the FBI to find the individual committing these horrific crimes. That's when Dr. Amanda Hertzel began to break away from her mentor's theories. Against the objections of Feller, the young profiler, only a few years removed from college, suggested a new tactic.

By looking at the physical makeup of the girls taken from a different angle as well as the killer's type of ritualistic behavior, she made entirely new determinations. She came to the conclusion that the sexual assaults were not the prime motivation, but rather a cover behavior of his other compulsions. This revelation led to a change in tactics. Three weeks later, a suspect was taken into custody just outside of Cooperstown, New York. Seven young girls were found, scared and filthy in the basement of his home, and a new star in the profiler department was born.

The press lauded over the miraculous recovery of the teenage girls and Dr. Hertzel's amazing ability to decipher the clues that led to their return to safety. The *New York Times* claimed her a "hero," and articles in *Newsweek* and *Time* magazines gave her accolades most FBI agents could only dream of. She even received a commendation from the governor.

When Katney finally stepped down, Amanda was offered the position, passing over Feller. Enraged and humiliated at losing his promised dream job to his young protégé, Feller was left with nothing to do but lick his wounds. Although the department requested him to stay on staff, his pride would not allow him to work underneath "a kid."

He stormed out of the FBI offices carrying a cardboard box with his belongings and a grudge that could fill Madison Square Gardens. His parting words, "You'll regret your decision," echoed in the halls, followed by the sound of his stomping feet as they charged out the lobby doors.

CHAPTER 25

SHE DIDN'T MOVE a muscle, transfixed by the mature man approaching her. Des, not realizing their past, immediately sensed the extreme tension. He knew there must be something of significance between them.

"Hello, Amanda," Feller said brazenly. "How are things at the office? There are rumblings that you're getting busy."

She stood in disbelief. The last time she saw him a year ago, he looked old and tired and was forty pounds overweight. That image stood in stark contrast to the man now standing before her.

He was lean and muscular. The shorts he wore showed legs displaying rippling definition. His arms looked as if they had been chiseled from granite. Feller's face, once pudgy, revealed pronounced cheekbones and an angular chin no longer softened by fat. The only past feature that remained in helping distinguish him from his current self were his eyes. The steely blue irises still had their recognizable stare, the one he always had when he was nearing the end of a chase.

"Dr. Feller, oh my god! You look fantastic! I hardly recognized you."

"Thank you, Amanda. I've been preparing to change the direction of my life. I needed to be fit in order to do so. Hello, Mr. Cook," he said, looking directly at Des.

"I'm sorry, do I know you?" Des asked confusedly.

"No, but I know you."

"I'm sorry, Des. This is Dr. Feller. He was assigned to the Arlington Case. We used to work together…"

"Before she took my job," Feller said curtly.

Amanda looked down, not wishing to experience his glare. "Dr. Feller, I didn't—"

"You don't need to apologize or explain. You did what anyone in your position would have." Then there was an awkward pause as Feller waited for Amanda to meet his eyes. "I have to go, Amanda. You be careful though. This new case you're on, I have a feeling… may get dangerous. You don't want to be the one held responsible if it slips through your fingers. Trust me, you don't want that kind of accountability."

Amanda was stunned. "How did you know about the case?"

"Oh, come now, Amanda, you know me better than that."

With that final quip, he smiled and gave Des a wink before proceeding down the sidewalk. Des turned to watch him. He walked with a confident, almost defiant gait, like a man who knew a valuable secret to which only he was privy.

He then turned to look at Amanda. She was visibly shaken. "Are you okay?"

She did not immediately respond, instead standing silently, still trying to comprehend the metamorphosis of the individual she once worked with side by side. His chilling warning was making her stomach do somersaults.

"Yeah, I'm okay," she said, shaking herself. "He just caught me off guard."

"What was that all about? He sounded very resentful."

"He was in line to get the job I was given. He quit in protest."

"What's he doing now?"

"I have no idea. But he's obviously still pissed," she said, staring in the direction that Feller had disappeared into the crowd. "We better get going. We have a plane waiting for us." She raised her hand, and within seconds a cab pulled up.

"How did you do that so fast? I couldn't get anyone to stop."

"After you," she said, holding the door open for him. "Ah… tourists, they never learn."

CHAPTER 26

Washington, DC

THE MESSAGE CAME in on Thursday at 11:13 a.m. It was official. Robert Cantwell's efforts had failed again. The bill that was supposed to fly through both Houses of Congress and land on the president's desk before he left office was in a stall. It was being held in committee, frozen in a sort of cryostasis, only to be brought back to life at the end of the president's term.

Cantwell had been playing an impossible game. He had been trying to convince the bill's author, Senator Wayman, that he had the president's ear. He tried to make him believe he could sway his boss into signing the bill into law, knowing full well the president would never do such a thing. That's exactly what he wanted to happen, get it through Congress and then let it die on the president's desk.

Yet Senator Wayman read the field too well. Cantwell's encouragement could not convince him to release the bill to a vote, making it a very real possibility that it could land on a friendlier field. If that happened, it would all come crashing down. The pressure had just increased a hundredfold. If he continued to fail in his attempts, the only way to save the situation was to win the election.

The odds were decent, it could be accomplished, but not without risk. It was supposed to remain contained. But men got greedy, and it had become a leviathan with its tentacles into everything.

The scrutiny would be great. Could it be covered? Were there enough fingers to plug the holes in the dam? *Maybe it could be dismantled.*

Yet how was that to be accomplished? How do you break something up that never really existed? How do you deconstruct a figment of someone's very creative imagination? It was one thing to take apart something of substance; it was another issue to grasp at the wind.

He walked to his window overlooking the city. Gray clouds had gathered over the capital, and the once-gleaming white monuments of Washington, DC, took on a gloomy and foreboding appearance. Traffic was in mass gridlock. It reminded him of what seemed to be the constant state of Congress, always in a rush and always going nowhere.

He knew a plan needed to be formulated. There was no way in hell he would take this risk without at least some kind of backup.

Once again, his phone rang. It was Adam. It was time to break the bad news. He took a deep breath and answered the call.

CHAPTER 27

New York, New York—en route to Louisiana

WHEN THEY ARRIVED at JFK airport, the experience was much different from what Des had encountered a few days earlier. No long waits, no time-consuming security measures or annoying gate attendants. Instead, they were hustled through the chaos to an awaiting jet. Their instructions were to meet field agents in Louisiana when they arrived. But after that, their path would be dictated by what they could decipher on the way there.

The small and sleek plane had twelve seats covered in gray leather. A red carpet ran down its aisle. Spacing was well thought out to allow room for passengers to work, including a built-in table. In the back was a mini-kitchen, with an industrial-style coffeemaker to make sure everyone had their caffeine infusion at the ready. The aircraft was designed to be a small office in the sky.

"We have a little over two hours to work on this," Amanda said as they boarded the plane.

She was in full investigative mode. Des could not help but notice how she emanated a kind of radiance when that intensity grasped her.

Sitting next to him, the flowery scent of her skin was just detectable as she opened her laptop and moved in closer. Her expression was hard to discern as it bounced from one of concentration to one of peace, as if she was most at home when attending to these types of tasks. Her auburn hair fell around her shoulders with a wisp dangling delicately on the left side of her forehead, coming to rest on her pink cheek.

"I know a lot about psychology, but I suck at history," she said, pushing the computer toward him.

"It honors the one who was a hero and then became a tyrant of tears," he said while opening up a search page.

"Where do we honor a tyrant, and why would we do that anyway?" she asked.

"I don't think that's the important word here. History is not so clearly divided. There's a lot of gray matter. 'Tyrant' is relative to perspective. I mean, look at General William Sherman. In the North, many revere him as a Civil War hero, while in my part of the country, he is seen as a war criminal. The killer is using their perspective here, which may be different to what you and I might think."

"So, what should we look at then?"

"I think significant events would create such an individual," he answered as he entered various search words into the computer.

"Well, what major events have happened in Louisiana?"

"There's a lot of them, most during the Civil War. But I think we may have to go further back."

Amanda gave him a look that was part perplexed and part admiration. Yet she was pleased she had been provided such a gifted intellect to challenge and aid her. It was not often she had the opportunity to work with someone who operated on such a high level of thinking.

"Further back?"

"Yes, one of the most famous battles that ever happened in the state was during the war of 1812, the Battle of New Orleans. The war had already been decided, but it made a hero of a newly appointed general by the name of Andrew Jackson," Des responded.

"But Jackson became president. He was obviously tough, but I don't know if you would call him a tyrant," she rebutted.

"That depends on whom you ask," he said, clicking on more information.

Andrew Jackson was one of the true paradoxes of American history and was an original in many ways. Unlike his predecessors, Jackson was not from the aristocratic class. He was born into poverty in 1767 in South Carolina, having no parental inheritance, which was so common among most colonial leaders.

At the tender age of thirteen, Jackson joined the mounted militia of his birth state during the Revolution. When he was caught by the British, his disdain and disobedience led to him receiving a slash from a sword on his forehead from an English officer. It left a scar, which he would carry along with his incessant drive and combativeness for the rest of his life.

Upon the death of his grandfather, Jackson did receive a small amount of money and used it to begin his study of law. At the age of twenty, he was admitted to the bar. His aggressive tactics gave him enough notoriety that he was appointed as a delegate to represent the state of Tennessee during their admission process to the Union.

Yet his greatest fame was the result of his efforts on the battlefield as he served as a major general, beginning in 1802. His controversial role and relationship with the Native Americans also commenced at that time, as well as many of his attacks, which were so devastating on their population. However, in an almost tragic irony, he actually adopted an orphaned Indian infant, caused by one of his military operations.

But his most notable military accolades were showered upon him in 1815 at New Orleans. Even though a peace treaty had been signed with Great Britain, officially ending the War of 1812, the news had yet to reach Jackson and his army, who were entrenched in the city. The ensuing slaughter of the British troops left a definitive stamp on the end of the war and saw Jackson rise to national prominence. This wave of popularity would attach itself to the war hero, eventually elevating him to the presidency.

"So, what about the word *tyrant* leads you to believe it may be Jackson?" Amanda questioned.

"I don't think the operative word is *tyrant*. I think it's *tears*," he answered.

"But all tyrants cause tears. Why would that be significant?"

"I'm not positive, but I have a hunch." Des was typing furiously, entering more key words into the search engines as he delved deeper into the riddle. "Jackson was known for his ability to gain control and wield the power of the executive office like no one before him. He seemed to battle everyone—political rivals, financial institutions, and even the Supreme Court. In one particular case, he defied a court order to not relocate the Cherokee population from Florida. Instead, he forced them out onto a horrific march across the country. Many died on the way. It became known as the Trail of Tears." Des turned the computer toward his investigative partner. It showed the famous painting by Saunders portraying the agony of the Cherokees being expelled from their homeland.

Amanda had a look of awe as she took in the moving artwork.

"It's got to be New Orleans," said Des.

"New Orleans is pretty big. Where do you suggest we start looking?"

Des pulled up a map of the famous city. Scanning it, he looked for anything honoring the former general and president.

"Are there any statues or memorials honoring Jackson that you know of?" she asked.

"Maybe, but that number he left us almost sounds like an address," he answered.

Des continued examining the map, looking for any famous landmarks that would indicate some connection. His eyes kept being drawn to the most famous area of New Orleans, the French Quarter. He looked at the labels marking the section. There was La Petit Theatre, Absinth House, the St. Louis Cathedral, and a plethora of other historic sites. Then he saw it. Just across from the French Market was an area simply known as Jackson Square.

He smiled and said, "I think I know where to go."

CHAPTER 28

Savannah, Georgia

HER GUILT WAS nearly consuming her, but the worry and fear had finally overwhelmed that feeling. She had to know what was going on. She could not sit idle any longer. She couldn't become a victim again. Madison needed some control in her life.

"Hi, this is Des. I'm sorry, I'm not here right now, but leave a message and I'll get back to you."

There was a pause. It was the final bridge to cross, and she felt awful that she had let it get this far.

The words first stuck in her throat, but then she forced them out. "Hi, baby, it's me… I… I know you said not to call… but… but I'm worried about us… you. Please let me know you're okay."

She put down the phone, disgusted with her Freudian slip. *He'll see right through that.*

Now, instead of worry, she was filled with regret, and for a moment, she hoped she would not receive a response. She realized that her insecurities might have jeopardized the whole situation in more ways than one.

CHAPTER 29

New Orleans, Louisiana

NEW ORLEANS HAS been one of the cultural centers of the South nearly since its founding. Covering just over 360 square miles, the historic metropolis has been a hub for trading and commerce for three centuries. With its access to the Mississippi River and the Gulf of Mexico, countless riches have been moved through her ports.

Founded in 1718 by Sien de Bienville, he made it the capital of the French territory of Louisiana. While it's most famous area today is known as the French Quarter, ironically, there is as much Spanish influence as French. This was the result of Louis XV gifting the region to his cousin King Charles III of Spain. Spanish rule, however, was short-lived, as a few years later it was reclaimed by France. The transfer was made just in time to broker a deal with Thomas Jefferson to acquire the entire Louisiana Territory for the new American nation.

But even with the changing of hands, New Orleans continued to be an area heavily touched by its European lineage. That flavor mixed with an array of different ethnicities and cultures from around the globe. People from Africa, the West Indies, and Latin America morphed the great city into the Mecca it has become for music, cuisine, art, and literature, which is now uniquely American.

As with a great number of historic cities, its most iconic parts only comprise a small section. While many envision New Orleans with its Antebellum South architecture and parading jazz bands as a throwback to times long since passed, it is truly a dynamic and modern enclave. Adopting all the most recent trappings, both good and bad, it resembles any of its major metropolitan contemporaries.

After being picked up at the airport by two FBI field agents, Des and Amanda were whisked away toward the historic part of the city. Within minutes, skyscrapers as well as the Superdome came into view. They were surrounded by a webbing of highway overpasses giving its many cars the appearance of ants descending into a hole. Water completely encased its borders with the Gulf of Mexico greeting the Mississippi River like a mother welcoming a child into her bosom. It was a vibrant scene, and from a distance, one could hardly tell of the damage wrought on this American jewel just a little over fifteen years earlier by Hurricane Katrina.

As they traversed from the highway into the heart of the business district, it was easy to observe the contrast between old and new. Office buildings featuring companies in computers, communications, and other of the latest technological fare were organized into blocks of cold exteriors and sterile atmospheres. It was very twenty-first century and maintained a stern impersonal demeanor.

This was in stark contrast to the touristy but soulful French Quarter. There, the feelings of the visitor would move away from heartless modern to a fantasia of mesmerizing and enriching colors, smells, and sounds.

Everything seemed to transport one to an eighteenth-century European village. Beautiful three-story structures cut the future off from the past. Their graceful lines, lacey iron grill work, and French-Spanish flair served as a reminder of a time when utilitarianism was not the only goal considered during construction.

Old homes, some built as far back as the early 1800s, lined many streets. Structures hearkening to the Antebellum South were still being used as their designers intended. In this tiny area only a mile long and a half mile wide, the old New Orleans came to life. It was a vestige to a period when the burgeoning mix of cultures, ethnicities, and religion changed this city into one unlike any in the world.

As they parked on the outskirts of Jackson Square, Des's and Amanda's senses were immediately overloaded upon exiting the car. Jazz music seemed to be coming from all directions. Delectable smells poured in from the French, Spanish, and Cajun restaurants dotting the streets. Although it looked more docile than Des had imagined, the famous Bourbon Street displayed definitive hints of its upcoming nightlife as laughter and cheer could be heard emanating from its massive collection of bars. Tourists walked up and down its pathway wearing cheap plastic beads and carrying gigantic insanely decorative cups filled with exotic alcoholic concoctions.

Des and Amanda continued to head east until they came to the location known as Jackson Square. Des stared at the space as all hints of America appeared to dissolve. This, of course, was the intention of its designer, Louis H. Pilie, who took inspiration from the Place des Vosges in his hometown of Paris while creating his vision.

Just about a city block in size, the popular gathering point in the French Quarter still maintains its original Parisian landscaping. The pedestrian space is bordered by three streets—Chartres, St. Peter, and St. Ann—and is a haven for artists, musicians, tourists, and city regulars.

Its most prominent feature is the extraordinarily beautiful St. Louis Cathedral, which has European, colonial, and Old South influences. Its three towering spires overlook a perfectly manicured green expanse showcasing the famous statue of Andrew Jackson for which the square is named.

They walked along the borders of the space. Artists tracing designs on easels sat in small areas displaying their work. Musicians playing everything from Mozart to Louis Armstrong filled the square with sound. People wandered through the area enjoying foods, taking photographs, shopping, and admiring the red brick décor of the mid-nineteenth-century buildings.

"I don't know what we're looking for," Amanda stated as she turned a full 360 degrees.

"The number has to be significant," he replied.

"Is it an address?"

"Possibly, I'm not sure."

"This is so out of my realm. The killers I investigate leave clues to their personalities and motives, not historical treasure hunts."

Des continued to move forward, trying to locate something that stuck out, but the whole place was historical. From the Cathedral to the Pontalba Buildings to the scenic path on top of the levee named the Moon Walk, everything was significant.

"So where do we go? What's the most historically important thing here?" Amanda asked dismayed.

Des continued eyeing the plaza, trying to take in the entire tapestry of his surroundings. *Historical… historical… What's important? Come on, Des, slow down. Don't try and take in everything at once.*

"Wait a minute, what if one-eight-five-six is not an address but a year?" he asked.

"Okay, what if it is?"

"Well, what are some of the historical years concerning this location?"

Amanda grabbed her phone and pulled up a webpage. "Okay, let's see here… It says that the square got its name in 1815 after the Battle of New Orleans. So obviously that doesn't work."

"Keep going."

"Alright… the landscaping was from 1951 and the Cathedral," she said, pointing in the direction of the enchanting structure, "was built in the mid-eighteenth century… so I guess that doesn't help much."

Des followed her finger toward the church before his gaze became fixated on what was before it. "Amanda… the statue… when was that put here?"

"Eighteen fifteen."

"The statue couldn't have been here in 1815. There wouldn't have been enough time to have it commissioned. The war had just ended."

Amanda scrolled through the webpage, searching the information. She then looked up and smiled, "Eighteen fifty-six."

"That has to be it!"

They ran to the statue and onto the dirt trail encircling the bronze edifice. The magnificent sculpture displayed a confident and determined General Andrew Jackson, valiantly posed on his rearing horse as he prepared for battle. It stood on a rectangular granite slab, adding height as well as grandeur to the impressive display. The background of the cathedral only enhanced its beauty and raw power.

They moved around it, searching it up and down, looking for any markings or symbols of significance. They walked separately and slowly, making them appear like they were in some ritualistic dance.

"Des, over here!"

He ran over to the other side. There at the base of the statue was a piece of metal stuck in the soil. Des jumped over the small railing and trimmed brush surrounding it.

He hovered over the object, hesitant at first to grab it. His fear of what it might be or contained clearly bothered him. He knelt down and peered closer, looking at it much like a golfer examining a putt.

"Oh, screw it!" he said, reaching for the metal square.

It extracted with little effort. He then looked down into the slight hole it had created. But in his examination, he noticed an envelope taped to the backside of the small piece of sheet metal. "There's something here."

He ripped it off and hopped back over the railing. When he turned the envelope over, he saw, in red ink, "Enemy." Pulling out its contents, he gingerly unfolded it.

> 54.6 miles northwest from this point
> 323 Jackson Street
> Large oak, end of north fence
> She's waiting.

They jogged back to where the other agents were awaiting them at the car.

"Call the local authorities and tell them to go here," Amanda said, pointing to the note. "Tell them not to touch anything. We've got to get there quickly."

As they sped off, the fantasy-like setting of the Old World vanished. Once again, Des was shaken by this very modern terror.

CHAPTER 30

LOUISIANA IS A state defined by water. Its topography is not only crossed and bordered by famous bodies like the Mississippi River and Lake Pontchartrain but is also home to hundreds of streams, bogs, and pools. The role the life-giving liquid has played has shaped not only the lives of its human inhabitants but also the abundant wildlife and foliage that make the state their home.

Des looked out the car window at the lush growth of trees and grasslands that were very different from what he was accustomed to seeing in Georgia. Small wells of water were everywhere, nourishing the unique plant life surrounding them. The humidity, which added to the variety of growth, seemed to emanate from the earth itself rather than from the air. It held a malt-thick atmosphere containing a heaviness surpassing that of Atlanta and New York. So much so the chief formative element of the environment did not appear to be liquid or solid, but gas. In this case, steam.

Yet while he appeared to be taking in his surroundings, he was actually seeing little of it. His mind lay on what was ahead and what the local authorities would find.

"Hey," Amanda said, patting his hand. "Des, I don't want to be the bearer of bad news, but you need to be prepared."

"What do you mean?"

"I don't want you to get your hopes up that we're going to find anything encouraging. It's most likely going to be a body."

"But he said 'she's waiting,'" Des stated, desperately wanting to believe otherwise.

"That doesn't mean much. I just don't want you to get your spirits crushed. He gave us a lot of time, and you add that to what he told you on the phone... It just doesn't look good."

Des turned back toward the window. He wanted to have hope that some innocent person would not pay for his earlier failure. But he knew Amanda spoke the truth. It was about fifteen minutes later when her phone rang.

"Hertzel... Yes... Okay... We should be there shortly. Make sure they don't disturb the scene until we get there... Alright." Amanda clicked her phone off, turned to Des, and shook her head.

He did not say anything, simply inhaling, and then returned to staring out the window. He felt Amanda grab his hand and squeeze in a sign of support. Des tried to remain calm, but internally, he was feeling a type of turmoil he had only experienced in Afghanistan.

They drove for about fifteen more minutes until they hit a rural area near the banks of the Amite River, about twenty miles southeast of Baton Rouge. Small homes and farms were spread out across the area divided by their fields of soybean, rice, and cotton. Many of these places seemed to have ignored the passing of years and, in some cases, centuries. Other than some modern farm equipment, there was little that would distinguish these places from fifty or even a hundred years ago.

Streets were desolate, most allowing for only two opposing lanes of traffic. Small ponds could be seen on both sides of the thoroughfares with the state tree, the bald cypress, soaking in their depths.

As they continued to journey deeper into the farm country, the roads narrowed and took on names of old Southern heroes, such as Stuart, Lee, and Davis. Though long since over, the Confederacy was still unabashedly showcased. Jackson Street looked no different from the previous ones. Its fields were marked with sugarcane and dairy cattle, and the houses occupying the land were usually simple one-story structures.

However, the tranquil scene was soon broken when three police cars appeared. As they pulled up, Amanda could tell by the looks on the local law enforcements' faces that this was not something they were used to.

"Hello, I'm Kyle Huffings," a mature officer said.

"Hi, I'm Dr. Amanda Hertzel with the FBI profiler's department in New York. This is Desmond Cook. He's assisting us."

"New York? You're quite a ways from home. I know why you're here, but why are you here from the Big Apple?"

"We have reason to believe the same individual is responsible for a recent murder in California."

The officer shook his head in confusion as he was trying to contemplate the situation. "Well, follow me," he said, motioning in the direction just behind him. "The body looks like it's been sitting here for a couple of days. My officers have been questioning some of the local residents, but no one seems to have seen anything."

They walked for about a hundred yards before they came upon a grove of trees. Two officers were standing next to the area waiting for them.

"We haven't had a coroner out here yet, but the cause of death is pretty clear," Officer Huffings said as he walked up and pulled aside the brush.

Des turned away in disgust.

The officer, noticing his reaction, said, "It's not easy to look at, I know… You going to be okay?"

Des just whispered, "Yes."

There on the ground lay a woman who appeared to be in her early forties. She had been stripped nude from the waist up, left only with a long blue skirt to cover the rest of her body. Her hands were bound above her head with chain, and she was blindfolded. Her skin was a ghostly white, which highlighted with great clarity the purple reddish-brown gash across her throat. The smell was ghastly as the flies had already started the decomposing process.

Amanda turned on her professional demeanor and pulled out her digital voice recorder to describe the scene. "Female… late thirties, early forties. Cause of death appears to be a knife wound across the throat, severing the jugular. No evident additional bruises or cuts. There are no cuts or signs of trauma to the hands… which may indicate there was no struggle. The victim is completely exposed from the waist up, blindfolded with a white cloth. Hands are bound above the head. Same layout as the victim in California. Although, this is preliminary," she said, lifting up the skirt, "but it doesn't appear the victim had been sexually assaulted…

"Officer, did you find any ID on the victim?"

"Strangely enough, we did. Her driver's license was left just a few feet away from the body. Hey, Nick, can you bring that ID here?" he said, waving.

The officer came over and handed Huffings a clear plastic baggy, which contained the license.

"It says here that her name is Emily Claude, from Baton Rouge, and she was forty-two years old. What's weird is that whoever did this seemed like they wanted us to know who she was."

"Why do you say that?" asked Amanda.

"We found the license in this baggy. They were trying to protect it from the elements," Officer Huffings replied.

"Hey, Amanda, look at this," Des said, motioning for her to join him.

When she arrived, he pointed to two brass plates beneath some brush about ten yards from the body. In each one was a small mound of grayish black soot.

"Same as California," Des said regretfully.

Officer Huffings walked over to investigate as well. "What the hell is that?" he exclaimed.

"I'm not sure, Officer Huffings, but I know we're dealing with the same perp," Amanda answered.

"You've seen this before?"

"Yeah, and unfortunately, I think we'll be seeing it again."

CHAPTER 31

En route to New York

THE PLANE RIDE back to New York was a sullen one. Although he had promised himself he would not focus on his own guilt in this woman's murder, Des was finding it a promise impossible to keep.

Amanda was sitting at the front of the small jet, talking on her phone with Keller, while Des continued to gaze at the darkening sky, feeling more helpless and confused than ever.

"Well, I got a little more info on our victim," Amanda said, walking back and sitting next to him. "Unfortunately, it's nothing significant. Let's see here… Okay… Ms. Claude was born in Norman, Oklahoma, and moved to Baton Rouge after graduating high school. She was married in 1998 to a Raymond Claude and divorced four years later… no children."

"Thank God," Des interjected.

"Yeah, really… She worked at various odd jobs and most recently worked as a seamstress in a local dress store."

"Sounds pretty mundane."

"You're right, it doesn't give us a whole lot to go on."

"Does she have any connection to the one in California?"

"Not that I can tell."

Des ran his hand through his hair in despair. "I don't get this. We have two victims with no relation to each other or to me, but this guy claims that I'm the enemy."

"I understand your frustration, but I still think we'll find a link."

"But what if we can't? What if he's just picking people at random? What then?"

"Most serial killers don't pick at random. There's always a pattern, a twisted logic they use."

"So, you think there's a connection?" he said with hope.

"Maybe… It could be a type of connection we haven't thought of."

"Like what?"

"He could be picking them based on a certain aspect of their bodies… or he could have a personal connection with both of these women, or…"

"Or what?"

"Or he could be picking them based on what they represent to him."

"But one was an attorney, the other a seamstress. What could they possibly represent?"

"That's my job to figure out."

"I'm glad I don't have your job."

"I'm glad I don't have yours," she responded emphatically.

Des smiled at the comment. At this point, he would much rather have her job than be in the position he was now. "So where do we go from here?"

"Keller will run all the evidence through the lab to see if anything new can be found. I'll continue to analyze both murders and see if I can find some pattern of behavior that would indicate his motives."

"And me?"

"You have the hardest job. You have to wait until he contacts you again."

"I was hoping that wouldn't be the case."

"I'm sorry, but it's almost an absolute certainty." Des looked down with her response. Noticing his disappointment, she added, "I'll only be a phone call away."

"Wait… where are you going?"

"I should have told you earlier, but I'm going to Connecticut for a couple of days. I'm giving a lecture at Yale… and I'm receiving an award."

"Do you have to go? You can't postpone it?"

"It will only be for a couple of days, and if you need any help, Keller will be there."

"But what if he contacts me again?"

"Look, Des, I'm a profiler. I will not stop analyzing. But until something new comes up, it's going to be mostly in other agents' hands."

He nodded in acknowledgment. What she said made perfect sense. "Congratulations."

"For what?"

"Your award."

"It's nothing really."

"I'm sure if it's an award from Yale, it's something… and I'm sure it's well deserved."

"Thank you," she said, smiling and squeezing his arm.

Des knew he was in capable hands with Agent Keller. The man was the head of the whole damn department. However, he never felt more alone than he did at that moment.

CHAPTER 32

Location unknown

THE KILLER TOOK satisfaction in the intricate art of torment. The pain being caused to The Enemy must be intense, so intense it was palpable. The Enemy was useless, failing in each attempt to prevent another calamity.

It wasn't as if the playing field was not level. Every item The Enemy could use or need was at their disposal. If there was any responsibility, it rested with his shortcomings, his ineptitudes, his failure to interpret the message being laid out for him.

Nonetheless, there was comfort to be felt in The Enemy's emotional roller coaster. The gamut of feelings had to be moving from fear to terror to sadness and self-loathing. Each of which the killer had experienced every day since the betrayal.

However, the emotion The Enemy needed to encounter the most was helplessness—the utter degradation one feels when the normal pattern of moments is interrupted and then goes astray. It's a feeling that can only be produced when tragedy goes unabated and every attempt to reverse the swing of the cosmos is in vain. If anything was accomplished, this had to be it.

CHAPTER 33

New York, New York

IT WAS IRONIC. For years, Des wanted to explore the great city of New York. It was America's London, America's Paris, its Rome, the heart of New World culture. He had always dreamed of coming to the metropolis, even flirting with the idea that he and Madison might go together. Yet now the favored destination had turned from a dream into a nightmare. Its expansiveness, at one time looking endless, felt as confined as a prison cell.

He wanted to get out of his hotel room. However, for the last couple of days, he would limit himself to short excursions, fearful the killer might contact him at a moment's notice. It left him in a constant state of preparing to walk on hot coals.

He agonized about everything. The killer's next challenge, another possible victim, Amanda's absence, and Madison's safety were pulling him in multiple directions toward a breaking point. He hated being at the mercy of the situation. Des had always taken solace that he had control of his own life. But current conditions had deteriorated to where he was in charge of nothing. He couldn't even call Madison to tell her of his worries and woes. His two greatest phobias, being useless and helpless, had merged into a noxious ball that was choking him.

All he could do was wait… for everything. The only thing he was certain of was this was nowhere near over. The only possibility for any relief was that Amanda would be home tomorrow. Hopefully, she would have some new insight into this madness.

The night felt like it was dragging on for an eternity. Lying on his small hotel bed, he flipped through the television channels in an attempt to lead his mind somewhere else. Anywhere would suffice as long as it did not include the predator.

As he continued to explore the wonders of cable television, he started to drift. The colors on the screen began to blur and run together, until he had lost track of his senses. The border between the real and surreal had been crossed.

"You have the answers," a voice whispered.

"I don't understand," Des responded.

"It's all in the presentation."

He could not see clearly. The vibrant colors he had viewed a moment earlier had dulled into a lifeless beige. All was desolate. There was nothing to break the ceaseless barrenness.

"I don't understand," he cried.

At first it was silent, but then the sound of distant gunfire began to creep in. It was followed by explosions, which began to increase in volume until it was nearly deafening.

He wanted to turn, but there was no need as the earth spun around him at blinding speed. It caused intense dizziness, and just when he thought he could no longer stand it, it stopped.

He tried to ascertain where he was. It looked to be some type of extensive hole. Soldiers were scurrying back and forth, firing their guns and mortars and then taking cover when the whiz of another incoming shell could be heard. Like a train, the realization plowed into him. He was back in that trench, back in Afghanistan.

"What's going on?" Des yelled. But he was ignored. Soldiers ran past him and even through him like he was some type of ghost.

"Grayson's been hit!" yelled a soldier. "See what you can do for him!"

Des was horrified. It was those words that had thrust him into his greatest terror and his greatest shame. He was in that same trench on the worst day of his life.

He saw a young soldier turn and run toward the injured man. The infantryman moved clumsily, tripping over a munitions pile on his way to aid his friend. Then, in a split moment, he glanced back. Des caught the boyish face. It was like looking into a mirror. But it was a mirror of the past, as he had just caught a glimpse of his younger self.

Des hustled in pursuit of his youthful incarnation. He wanted to warn him of the events about to occur. He wanted to keep himself from repeating the dreadful mistake. Des screamed, but his voice was drowned out by a shell striking the ground just yards away. When the dust began to clear, he could see his younger self covering the injured soldier's body with his own and then, in horror, lift up, only to realize the soldier he tried to protect, his friend, had died.

Des turned away, not wanting to relive his failure. But he was compelled to look again when he realized the bigger tragedy was about to happen.

"Don't do it!" he shrieked.

It was too late as his young naive self grabbed his rifle and fired over the ridge of the trench. Then all fell silent.

A trickle of dirt started to fall back into the trench. It was immediately followed by a small child's lifeless body crumpling into the pit. His past self bowed his head and leaned against the trench wall. Des felt the anguish all over again but now found he was in a position to console. He slowly approached; his desire to heal was nearly overwhelming. He reached out and placed his hand on the shoulder of his youth. He was rocking in what appeared to be convulsions of sobbing.

However, the sound being produced was not one of sorrow, but uncontrollable laughter. Des stepped back in confusion, not remembering this being his reaction. The laughter continued until the soldier slowly turned his head.

Des was repulsed and fell backward. The face glaring at him was not his own but William Hatton's.

"What is this? You weren't there. How could you be here?" Des cried.

"It's all in the presentation," he responded as he continued to laugh.

Des was mortified. He looked down at where the child had fallen, but all that remained was a pile of soot.

Then Hatton raised his rifle and pointed it directly at him. His laughter's volume had increased to painful decibels. Then he pulled the trigger.

The phone rang and Des rocketed up out of his bed, panting like he had been sprinting. He was disoriented and emotionally drained. It took a few more rings before he finally grabbed his phone.

"Hello."

"Hello, Desmond," the computer voice responded. "Sorry to disturb you so early."

"Early? What time is it?"

"Seven a.m."

"What do you want?"

"I want to help you."

"How the hell do you propose to do that? You think it helps me when you kill innocent people?"

"They were hardly innocent. But if you think so, that is fine."

"What do you want from me?"

"I want you to try and prevent another so-called innocent from meeting the same fate as Ms. Claude."

"I'm listening."

"In the place of the brilliant sapling, the death of heroes on the day marking its birth… saw a century pass before the death of its meaning in the same place. It's the second step. You have twenty-four hours."

The phone went dead, and Des tossed it to the side in anger. He knew in a few seconds Keller would call and he would be summoned to meet him and Amanda at their office.

CHAPTER 34

KELLER SAT QUIETLY behind his desk, while Amanda stood just to Des's side, only leaving her post to pace across the office.

"I went over the evidence several times when I was gone. This guy is definitely not going to be delayed for any reason. Deadlines are obviously of prime importance to him. I think he wants to give us just enough time to fail," Amanda said as she read the text from the earlier phone call. "You know… he's sending a message in two parts."

"What two parts?" Keller asked.

"The way these two women were presented is significant, as well as the way they were murdered. They were killed quickly and displayed not for his purposes, but for ours."

"So, you're saying this defines something."

"Yes, but he's not defining for himself."

"I don't follow you."

"Most serial killers have compulsions that lead to the very specific ways in which they kill and then present. Those compulsions are usually dictated by their own inner demons, and often times what makes perfect sense to them makes little sense to the sane individual."

"Okay, but…"

"But this one is different. He's not killing because he is falling prey to his compulsions. He's using his methods to allow us to fall prey to ours."

"So, you think he's exploiting us?" Keller asked.

"Not only that, but he gets his kicks, his fulfillment, not by satisfying his needs, but ours… our insatiable need for the hunt."

"And the second part?"

"Something in your background, Des, pissed this guy off," she answered.

"But the only thing significant that I've been a part of is what happened at Arlington… and that was never released to the public," Des stated.

"We can't concentrate on that now, Amanda. We have less than twenty-four hours," Keller interjected, trying to redirect them.

"I've got to have more time to figure this out," Des pleaded.

"We don't have more time, Des. We've got to get this done now."

Des's shoulders were tense, and his brow furrowed. He began repeatedly running his hand through his hair. A strand defied the motion, falling gently across his forehead. "Okay, he said in the place of the brilliant sapling. What places near here are known for brightly colored foliage?"

"There are a lot of places with bright foliage. Hell, the entire New England area is known for that in the fall. It could be anywhere," answered Keller.

Des pondered this reality. He was right. Up and down the northeast, tourists come from all over the country to take in the magnificent fall colors of the trees that form a canopy of beauty over the terrain. "Wait, you said fall."

"Yeah, the trees change in the fall… so?" Keller responded.

"It's not fall."

"Yes, I realize that," Keller said sarcastically.

"We're looking at the wrong connotation of the word." Realizing they were not following him, he continued. "Look… we recognized there's a definition for the word *sapling*. It means a young tree."

"Okay… that's the correct definition," Amanda added.

"Well, maybe he's telling us to look at the different definitions of the word *brilliant*. We're assuming it means brightly colored. What if it's referring to intelligence?"

"A smart tree?" Keller questioned with doubt.

"Think about it," Des encouraged. "He's leading us to a place… a location. The word *sapling* is singular. I think he's giving us a clue to its name."

"So, you're saying, he's spelling it out for us?"

"Yes… exactly. Amanda, what's another name or word for intelligence?"

"Sharp… smart… genius," she said, throwing out guesses.

"Those don't sound like any places I know," said Keller.

Des was then struck by another possibility, but the word he was looking for eluded him. "Agent Keller… what are those people called who work for the CIA who just think up strategies? They're not spies. They just come up with ideas."

"Brains… why?"

"That's the word I was looking for!"

"What are you talking about?" asked Amanda.

"There's a town in Massachusetts called Braintree. But much of it was incorporated into other townships."

Des ran over to Keller's computer and started typing. He entered the keywords "Braintree, Mass" and then sent it into the search engine. Immediately the search results displayed.

"Quincy—Braintree, Mass."

Clicking on the link, he was able to bring up the latest news on Braintree, as well as its adjoining township of Quincy. Upon reading the first few words, Des was confident he had found the correct answer.

Braintree was a very early settlement of the region and served as the birthplace of two American presidents, John Adams and his son John Quincy Adams. Contrary to popular belief, the town did not derive its other name from the second Adams, but rather from the Revolutionary War colonel John Quincy.

"Okay, but what did he mean when he said 'the death of heroes on the day marking its birth'?" Amanda asked.

Des knew the story well. There were two founding fathers of the nation who passed away on the same day. As if fated by the heavens, John Adams and Thomas Jefferson both died on the fiftieth anniversary of the birth of the American nation, July 4, 1826. While on his deathbed, Adams recognized the significance of the moment and their places in history. His last words were "Jefferson still survives!" not realizing that his colleague and good friend had succumbed to a prolonged illness just hours before.

Des turned the computer screen toward Amanda. "Look at the date he died!" he stated, smiling, his face showing an expression of accomplishment.

"He said a century would pass before we saw the death of its meaning… death of the meaning of what?" Keller inquired.

"Well, obviously a century later would be a hundred years. We need to find out about important events that happened in Braintree somewhere in the 1920s," Des said.

"That still doesn't answer my question. What death of what meaning are we looking for?"

"I'm not sure, but there should be a link to Jefferson and Adams. I guess we have to ask what or who they were."

"Well, they were both presidents, that could be significant," Amanda stated.

"Yes, that's true, but I'm not sure the presidency means only one thing since they often come from different political viewpoints. Although he could be talking about the death of what the office is supposed to do," Des responded.

"What else do we know about Jefferson and Adams?" asked Keller.

"Jefferson believed in a limited federal government. He focused on states' rights. But from what I know about Adams, he was a moderate. He certainly did not go the way of Alexander Hamilton, who was a true federalist."

Amanda's eyes lit up. Placing her hand on Des's shoulder, she said, "I think that may be important."

He could not help but notice how beautiful she appeared when she was struck with a revelation. Her reddish-brown hair cascaded down her shoulders. Her hazel-colored eyes opened to the size of saucers, and a flushness entered her cheeks. "This may be a dislike of our government or one facet of it."

"Well, there are three branches of government—the executive or president, the Congress, and the Supreme Court," stated Des.

"So, what are the president's main responsibilities?"

"Well, are we talking as described by the Constitution or by tradition?"

"I don't think our killer is someone who deals in ambiguities. I would say as defined by the Constitution."

"According to our design, the executive branch is supposed to enforce the laws."

"With the Congress left to write them and the Supreme Court to determine their constitutionality."

"So, failure to enforce those laws could indicate the death of its meaning," said Keller.

"Okay, we may be on to something. But what happened in Braintree a hundred years later that made this guy so angry?" asked Amanda.

"I don't know, but you two will have to figure it out on the way there."

CHAPTER 35

En route to Boston, Massachusetts

IT WAS A travesty, one of the most shameful chapters in American legal history. In 1920, in Braintree, Massachusetts, an armed robbery of a shoe factory resulted in the murder of two of its employees. Shortly afterward, Italian immigrants Nicola Sacco and Bartolomeo Vanzetti were arrested for the crime and put on trial the following year. But what started out as a standard criminal trial soon degenerated into negative ethnic stereotypes and primal fears relating to foreigners and their political beliefs.

Both Sacco and Vanzetti were avowed anarchist at a time when political unrest in Europe was causing great concern and heightened nerves in the United States. For years, immigrants had been flooding into America from Europe, mainly through Ellis Island in New York. However, the migration patterns changed, morphing from mostly Western European Protestants to a constant influx of Eastern European Jews, Southern European Catholics, and Russian Orthodox. This sudden alteration in the immigrant cultural and ethnic makeup caused many citizens to become suspicious of these "outsiders."

Although the courts are supposed to keep biases at bay, the one handling this case did a miserable job. Evidence was ignored. Illegal and prejudicial pretrial statements by the jury foreman were allowed.

Even a confession by an alleged participant in the robbery vindicating the defendants was thrown out.

The trial garnered national and international attention as people across the globe protested the shoddy proceedings. In the end, however, they failed. Sacco and Vanzetti were both executed via the electric chair on August 23, 1927. It was one hundred and one years after the deaths of Thomas Jefferson and John Adams.

As they flew to Boston, Des and Amanda were entrenched in the story of the infamous case. Yet they were even more fascinated as to why the killer had chosen it as his latest clue.

"Okay, I understand the Sacco and Vanzetti trial was a gross miscarriage of justice, but why did he use it this way?" Des asked.

"Well, I think if you combine it with the first task he sent you on, there's a definite dislike of government," Amanda stated.

"How did you come up with that?"

"Think about it. In the first set of instructions he gave you, he referred to Alexander Hamilton as the 'problem' and the source of our 'misguidedness.' He also referred to Andrew Jackson as a 'tyrant.' As you stated, Hamilton was pro federal government and Jackson wielded unprecedented executive authority. Now you have this farce of a trial."

"Okay, so this is just some antigovernment nut?" asked Des.

"Possibly, but I think there's more to it than that. I think it mostly has to do with the executive office. In the Sacco and Vanzetti case, the Massachusetts Supreme Court failed to grant a new trial for these two men. Who would be the only one left to pardon them?"

"The federal branch… possibly the president."

"Exactly."

"But that still does not tell us where we need to go in Braintree," Des lamented.

"You're right, it doesn't."

Des turned his attention to the clue once more. Reading it and rereading it, he tried to gain new insight. *In the place of the brilliant sapling, the death of heroes on the day making its birth, saw a century pass before the death of its meaning in the same place. It's the second step.*

"I doubt the shoe factory where the crime took place still exists," said Amanda.

"And there's no indication he's referring to a certain place directly that I can see."

"There has to be something here," she said, staring at the clue.

Des looked out the plane window. He eyed the puffy cotton-like clouds floating beneath them, trying to concentrate. He started to become lost in the expansive blueness. It looked as if it stretched on forever. The perspective was so different from the ground, when often a blanket of gray would cut one off from the sky. It seemed to restrict the possibilities of what once was… *once was… once was.*

"Amanda, could you look and see where the Sacco and Vanzetti trial was held?"

"Why would that matter?"

"We're focusing on the crime itself. But where would all these transgressions of the government take place?"

"Ah… the courtroom." Amanda typed quickly. "It says the first trial for Vanzetti was in Bridgewater."

"That won't work."

"Why not?"

"Because only Vanzetti was tried there. Where was the first place they were tried together?"

"Hold on… it's… Norfolk County Courthouse in Dedham. But how does that help us? It's not in Braintree."

"You have to remember that when Braintree was originally founded, it encompassed much more land than it does now. Many towns on the East Coast are smaller now than they once were."

"We've got to get to Dedham."

As the plane made its descent into Boston, Des, although distracted, was excited to be in the historic city. Home to such important places and events as Plymouth Rock, Concorde and Lexington, Bunker Hill, and the Boston Tea Party, it held a special place in the American experience. Its independent nature led to this part of the country being labeled the "cradle of liberty." This influence still holds strong today, with political groups like the Tea

Party using part of the state's history as its name to signify those values in modern times.

Like most of the Eastern Seaboard, everything along the perimeter of the state is also fairly close together. Dedham was less than twenty miles outside the center of Boston. Boston, and the area that surrounds it, seemed to be a place without zoning laws. In many areas of the South, distance and less population density separated historic places from much of the modern world. In the Boston region, this is not the case. Colonial period buildings are often dwarfed by modern high-rises, which are nestled upright against them. The old is interspersed with the new.

Bostonians cling to their history with tremendous pride in everything from politics to sports. They often choose to mix the past with the present. Even their beloved Red Sox play in the second-oldest stadium in the Major Leagues, when other franchises have chosen more modern amenities.

Taking Highway 1 south, they passed the towns of Brookline and Dorchester before arriving in Dedham about fifteen minutes later. The town looked to be a mixture of colonial and Greek-style architecture with quaint homes and picturesque streets lined with majestic trees.

It only took a few moments before they located the courthouse. It was not a large structure, but attractive and charming. It featured a colonial-style base with two stories and six windows on either side of its center. A Greek-style entrance with four modest columns held up the triangular roof. Rising above it all at its center was a white colonnaded dome, crested with a point where the American flag was flown. It was dignified and rustic at the same time.

After parking, Des and Amanda exited the car and walked to the front of the building. The structure was framed by large trees towering over its manicured lawn.

"Where do we start to look?" asked Amanda. "It said something about it being the second step, but he never mentioned a first step."

"Yeah, that's a problem." Then Des realized what they were doing. "You know, we're making the same mistake we made before.

We're only looking at one connotation of the word. He said it's the second step, so…"

"The courthouse steps!"

They jogged over to the two levels of steps leading to the entrance. Simultaneously, they walked the top of the second stair, searching for anything that would catch their eye. But they saw nothing. Des hopped down and moved back, trying to see if he could locate anything underneath. It didn't take long before he saw a small square piece of sheet metal attached beneath the step, which looked just like what they had found at Jackson Square.

"Amanda," he said, pointing to the object.

She went to the place he indicated and knelt down. Smiling when she saw it, she gave Des an excited look. He gave her a slight nod of encouragement in return before she pried it loose. Like before, an envelope was attached to its other side with the word "Enemy" emblazoned on it. Des moved quickly to her to see the message.

His heart jumped into his throat as Amanda pulled out the paper from the envelope and began to unfold it:

> Your knowledge of history should be your guide.
> Your prize awaits at the end of the journey.
> A realization will be reached.
> Just northeast of Springfield in Southbridge.
> The Farm of Bannister.
> Two hundred yards west of driveway.
> I made the calculations.

"I'll contact the local police," she said, checking her watch. "We still have enough time. It's about thirty minutes away."

CHAPTER 36

THE CONNECTICUT LOWLAND is a valley stretching across the middle of Massachusetts and continues through its neighboring New England states. Home to generations of families, its fertile fields have served as one of the state's agricultural centers for nearly two centuries.

Des and Amanda drove the roads transecting its green pastures. As they began to near their destination, Des's stress level was nearing a boiling point. They had not heard back from the local police and were already pulling up to the Bannister farm by the time Amanda's phone rang. The scene mirrored what they had encountered in Louisiana.

"Dr. Hertzel?" a young officer said as she and Des approached. "We found what you were looking for. Sorry it took us a while. The body was hidden under quite a bit of brush."

"Body?" Des said.

"Yes, I'm afraid so."

"But we met the deadline."

The officer led them over to the area. It was being watched by one other officer. Hardly a difficult duty, as the only people aware of what was going on was Mr. Bannister and his wife.

When they reached the deep grass and brush, the officer moved slightly ahead to pull away the obstructing growth. Imbedded in the mud was the body of a female who looked to be in her late fifties.

Like the two previous bodies, the victim was nude from the waist up, hands bound above her head with chain, and she was blindfolded with a large tear across her throat.

"We have an ID on the victim," said the officer. "Her name is Linda Richardson. She lived in Boston. She was a retired probation officer for the Feds."

"I don't understand," Des said to Amanda. "We got here before the deadline. Why did he kill her?"

"To show he's in control, not us," she responded. She then took out her voice recorder and began to document the scene.

"How long has she been here?" asked Des.

"At least thirty-six hours," answered the officer.

"Thirty-six hours? But that would mean he killed her before he even contacted me. How can you tell it has been that long?"

"From that," he said, pointing to two brass dishes filled with a grayish black water. "It rained about a day and a half ago. That's why those things got water in them."

Des walked over to the dishes and touched one of its edges. The tip of his finger was turned black by the wet soot, which had become sludge.

There was no chance to save this one. The deadline was a ploy, nothing more than a way to rush him to another murder scene. Des dropped his head in despair. He knew if this was the way the killer played the game, he didn't stand a chance.

As they flew back to New York, Des could already feel the situation spiraling out of control. Amanda had formulated a theory of who the individual might be, but with so little to go on, it remained just a theory. The killer definitely had the upper hand.

The plane began its approach into New York, and as it dropped in altitude, Des felt like he was descending into the pit of hell. He understood he had only one job to do, and that was to wait to be contacted again. It was a job that he didn't want and couldn't quit.

CHAPTER 37

Location unknown

IT WAS ALWAYS the same—rage followed by peace, sadness followed by contentment. The eyes were the telltale sign, with the glare that could burn a whole in its receiver.

The killer woke up in a cold sweat. It seemed like such a long time ago that their dreams had been dashed. Yet the nightmares were always the same, a betrayal beyond anything experienced.

Walking slowly to the bathroom and leaning over the sink, there was hope for relief by splashing water onto the face. But it did not hold back the nausea. Even though it needed to be done, it never came naturally. Feeling increasingly sick, it was only a sidestep to the toilet to vomit up the illness of the latest kill. It was nothing personal, but it was necessary.

They had to be taken. It was the only way to get their attention. They needed to see the fallacy of their decisions. The whole system was failing, and in the process, it left everything in ruins. It punished those who tried to achieve, who put those around them before themselves.

After wiping away the expelled bile; it was a short reach to the shower to turn the knob. Piping-hot fluid rained down, filling the air with vapor, shrouding the image in the mirror.

The water was nearly scalding, and when it hit the body, there was pain before relaxation. It poured over the killer's toned back as the muscles began to release the tension of their latest savagery. The hands began to wander over the body, across the shoulders, down the chest, below the waist and between the legs.

Reaping the pleasure of this finely honed machine, the expression was one of ecstasy at exploring this creation. It had been tuned, designed, and dedicated to the purpose. The physical requirements of the task demanded such an artwork. The body as a tool needed to change, and once the metamorphosis was complete, it had to be maintained.

Now, sharpness had to be reinstituted; awareness needed to be heightened. Turning off the hot water, leaving only the cold; the temperature soon deteriorated to icy depths. Muscles once relaxed became taut with the shock of the frigid liquid. It was necessary. There was a need to be prepared, to always be one step ahead of their adversary.

After patting the livened body dry, the towel fell to the floor, allowing the bare skin to feel its environment. There was a freedom in nudity, a pureness that washed away all evils.

Dropping to the floor, the exercises commenced. Pushups filled the chest with blood. With each set, the killer admired the sculpted arms the effort created. Crunches made the torso defined, and the hips showcase their power, while lunges formed legs of immense strength.

The rhythmic breathing as the body expelled carbon dioxide and then took in enriching oxygen brought on a hypnotic state until the rapture was too much, causing a surrender to this orgy of exercise.

Taking in a few more nourishing breaths, the creation lifted off the floor and walked to the mirror. The blood-filled cavities turned the complexion pink, a precursor to the fury flowing from within.

Once again, the palms ran over the body, caressing the skin as if to praise what this object had become. Only one thing remained.

The fingertips touched the area just above the nipple. This is where it would go, and then the Leader of the Enemy would understand their betrayal.

CHAPTER 38

New York, New York

AFTER RETURNING TO New York, Des was more dismayed than ever. With Amanda out of town the last couple of days to share notes on the killer with a fellow profiler, he also felt more alone. *Thank God she is back tonight.*

New York, with its endless buildings and teeming masses, at times, could make one feel isolated beyond description. He had no plan of action; there were no more messages or instructions to deconstruct. All he could do was wait.

Since departing Massachusetts, he had tried to pass the time. Taking walks through Central Park, going to various museums, and even walking the streets of Greenwich Village were activities he indulged in to relieve his mind. Though he tried to take some pleasure in the wondrous city, little was derived from these excursions. He knew he was only a phone call or letter away from another frantic chase and another dead body.

As he sat in his hotel room, the stillness, the inactivity, the useless idling, was almost as torturous as the innocuous clues and excruciating time limits. He felt helpless and longed for comfort, some soothing to regain his balance.

His thoughts started to wander to Madison. He wanted to tell her everything; he wanted to confide in the person he felt closest to.

But he was forced to keep up the wall of silence, being threatened by the killer and sworn to secrecy by the FBI until this episode came to a conclusion. However, that possibility, as things stood now, was a long way from happening. This realization only made him fall further into despair.

He now contemplated whether his caution in their relationship would leave things left unsaid that needed to be confirmed. With this psychopath set on his mental torture and ultimate demise, would he ever get the chance?

He could feel her embrace, her soft lips and skin pressed against his. Des could see her deep brown eyes gazing at him as they made love. How he wished he could get lost in those eyes again.

It shook him out of his daydream. A voice calling from the other side of his door, followed by a polite knock.

"Mr. Cook, I have something for you," the young bellboy said.

Des walked tentatively to the door. Peering through the peephole, he could see the babyface kid standing astutely. Opening the door, he was greeted with a tepid smile.

"Mr. Cook, a gentleman asked me to deliver this to you," he said, handing Des an envelope.

"How long ago?" Des asked urgently.

"Oh, I guess about ten or fifteen minutes."

"Do you remember what he looked like?" he asked, hoping a description of the killer might be had.

The kid looked up trying to access his memory. "Uh… he's white. I think he was in his forties or fifties. He had brown hair… and a regular build."

Des disappointedly handed the bellboy a tip. The kid had just described someone who fit the description of about a million men in the city.

He hated this moment. It was going to be another delve into panic, and at the end of the journey, another corpse. Turning the envelope, he was struck by an immediate difference. There was no blood-red ink, no threatening reference, just a simple, clear, and polite address of "Mr. Desmond Cook."

Perplexed, Des opened the envelope and removed the letter. Taking one last breath, he unfolded the paper. It was a typewritten note that looked to be as dangerous as the envelope it came in.

Mr. Cook,

Forgive me for contacting you in this manner. I think I may be of some service in the predicament you now find yourself as I have some comprehension of what is motivating the maniac you are now tracking. I'm sorry that I cannot reveal my identity.

I realize these unusual circumstances must cause you reason for concern or mistrust. Yet, the unorthodox approach I am taking is for your protection as well as mine.

I strongly urge you to put away that mistrust as you will need the information I can provide. Please meet me tomorrow at 11:00 a.m. near Lafayette Statue in Union Square. Come alone and tell no one. Our lives depend on discretion, and nobody else can be trusted!

Go Orange!

Des was stunned. His first inclination was it must be an attempted trick by the killer. But that thought was quickly abated. The meeting would take place in a very public area. If the killer wanted to take him down, he chose one of the busiest places in the country to do so. It was not a likely scenario. Still, he had no way of identifying who this individual was as they left no personal description… *And what the hell does "Go Orange" mean?*

His next urge was to contact Agent Keller. But the warnings in the note squashed that desire as well. But who could this be, and how did they know of his involvement? There had been no press releases, nor had he or the FBI told anyone who would distribute such information. Yet obviously this individual had some reliable sources.

Des walked to the bed and sat down, locked in his own mental debate at which option to take. Slowing his thinking process down, he calmed himself to come to some logicality. Then, as if struck by a blow, he came to a revelation.

Anger swelled inside him. Since this whole thing initiated, he had been at someone else's whim, chasing a rabbit who taunted him before ducking into holes, only to resurface and start the process anew.

No more! He was not going to just sit and wait to be led around by the nose. He was going on the offensive. *If this is some kind of trick, so be it! The game changes now!*

C H A P T E R   3 9

New York, New York

PRESIDENT AND CEO of Trans International Bank, James Gertig, prepared to close shop for the night. The slightly pudgy and balding man was ready for some pleasure. Over the last five months, he had been dealing with the latest allegations thrown at him by the US Attorney's Office. It didn't frighten him in the least. He knew he held the cards, and it was all for show.

His large office in Manhattan overlooked the inspiring panorama of the city, with its canopy of lights laid at his feet. It was breathtaking, power inducing, and gave him the feeling of a coronation.

His massive oak desk stood at the center of the back wall like a throne. An elegant black leather couch cozied up to a coffee table glistening with the reflections of its inlaid crystal. Across from the table was an equally impressive oak bar with a polished black granite countertop. The shelves behind it were adorned with thousand-dollar bottles of cognac and single-malt scotch. The amber color of the liquids was backlit by a soft white illumination, which made them glow.

Plaques commemorating accomplishments coupled with photos of him glad-handing Washington heavyweights covered the walls. It was truly a space to make guests gawk and at the same time feel humbled in his presence.

Standing by his desk, he glanced down at the file filled to the brim with details of his client's financial condition. He kept the information on a thumb drive as well, but his superstitions always had him keep a hard copy locked in his office wall safe.

As he packed his briefcase, he glanced at the files once more, adoringly, like a parent doting over their child. While putting them in the safe, a deep sense of accomplishment came over him. The bank's as well as his profits would grow to astronomical levels.

For years Trans International had been generating money, handling billions of dollars for clients in businesses considered less than savory. Fronts for terrorist groups and organized crime and drug cartels were some of their largest clients. Those entities had been using the institution not only to handle their profits but also to add an appearance of legitimacy to their operations.

Accusations did fly. But they were impossible to prove, leaving the US Attorney's Office to lead only halfhearted litigation. The most they could muster were slight rumblings amounting to nothing more than a disgruntled elder scolding a youth.

Yes, the bank during the previous administration was indicted on breaking federal law. Yet it went away with some promises to be good and a fine equal to a slap on the wrist. Once it was over, the bank was re-engaged in its previous activities. Gertig and his associates learned the lesson that they would never pay for sidestepping the law.

There was public outcry, and once again Gertig and other high-ranking bank executives were dragged before a Senate Judiciary Committee. Volumes of evidence was presented against them. It was like reading a manual on how to break federal statutes. Billions of dollars funneled to Iranian terrorists and Mexican drug lords was documented. Testimony from past clients and even former employees who admitted to being instructed to look the other way was also shown.

However, in the end, in spite of the evidence, this bank, who helped fund some of the world's greatest criminals, was not held accountable. The US Attorney's Office put on a big show but put in little effort. The result was not a single high-level employee, board member, or administrator spent a day in jail. Another fine was levied, and the Department of Justice closed the books. It was business as usual.

Some were shocked and others infuriated by the lackluster performance put forth by the Department of Justice. The official statement from the US Attorney's Office was that Trans International Bank was too vital to the world's economy, dissuading them from handing out harsher penalties. Their stance was if they did take such punitive action, they would in essence be punishing the innocent.

The terrible storm the media had predicted for Gertig and his associates turned out to be a slight drizzle. The message sent to the nation was that money and power equaled no accountability.

Turning out the lights of his office, Gertig said good night to his secretary and headed to his awaiting limousine, which would whisk him to the airport. The driver opened the door and tipped their cap as Gertig knelt into the back cabin of the luxurious automobile.

Once the door closed behind him, he put his briefcase down and reached for a glass and the fifteen-year-old scotch placed there per his request. As the warmth from the drink gradually matriculated down his throat, a calmness and joy set in.

This was going to be a celebratory time. The record profits the corporation had enjoyed had resulted in a sizable cash bonus for him. He was now only a few hours flight away from joining his mistress in the Bahamas for five days of sun, surf, and his Latin goddess's legs wrapped around his waist.

"Just another business trip to Tokyo," he told his wife before leaving his home that morning. He put on a fine display, as he convinced her of his exasperation of having to leave her again.

Opening his briefcase, he pulled out the day's copy of the *Wall Street Journal*. It had been so busy he didn't have a chance to perform his ritual. However, while he perused the articles, he was finding it difficult to concentrate. The upcoming five days were distracting him as all he could do was picture the beautiful curves of his mistress's nude form. *I may not get out of bed all week.*

He leaned back against the supple leather seats and closed his eyes. The hum of the motor, calming vibrations, and fine alcohol only added to the relaxation.

About twenty minutes had passed before he awoke. Looking out the car window, he realized that none of the familiar landmarks were around. He recognized nothing. Instead of bright lights and the stream of traffic coming and going from JFK, only abandoned buildings and warehouses were in his field of view.

"Hey, driver, are you lost? I don't remember any of this, and I have a plane waiting for me," Gertig said agitatedly.

The driver did not respond, only holding up their hand in acknowledgment the question was heard.

"Look, I can't be late. They expect—"

Before he could finish his sentence, the black partition separating the driver from passenger quickly slid up. Then the locks on the doors snapped down with a definitive click as the limousine jerked to a sudden halt.

"Hey, what the hell are you doing? Why are we stopping?" Gertig protested, knocking on the partition.

At first, there was silence and then the clearly audible sound of the driver's door opening and then being slammed shut. Gertig reached over and tried to unlock the door, but to no avail. His attempt was suddenly interrupted by a cold computer voice filtering through the passenger cabin speaker.

"Good evening, Mr. Gertig."

"Who the fuck are you? Open this goddamn door!"

"We have something to discuss. There's something I need from you."

"Let me out of this car now!" he demanded.

"You have not heard me out."

"I don't need to hear you out!" he yelled as he pounded against the window. He tried to see who it was he was talking to, but there was no one in sight.

"That attitude is not helping, Mr. Gertig."

"What the fuck do you want?"

"It's a shame you still don't recognize it."

"What the hell do you mean? Recognize what?"

"That you're part of the problem. You see, Mr. Gertig, I don't want money or favors, and I don't even care that you were on your way to fuck that Colombian whore in the Bahamas. I only want one thing."

"And what the fuck is that?" he angrily replied.

"I want you to take responsibility. I want you to be accountable."

"What the fuck for?"

"For the label you carry."

"I don't understand. What do you mean? What fucking label are you talking about?"

"Felon."

It sounded like a cap gun being fired. Gertig looked for the source. Yet within moments, that search ceased as he noticed the grayish-white smoke pouring into the cabin from below his seat. It was quickly followed by a pungent acidic odor.

The coughing attack initiated soon afterward, and then panic ensued. He struck the window with his fist and kicked at the door, but the gas was already beginning to overwhelm his senses.

His breathing began to feel heavy as the burning poison filled his chest cavity. Soon his lungs were becoming deluged with fluid. He tried to scream, but only a gurgling sound exited his mouth. With his strength waning, he struck the glass one more time, but with the remaining power he possessed, he could only manage a tap.

The killer stood just outside of the vehicle, the deadly vapor obliterating the view of the death struggle in its interior. The final indication of the escaping life force was Gertig's hand pressed against the window as it slowly slid down its smooth surface.

The killer's mouth rose at the corners, giving the slightest hint at the satisfaction with the result. Inside the vehicle, Gertig's mind flashed in brittle segments as the synapses in his brain fired their last images. They were of his mistress waiting for him at the airport and the loins he would never feel again.

CHAPTER 40

New York, New York

DES WOKE UP feeling more tired than he did the previous day. Tossing and turning over concerns about the upcoming meeting, his sleep was more like a series of intermittent catnaps.

Even after showering and doing his best to polish his appearance, he was still astonished at the figure staring back at him in the mirror. It looked as if he had aged thirty years in the last week. His eyes were bloodshot with dark circles hanging beneath them. The creases in his forehead had not faded from the day before due to his terrible nervous habit of raising his eyebrows while under stress. His sandy-brown hair looked like withered sage brush.

It was 8:55 a.m. and he had just enough time to grab a bagel and coffee and do a little research on Union Square where he was to meet his mystery informant. Des exited the motel and immediately felt the higher concentration of humidity. As he went to the deli about three blocks away, two construction workers walked past, wearing their yellow hard hats and arguing over who the Yankees should trade to get another pitcher. Summer was definitely near.

Stopping at a news vendor, he bought himself a *New York Times* and sat at one of the outdoor tables with his coffee and cream cheese-smothered bagel. The newspaper provided very little of interest. The New York City School Board was preparing for another battle with the teachers' union over their latest contract offer. The mayor was dealing with some issues concerning street performers in Times Square. There was also another article at the bottom of the page where the police were investigating the disappearance of the CEO of Trans International Bank. Apparently, he was last seen leaving his office at about 7:00 p.m. the previous night. According to his wife, he was on his way to Tokyo for a business meeting.

By 10:15, Des had hailed a cab to take him to Union Square. He was relieved that this time he did not have to travel by foot as the increasingly warm and humid weather would make it an uncomfortable trip.

As he passed by the edges of Central Park, doubts started to creep into the back of his mind. *Is this really a good idea?* While the cab traversed through Columbus Circle, he noticed how his perspective had changed since viewing this same scenery a few days earlier on that first chaotic trip. He was still nervous, but not panicked.

Moving through Times Square on Broadway, he caught sight of the Garment District with its vendors rearranging their racks of clothing and colorful cloth. Passing the famous Macy's Department Store, he marveled at its size. It was almost a city unto itself, being so large it literally had its own zip code.

Traveling farther south, he could see the outcropping of Madison Square Park as they bypassed Chelsea. Signs marking other historical locations, such as Teddy Roosevelt's birthplace, came into view.

Within a minute, Union Square entered the scene. Des checked his watch as he handed the driver his fare. It was seven minutes before his appointment. As expected, it was a cluster of humanity. *Thank God.* He scanned the crowds, hoping to catch a glimpse of the individual or at least be able to identify him before he reached the statue but could spot nothing among the bobbing heads. *How am I supposed to do this? He didn't tell me what he looked like.*

As he weaved his way to Lafayette Statue, he caught a man wearing a Syracuse University baseball cap. *The Syracuse Orangeman… Oh, right… Go Orange!*

CHAPTER 41

EVEN THOUGH HE was in an area swarming with people, his days in Afghanistan made him weary. He had seen too many horrific things happen in such public places. Looking to the right and left of the baseball cap marker, he cautiously approached, wanting to be ready for any surprises, as well as not to cause alarm.

As he drew closer, the features of the individual came into view. He was a distinguished-looking man who appeared to be in his early fifties. Brown hair that faded to gray by his sideburns could be seen peeking beneath his cap. He was trim, but not particularly athletic looking. His faded blue jeans and gray New York Athletic Club T-shirt seemed to be trying to hide a more uptight personality than what his casual dress implied.

"Hello," said Des.

"Thank you for coming. Walk with me."

His gait was slow but deliberate as they headed toward Fourteenth Street. The tension was very present as Des could see the man spying his surroundings in a paranoid exercise of nerves. They left the confines of Union Square without saying a word as they headed in the direction of the East River.

"Forgive me if I don't introduce myself, but after what I tell you, I think you'll understand," said the mysterious figure.

Des didn't know quite how to respond. He felt vulnerable yet intrigued with this serious-looking gentleman. "How did you know who I was and that I was involved in all this?"

"I'm not going to be able to tell you everything I know or how I came by certain information. Understand, I'm taking a huge risk in meeting you," he stated while looking over his shoulder.

"Why did you contact me?"

"I've been following the story in the newspaper and online. I also have a contact who has access to more detailed information."

"But I was told they put a lid on it."

"You'll find that many things you're told are not entirely accurate. There's always ways to get information."

As they made their way down Fourteenth Street, the buildings encasing them took on an almost-ominous look, like sentinels eyeing a suspicious visitation. It was a claustrophobic feeling, which only added to the already tense atmosphere.

"I'm not even sure how I'm involved in all of this. Nothing about this situation makes sense," Des responded.

"I'm not either, but I think I know what motivates the individual you're chasing."

"Well, if you have that info, why don't you go to the FBI and give it to them?"

The man scoffed. "They can't be trusted and would discredit me anyway. Plus, they would make sure I'd lose everything if they knew I was talking to you."

The man sped his pace, almost like he was trying to evade a pursuer. The stress he was under was etched on his face. He did not speak another syllable until the East River came into view. Its murky brown water was balancing a myriad of boats and ships. Placing his hands on the railing by the docks, he turned around with the look of someone trapped against a wall. "I couldn't live with myself," he said with a deep sense of sadness.

"I'm sorry. I don't understand what you mean," answered Des.

The man looked down and said, "Your killer is motivated by something that borders on obsession."

"Most serial killers are."

"You don't understand what I'm saying. This is a different kind of hatred, and I don't believe he's crazy."

"Hatred? Hatred of who?"

"It's not a hatred of who, but of what."

"You mean like the government?"

"I should have figured you guys would lump him into that crazed radical antigovernment bullshit category. Believe me, this is not some nut running around the hills talking about Armageddon or a governmental dictatorship or any of that nonsense."

"You've lost me," Des responded, still not grasping what this man was trying to convey.

"The first victim was an assistant US attorney... right?"

Des just nodded, still bewildered.

"The third victim was a retired federal probation officer. But it was the second victim who caught my attention."

"She was a seamstress," Des said perplexed.

"I bet they didn't look any further into her background, did they?"

"Should they have?"

"Those fucking idiots at the FBI are still looking at this as your typical serial murderer of women. They're ignoring the bigger picture."

"But they were all women."

"The fact they were women has no bearing on the reason they were targeted."

"But they were all in different states and had no connection to one another."

"Not on the surface they didn't. I recognized the name of the second victim you found in Louisiana. She served on a grand jury I presented evidence to for an indictment."

"You're a US attorney?"

"I was a US attorney," the man said almost embarrassedly. "An assistant US attorney, a former grand jurist, and a retired federal probation officer, all killed in the same manner... It made me realize the connection. They represent three of the most prominent parts of the system. Your killer is attacking the legal system—the federal legal system."

"What? That makes no sense. Why would someone kill to protest the federal legal system? I mean, I've heard of killers taunting the police with their crimes, but not the entire legal system."

"You don't get it. The federal legal system in this country is the most corrupt legal system in the modern world, and most Americans are completely oblivious to it. I believe the person who is committing these crimes is protesting what that system has become."

Des was startled by the revelation. The idea someone was killing people based on a hatred of the federal legal system was nearly impossible for him to conceive of. "But the federal courts deal mainly with constitutional issues," Des replied, recalling his government classes.

"You're doing what most people do. You're thinking of the Supreme Court. Those are mainly civil cases, and that's just a small cog in the wheel. You're still missing the big picture. He's not just protesting the courts, but the whole fucked-up machine from beginning to end—beyond the civil cases."

Des shook his head in disbelief. Seeing his confusion, the man continued. "Let me explain it to you this way. Do you know what the success rate of the US Attorney's Office is?"

"You're talking criminal cases… right?"

The man nodded affirmatively.

"I don't know the exact rate, but I know it's high."

"It's 98 percent… 98 percent! Now what government agency has a success rate of even 50 percent? But this branch of the government has a rate that nearly doubles that of many state prosecutors, and the amazing thing is no one questions how or why. It's one of the nation's greatest secrets, and it's hidden in plain sight."

Des took two steps back as if he were knocked astray by the information. He didn't know what to think. Was this man sane, or was this just the ramblings of some deranged lunatic?

"So, you're saying the entire system is corrupt? How could they get away with it if it's out in the open?"

The man shook his head as if to say "another disbeliever." "It's not as hard as you think. People are blinded by the numbers, and quite frankly, the general public is stupid. Most of the population gets their knowledge of law enforcement and the courts by watching TV shows, and even those usually only depict state courts. Federal courts are rarely shown, and they always put everything in a nice and neat format. You have the cops and the prosecutors who are the good guys and the evil criminals who always go to jail. In the real world, it's not that cut-and-dry, and how US attorneys get those convictions is never pristine."

"Well, aren't US attorneys like the top ones in their class? I would imagine it's hard to get a job with them."

The man chuckled mockingly. "There's an old lawyer joke. In law school, your A students become judges. Your B students go into private practice. Your C students become private investigators, and your D students become US attorneys. In other words, they get the attorneys no one else wants. Usually, the ones who do graduate at the top of their class choose to make more money with a big private firm."

Des was shocked. He still could not make heads or tails of any of this information. Walking over next to the man, Des still held doubt. "If that's the case, then how do they have such an incredible success rate?"

"Now you're asking the right question," the man said with satisfaction. "The answer is because the system is rigged. If you get charged with a crime by the US Attorney's Office, even if you're completely innocent, you're guilty and will be found as such. Hell, 25 percent of all people in the federal prison system right now are actually innocent—over fifty thousand people. I've sent people to prison myself who I knew were innocent."

"But why?"

"That's the directive. The only thing the US Attorney's Office cares about is getting the conviction no matter the cost. It's all about keeping the conviction rate up, and the ends always justifies the means. If you charge and don't get the conviction, there'll be hell to pay. I just couldn't do it anymore."

"You said the system is rigged, what do you mean?"

Once again, the man looked down ashamedly. He reached back and started to massage the knots forming at the back of his neck. "It all starts when the investigation begins. In most cases, the actual investigation is over quickly… a few months at most. But they won't charge someone with a crime until two, three… or even four years later."

"Why the wait?"

"They want to put as much emotional and financial strain on the individual as possible. We used to call it 'the grind.' They'll do things like notify his employer that he's being investigated with hopes of getting him fired. If he does get fired and tries to get another job, they'll notify the potential employer as well. Their goal is to make sure he's in financial ruin so he's forced to go with an overworked and oftentimes underqualified public defender who is much more willing to make a plea deal than a private attorney. Once the defendant has been drained financially, they'll finally take it to a grand jury so they can officially charge them. Since the grand jury only hears the prosecution's side, it's pretty much a slam dunk."

"A grand jury will indict a ham sandwich," Des responded, remembering the old adage.

"You're catching on, but that's just the tip of the iceberg. There's another reason why the grand jury is important. You see, once they charge the individual, his sentence is already predetermined."

"Wait, doesn't the judge determine sentencing?"

"In criminal cases at the federal level, judges are nothing more than ceremonial figures. In reality, they're just the US attorney's bitch. They have almost no power because they have pretty much eliminated them from the process."

"How?"

"With mandatory minimum sentencing. Most crimes they prosecute have set sentencing that judges can't go under. So, depending on how long they want the defendant to serve, they just manipulate the charges to fit what they desire. Take your standard drug case. In a state court, a first-time offender caught selling five grams of crack cocaine will most likely get probation. The judge has the power to allow this person to turn their life around. In the federal courts, that same person is going away for years because of the mandatory minimums. Since the laws are so vague and the US Attorney's Office has carte blanche to interpret them however they want, they can pretty much add almost any charge they dream up. You know, I once sent a nineteen-year-old kid to jail for two decades for selling a piece of crack cocaine the size of a nickel."

"But can't someone take their case to trial? If they're innocent especially, wouldn't that come out?"

"Don't you think they've thought about that?" he said annoyedly. "They'll make sure it will never come out even if it gets that far."

"But how do they do that?"

"Because they control all the evidence. Remember, once the FBI completes the investigation, all the evidence is sent to the US Attorney's Office who is handling the case. They're not required to turn over that evidence until the person is actually charged. By that time, it has usually been in their possession for years."

"So it…"

"Gives them time to manipulate the evidence… yes," he said, finishing Des' sentence. "Anything supporting the defense will magically disappear. Even the FBI will destroy evidence demonstrating a person's innocence or shows they violated a person's constitutional rights as a matter of basic protocol. They're under as much pressure to get the conviction. They both work for the same goddamn team— the Department of Justice. This is how they're measured."

Des couldn't believe what he was hearing. "But that's illegal."

"Of course, it's illegal, but no one will ever be held accountable, because the only way a US attorney or the FBI can be charged with a crime is by the US Attorney's Office itself."

"The fox guarding the henhouse."

"Exactly! Plus, you throw in the fact that US attorneys have absolute prosecutorial immunity, they're basically untouchable. You see, the whole process is designed to remove the judge from the equation. By controlling the evidence and with the mandatory minimum sentencing in place, they can essentially blackmail the defendant to plea out by dropping or adding charges, and that doesn't take into account the enhancements."

"Enhancements?"

"Before a defendant goes to sentencing, they go to what is called a presentencing interview, or PSI. It's basically an interview with a probation officer who gets your life history and then takes a look at the charges and gives a recommendation to the judge for the amount of time that should be served. That's what your third victim did for the DOJ. She looked at the enhancements for each crime. So, for instance, let's say you're charged with computer fraud. There's an enhancement of up to two years added if you used a computer in the commission of that crime."

"Isn't that kind of redundant? I mean, how else could you commit computer fraud if you don't use a computer?" Des said rhetorically.

"Of course it's redundant, most enhancements are. They're designed as another way for the DOJ to up the amount of time served. Believe me, it's not unusual for a crime with a mandatory minimum of five years to be teased up to twenty or even thirty years using enhancements. The probation officer is supposed to be neutral, but that's bullshit. They get paid by the same people to calculate the highest sentence possible."

Des looked at the man stunned. "What did you say?"

"They get paid by the same people to calculate the highest sentence possible."

"Oh, Jesus."

"What?"

"The killer left a note of where we could find the last victim. The last sentence in the note said, 'I made the calculations.'"

"Interesting choice of words… don't you think?" he said with raised eyebrows. Then he continued. "People just don't understand.

The power the Department of Justice wields is unbelievable. Why do you think that in 97 percent of all cases the defendant pleads guilty? All they need to say to them is that if you plead guilty to the charges we want you to, we'll only ask for five to seven years. But if you don't and attempt to take us to trial, we'll make sure you get twenty-five. Hell, they even have it written into the enhancements that if you don't plead guilty, you're not accepting responsibility and are mandated to have extra time added to your sentence."

Des immediately thought about the other words the killer had repeated to him about taking responsibility. "So basically, you're telling me that you're punished for practicing your constitutional rights?"

"Sickening, isn't it?"

"It's so hard to believe," Des said, looking out over the river.

"It's happening every day, thousands of times a year in our courts, and it doesn't stop there."

"What else do they do to them?" Des asked, almost afraid to hear more.

"Lots of things. For instance, if they feel a person is still resistant to plea, they'll convince the judge to remand them into custody until trial. Then they'll delay the trial for months if not years… keeping them in prison… keeping up the pressure."

"Hold on… wouldn't a judge eventually order their release based on their right to a speedy trial?"

"There are ways around that too. Even if the judge orders a release, literally as the defendant exits the prison, they'll have him arrested and thrown back in on a new charge. We, one time, kept a defendant locked up for seven years without trial doing exactly that… and the Department of Justice has even more tactics. If the convicted individual is thrown in jail but tries to reopen their case, the DOJ has designed the system to make it nearly impossible to do so."

"How?"

"Through the Federal Bureau of Prisons."

"What, are they worse?"

"Put it this way, if the DOJ is a cesspool, then the people who work for the Bureau of Prisons are the shit floating in it."

"I don't understand. I know prisons are bad, but aren't they just following the court's orders?"

"It's not that simple. They're a huge part of a system designed to exploit the people they incarcerate. You have to understand, the DOJ purposely divides its entities to increase their power over the people they prosecute and convict. Once a person is sentenced, they fall under the jurisdiction of the Bureau of Prisons, which is independent of the courts. The judges are once again diminished, because the BOP is given the power on how the sentence is to be administered. It's done to make it nearly impossible for a prisoner to do anything to reopen their case."

"Like divide and conquer."

"Absolutely. In over 90 percent of all requests to reopen cases based on new evidence, court procedure or whatever the reason, the BOP, at the direction of the Department of Justice and the US Attorney's Office, will deny them from seeing legal counsel. It's really incredible the lengths they'll go to. Mailrooms at the prisons will block vital time-sensitive documents from getting to inmates. The so-called counselors and case managers will tamper with and keep information from prisoners which might shorten their time. Guards will confiscate needed information from prisoners which informs them of their rights. The US Attorney's Office will coordinate efforts with prison staff to threaten, intimidate, and even assault inmates, and it goes on and on. It's all designed to keep them in as long as possible."

Des's knees felt weak as he was sickened to his core. He slowly walked over to a bench near the railing and sat down in a heap. All of his beliefs, all he grew up knowing about his country, which was supposedly built on laws and individual rights, had been obliterated. "I still question one thing. What's the motivation to do something like this? I mean, it has to be more than just conviction rates."

"What's the motivation behind anything? Money, of course."

"Money? Don't prisons cost society?"

"Yes, they do. But they don't cost everyone. The prison business in this country is a multi-hundred-billion-dollar industry. In order to keep that machine functioning at its highest level of profitability, you need prisoners."

"What do you mean prison business? You mean like private prisons?"

"Well… yes, partially. People use the term 'prison industry' but don't really understand what that means. You see, over the last thirty years, prisons have become increasingly privatized. Many prisons are now owned by large corporations who get paid unbelievable amounts of money to warehouse human beings. But as it became more and more lucrative, other corporations found ways to get in on the act in ways that most people don't even think about. Usually people, when they think of prisons, just think of the buildings and bars. But really, that's just a drop in the bucket. They forget about the real cash cow… all the goods and services they need to function—mattresses, blankets, pillows, food, clothing, sanitation, products for sale in the commissary, and all the hundreds of other items needed for a prison to function—are provided by the private sector and always at taxpayer expense. They have incredible influence in the halls of power."

"You're saying they have people in government positions or something like that?" asked Des.

"Oh yeah… All you have to do is look at what companies in the industry did last year to see how much power they yield. They spent over a quarter of a billion dollars on Washington, DC, lobbyists and campaign donations to encourage congressmen to vote for more mandatory minimum sentencing and even longer prison terms. They donate hundreds of millions to campaigns as well… and don't think for a moment that they're not giving personal donations… a lot of greased palms. Prison ceased being about justice or punishment a long time ago. It's all about jobs and profit now. In order to keep those up—"

"All you have to do is lock up more and more people," Des interjected.

"And they've been amazingly effective at doing so. Do you know how much the federal prison population has grown in the last thirty years?"

Des shook his head.

"It's gone up 800 percent. Now you don't really believe that's due to justified sentencing or that bullshit idea of deterrent, do you? It's big business. You can even buy stock in these companies just over there on Wall Street," the man said, motioning in the direction of the famous business district.

"Trading human freedom on the open market," Des added, shaking his head.

"And like any other business, they have projected growth. We have over a quarter of a million people in federal prisons right now, but they want to expand that."

"To what?"

"Between INS holding facilities, federal prisons, and other detainment methods, they're hoping for over two million in the next twenty years."

"Jesus, and no one speaks up?" Des said in amazement.

"There've been a few but not enough, and that's why it continues. The system thrives on people's ignorance of it. Most people have no idea what the federal legal system is, let alone what it does. The DOJ, Bureau of Prisons, the courts, the private prison industry, the prison guard unions, and the US Attorney's Office have become the largest human trafficking organizations in the world. But people believe what they're told."

"I don't understand why."

"Sure you do. Because it's presented as a win-win. Politicians get to campaign on how tough they are on crime while getting huge campaign and private donations. The corporations and unions get the legislation they need as well as taxpayer money to increase their profits and jobs, and the citizens get a false sense of security built on lies." The man stopped and inhaled deeply. "If the public only knew how they were being raped by the DOJ, the US Attorney's

Office, and the rest of these assholes, they wouldn't be able to stop throwing up."

"It's still hard to believe this has never been brought to light."

"Not really. People are only concerned with convictions and incarceration because they've been convinced that they're being protected… and they don't think of prisoners as human beings. In their minds, they're just criminals, and the harsher the punishment, the better. That's until it affects them personally, and with the way it's going, it's only a matter of time… They don't see the danger. They've been hypnotized by television shows that always portray the prosecutor as a person with a heart of gold, and the defendants and the defense attorneys as slime bags even though most of the time the opposite is true. They just go about their lives, working their jobs and paying their bills. They don't realize that in many of their everyday activities they break some ambiguous federal law that was influenced by a corporation to add to the books. They're clueless. They have no idea they're only one overzealous prosecutor away from having their lives completely devastated. I've seen it happen… I've done it," he said regretfully.

"I just can't believe people haven't noticed," Des said exasperatedly.

"You like baseball, Mr. Cook?"

"Yeah… big fan," Des responded, perplexed by this sudden change of direction.

"Me too… I love the game. You know, my friends are all Yankees fans." Then he smiled. "Not me though. The Mets are my team. I loved them since the '80s. Doc Gooden, Keith Hernandez, Gary Carter… those were fun days. But really, I'll watch any team. It's a beautiful game."

Then he paused for a few seconds, staring up at the sky before continuing. "You were probably just a kid back in '94 when the strike happened."

Des nodded, trying to follow this strange train of thought.

"I was a season ticket holder back then. You know when it started, I, like everybody else, thought it would be like previous strikes. The owners and players would trade some verbal jabs, some negotiation would take place, and then both sides would come to their senses and it would be over. So, you could probably imagine my shock when it didn't happen and they canceled the rest of season, including the World Series. But what I really remember most about that time was what happened afterward when play finally resumed. Shea Stadium was half empty. No one wanted to watch the games on TV. Hell, even some of my most die-hard friends hardly talked about baseball. The people had lost interest. It looked like they had finally killed the golden goose."

Des just looked at the man without a reaction or word. But inside he was beginning to question where this was going.

"Then there was the '96 season," the man continued. "All of a sudden, players started smashing the hell out of the ball. Home runs were flying out of ballparks like never before. Batting averages soared, and records that hadn't been remotely approached in decades were now being threatened not by one or two players, but hordes of them. Fans started to regain interest, ballparks began to fill up… It looked like the grand ole game was back. But when I think back to it, what amazes me now is not all of the incredible performances we were seeing on the field, but that no one asked how this was possible. How was it possible that so many players could perform at such a level? How was it possible that so many players who had never hit more than a dozen home runs in a season were now hitting over fifty? It made no sense. But nobody asked. Everyone just bought into the excitement… We bought into the fantasy. Hell, we even denied what was right before our eyes. We ignored the fact that players who just a year earlier were thin and wiry were now built like Arnold Schwarzenegger. Many of us knew something wasn't right, and you know the people who ran the game knew something was amiss."

"Steroids!" Des chimed in.

"Exactly! What we were looking at was nothing more than a farce, a cheap parlor trick, and when you look at the DOJ, it's the same damn thing. No one is asking how a government agency—with all its inefficient bureaucracy, red tape, politics, and below-average attorneys with little experience—is able to maintain a nearly 100 percent success rate. Just like that '96 season, people are caught up in the fairy tale. They're refusing to ask the simple question. How?"

"Why?"

"Because in reality, Mr. Cook, people don't want to know. They don't want to believe these cherished institutions and all these people with the prestigious titles that run them are that corrupt. They want to believe that only the bad guys go to jail and that it's the good people who put them there."

"So you think it's based on the desire to believe that everything's as it should be?"

"In a way, yes. But also, to believe otherwise makes us all complicit. By admitting that we're ignoring the problem, we've become willing accomplices in these crimes. It's just easier not to ask the question at all. Self-preservation, Mr. Cook… self-preservation."

The effect on Des was that of a delayed reaction as the influx of this new knowledge took a few moments to permeate. It was a range of emotions running from one end of the spectrum to the other, finally congealing and fermenting into a nauseating brew that emitted in one pervasive feeling—shame.

"It's so… so…" Des stammered.

"Evil?"

"Yes. I don't know how this continues."

"Mr. Cook, the spread of evil does not depend on the ideology or actions of the few, but rather the complacency of the many. The reason this is allowed to continue is the same reason people don't react to many tragedies or injustices. Because it doesn't affect them directly. But to me, what's really amazing is how the DOJ changed the definition of justice."

"Changed the definition?"

"It used to be that justice meant to find someone responsible for a crime and hold them appropriately accountable. But that ended when they began to claim that getting the conviction meant justice was being served. Once the public bought that argument, the word *conviction* had been substituted for *justice*. They were equated. So no matter how the conviction was obtained, regardless of the means, justice was being served. The more convictions meant the better the public servant, when in actuality, they were only perpetrating crimes. Unfortunately, people don't see the hazard. But at this rate, they will. It's a statistical certainty."

"And people are really in that much danger?"

The man nodded affirmatively. "You know, it's funny. We spend so much time focusing on terrorists overseas that we ignore the fact that we have created our own... and ironically, we pay their salaries."

"You make it sound like they're some kind of jihadist running around terrorizing and beheading people," Des responded, feeling like the man's point was being overstated.

"You don't need to behead someone to terrorize them, Mr. Cook."

"I don't understand how you know all this. The DOJ is huge. How could you possibly have access to this type of information?"

"Because I was one of the people who wrote the inner department manual on all of these methods. The one no one sees or will ever see."

"Wait, there's a manual."

"What? You're surprised the DOJ has actual classified polices on all of this? You think the CIA and NSA have secrets? They don't have shit on the DOJ. Of course, there's a manual. They keep track of everything. Every little tidbit piece of information on how to try, convict, and sentence people, including all the means, legal and illegal, to do it. All the crooked tactics... secret strategies to pollute and tamper with juries, coordination of efforts between the US Attorney's Office and the BOP to sabotage the rights of the convicted, the backdoor ways to tamper with evidence, payoffs from private prison corporations to wardens and other DOJ employees to ensure contracts and lengthen prison time... Hell, there's even quotas in there for prison populations that the DOJ has to maintain as a part of their agreements with the private sector."

"I... I..." Des choked as he didn't know how to respond.

"Oh, don't feel too badly, Mr. Cook. You're no different than the rest of the American public who doesn't have a fucking clue."

"This can't be everyone. I mean, every organization has a few bad apples," Des said, looking to salvage some part of the system.

The man winced. "I hate that fucking saying. It's just a chickenshit way of trying to mollify an argument by recognizing the problems but then immediately minimizing them as aberrations so they won't get any serious attention. Mr. Cook, the 'good apples' in the DOJ are the exception. The problem is systemic."

Des placed his hand against his forehead, trying desperately to contain the dizziness enveloping him. He took a deep breath, attempting to regain a little bit of his equilibrium. "You've got to go public with this. People need to know."

The man shook his head. "Not a chance in hell. I wouldn't be allowed to live long enough to make a dent. I guarantee you that. And they wouldn't stop at me… I have a family too."

Des felt exhausted. Justice as a business? People's freedom sold on the open market, not for punishment but for profit? If the public knew, they would be beyond outraged. He then suddenly felt another wave of shame come over him. He was a member of that foolish public who had believed they were being protected. He had bought into the idea that all criminals got what they deserved. Now he understood it was not black or white, that the separation of good and bad was murky at best and had flipped at worst.

"Why did you tell me all this?" Des asked.

The man then exhaled as if he was releasing a colossal burden. "About a year ago, I prosecuted a case involving a low-level employee who worked at a major bank. I was handed the case late… I wasn't even supposed to have it. Normally, a case like that would go to a much lower-ranking attorney. When I examined the evidence, I knew this man was innocent. He was just a pawn. The real guilty party were the bank's executives. I approached my superior about it and suggested we drop the charges and focus on the people above the defendant. He went into a rage and refused to let me. Then he forced me to destroy the evidence which would have exonerated him. 'Once we charge, we get the fucking conviction,' he would always say. Well, I got the conviction. He got thirteen years. He was married and had a seven-year-old son and a nine-year-old daughter."

"He was?" Des said, recognizing once again the use of the past tense.

"He committed suicide in prison. Slit his own throat in the shower. I didn't sleep or eat for weeks. I tried to perform my duties, but I couldn't. I resigned four months later. My heart was no longer in it. But it hasn't really helped either. I keep thinking of those children growing up without a father and how I'm to blame."

"You did what you were instructed to do. It's not your fault," Des said sympathetically.

"Yeah, I tried to tell myself that I was just following orders. Then I realized I was using the same excuse the Nazis did at the Nuremburg trials. It was wrong and I knew it. I wasn't strong enough. I knew I had perpetuated a system that had destroyed more children's lives than any other entity on earth. When I heard about these murders, I realized it could have just as well been me there with my throat slit… and you know, it would have been justified. People need to be made to understand."

"I think you're being too hard on yourself."

"No, I'm not, I was nothing more than a human trafficker, like the rest of them."

"Human trafficker? You were a US attorney."

"That was just a title. It wasn't indicative of what I actually did. I, like the rest of the DOJ, did nothing more than take away people's freedom to ensure profit for others. People can call themselves anything they want. It doesn't change the reality. A hooker can call herself an escort. It doesn't change the fact that she's a hooker."

"I'm at a loss. I don't know what to do with all of this. It's so beyond my capabilities."

The man stood up and faced Des. "Mr. Cook, I don't know why this killer has involved you. I wish I could help you with that, but I can't. However, to be honest, I'm doing this for me. This is my penance. I just wanted to point you in the right direction, and maybe you'll find some way to stop this person and expose all this."

"This is so much bigger than me. I don't know how. I'm not an expert or anybody of importance."

"Sometimes the people who seem the least significant are the ones who make the biggest difference. Good luck."

With that final comment, the man turned and walked away. Des remained plastered to the bench like an eight-hundred-pound gorilla was sitting on his lap. He turned his head and gazed out over the river, watching a modest-sized boat begin to edge its way into the adjacent dock. As it squeezed into its mooring, he could not help but feel the same tight grip on him. This had taken on a new dimension, one he was unsure he could handle.

CHAPTER 42

Location unknown

THE KILLER SAT in the backroom staring at the layout on the wall. It was all coming together. Everything seemed to be where it should be.

Opening up the briefcase, it was the treasure chest expected. It was all there, the pathway that would reap its terror on those who had denied what rightfully belonged to the worthy.

The papers were all neatly aligned, placed meticulously in order. Sitting in a pocket lining its side was the thumb drive that held the most intimate of business secrets, as well as a curious collection of photographs. They were of smiling faces, somewhere in tropical waters.

The predator recognized their significance immediately. It was better than expected and only increased the arsenal against those who promised one thing and then implemented another. Soon they would be held accountable. They would be made to understand that their conduct, their betrayal of ethics, would no longer be tolerated. There were only a few tasks left to accomplish, and once they were put into motion, it had no avenue but to be completed.

CHAPTER 43

New York, New York

IT HAD BEEN almost an hour and Des had yet to find the strength to lift himself off the bench. So many thoughts were racing through his mind he could hardly grasp one long enough to actually contemplate what to do.

Finally, he arose and began to trek back toward Fourteenth Street carrying his cluttered brain. If what this man told him was accurate, he had to look at these murders in a new light. But how was he going to explain where he came upon such knowledge? The FBI would have a lot of questions, number one being, how come he did not contact them before his mysterious encounter?

Yet there was another more pressing and disconcerting concern. The man had shown great distrust if not outright fear of the DOJ. If his information was correct, it was a rational emotion. Nobody in the Department of Justice would want such details out in the open, not to mention the companies and unions who were making such massive fortunes off the system. If he divulged what he knew to the FBI, would he become the target of two enemies?

Des reached Union Square but continued to walk rather than hail a cab. He always found solace in movement. When he was at a loss for answers, walking would release the grip of stress strangling his mind. *How do I approach this? What should be my next move?*

As he turned down Broadway and headed south, the bustle of the city slowly faded like the volume being turned down on a radio. He passed by the Washington Memorial Arch and New York University as the scenery slowly changed from towering skyscrapers to the quaint brownstone apartments of Greenwich Village. But he took little notice of any of it. Not even the delectable smells wafting in from Little Italy's array of restaurants, with their garlic seasonings drifting through the air, shook him from his trance.

You're rushing, Des. Slow down and let it come to you, he could hear his father's voice say. *Remember, it's about patience.* They were the instructions he always gave him when he was up to bat in his Little League games. *Patience, then react. Patience, then react.* It was his father's way of getting him to study the pitcher. The placement of his feet, the cadence of his motion, the angle of his arm as he released the ball, all had to be computed before deciding if and when to swing. *You have not done it, Des. You're not following procedure.*

Although this informant sounded believable, nothing had been verified. *You can't just take him at face value. His story needs to be vetted, but how? How can you confirm that the nation's legal system is in that state of corruption? Is it a condition so pronounced it would cause someone to kill?*

As a boy, whenever he became frustrated in any of his endeavors, his father would always repeat a story about the legendary UCLA basketball coach John Wooden. In the 1960s and early 1970s, UCLA was the giant of the college basketball world. National championships and undefeated seasons seemed almost commonplace as high school basketball stars from around the country would flock to Los Angeles to play for the revered coach.

However, when these prep school All-Americans arrived at their first practice, they were not given intricate drills to run, fundamental skills to practice, or even dramatic words of wisdom from Coach Wooden. At the first practice, these highly touted athletes were instructed on how to tie their shoes. They started at the beginning.

That's what Des needed to do, start at the beginning. The only way to confirm this man's theories was to go back to where this all initiated. It was time to return to the hotel and start the investigation anew.

CHAPTER 44

New York, New York

THE AREA HAD been cordoned off by yellow police tape, which had been tied to old pipes and shipping containers. The report came in about an hour earlier. A middle-aged man's body had been discovered a little after 6:00 p.m., not too far from the docks near the Hudson River. The description matched perfectly to the missing CEO of Trans International Bank, James Gertig.

The body was nude, except for a loincloth. Inexplicably, he had been propped up in a chair, a book had been fixed to his left hand, and he was fitted with what appeared to be a belt displaying some type of holster. Being off the beaten path, few people were attracted to the scene, even though the flashing lights of the many police cars made the area look like a 1970s disco.

Within the taped-off perimeter, Officer Kevin Sachi, a twenty-two-year veteran of the NYPD, was diligently taking notes when he noticed a familiar face on the other side of the tape. "Dr. Feller, is that you? Goddamn!" he exclaimed. "What have you been doing to yourself? You look like the freakin' Terminator!"

Dr. Feller smiled and gave a slight chuckle. "I just wanted to get in better shape."

"That's an understatement. I can't believe what I'm looking at."

"How's Janice and the kids?"

"They're fine. My oldest starts college this year. Hard to believe where the time goes."

"So what have you got here?"

"I think we found that big-shot bank president who went missing the other day. We're not quite sure of the cause of death, but there are burns around his eyes, nose, and mouth... poor bastard. Hey, whatcha doin' here? Back working with the Feds?" he asked in his definitive Long Island accent.

"No, once I walked away from that, I swore I'd never go back. I got wind of this through my sources. I guess my old professional curiosity made me want to check it out."

"We miss having you around. Things haven't been quite the same since you left. Dr. Hertzel is good, but kind of a cold fish, if ya know what I mean. So whatcha been doin' with yourself other than turning into the Incredible Hulk?"

"Oh, I've been working on a big project, but if I tell you, I'd have to kill you," Feller responded with a wry grin and a wink. "But I have a feeling, things are going to change for Dr. Hertzel soon."

"Sounds interesting... what—"

"Kevin!" a voice yelled from the other side of the shipping container.

"Damn, I have to go. You take care of yourself, Doc. It was good to see ya," the officer said, patting Feller on the shoulder.

"Good to see you too. Give my love to your family."

"Will do."

Feller turned and walked away from the scene. A contentment started to grow inside him. This whole process was nearing an end. Soon, he would bring it all crashing down, and those in charge would be made to truly regret their decision.

CHAPTER 45

New York, New York

THE SHOWER FELT wonderful and gave him the opportunity to slow down his thought process. Today had been a whirlwind for Des. The plethora of emotions he had been experiencing had left him drained.

How did this whole thing start? he thought as he allowed the water to rain down over his head. *It started with the note. "Find Des Cook, he has the answers."* The note the agent handed him upon their visit that fateful morning was what prompted his involvement. Yet it gave him no indication that the man's theory was correct. *Maybe naming me as the "Leader of the Enemy" can be connected?*

He continued this train of thought until it hit him. *Oh, Des, you idiot!* He shut off the shower and tried to dry himself enough to where he wouldn't drip all over the floor. He then wrapped a towel around his waist and scurried to the nightstand next to the bed. *Go to the beginning, Des.*

He realized he was being egocentric. He had placed himself at the center of the murderer's universe. But this thing didn't start with him; it started with the first victim, the assistant US attorney. He was part of the plan but not *the* plan.

Opening up the manila folder resting on the nightstand, he rifled through papers until he reached the photographs taken of the first victim. *Nude from the waist up… blindfolded… hands bound with chain… two metal dishes filled with soot.* The second victim and the third were presented in the same manner.

He laid the pictures out on the bed before him, comparing them to see any discernable differences. There were none. One could easily have been substituted for the other. The fact they were found in different states was the only difference.

"It's all in the presentation," he could still hear the cold computer voice taunting him. *It's all in the presentation… presentation. Protesting the federal legal system.*

His heart felt like it stopped beating, giving his chest the sensation that it was about to explode. The realization hit him with such a visceral effect he fell back into the dresser behind him. The man was not just giving him the wild paranoid theories of a guilty conscience—he was right! The way the bodies had been presented was meant to convey a clear message. These women displayed before him like some piece of twisted artwork were not picked at random. They did represent the various stages of the federal legal process. The final confirmation was who their bodies were designed to portray, the insignia of the Department of Justice, the Spirit of Justice.

Depicted in drawings and sculptures, the blindfolded women, holding the scales before her, was the symbol of a legal system that was supposed to be fair, balanced, and without prejudice. The killer had created his own depiction of the iconic symbol. Everything needed, down to the last detail of the chains and brass plates to form the scale, had been carefully attended to.

Although the soot in the plates was still an enigma, the victims' connection to the process coupled with this obvious symbolic representation left little doubt. The informant was right. All that was left now was how to break the news.

CHAPTER 46

New York, New York

GENERAL CORRECTION SERVICES was a massive corporation with thousands of shareholders and stretched out like an octopus with its tentacles into dozens of subsidiary companies. Each of them traded publicly on the New York Stock Exchange.

These companies were involved in the manufacture and sales of everything imaginable—from personal hygiene and grooming products to uniforms and various other clothing, to tables, chairs, and bedding to both the public and private sectors. But it was their numerous government contracts that ensured massive profits.

Last year was a banner one for GCS as its net worth between its main branch and satellite companies approached the one-hundred-twenty-billion-dollar mark. While many in the business world admired their success, the design of the company and the structure of its management seemed very unorthodox. Its spread over so many different entities, and its seemingly inefficient model did not make sense from either a business or practical level. The tax liability alone increased tenfold from its design.

It was not unusual for major corporations to diversify, especially in the products they provided. Nor was it unheard of for a company this size to spawn smaller corporations. However, for GCS, from the outside looking in, it made little sense. Many analysts were bewildered by its unusual setup and its failure to take advantage of what appeared to be obvious opportunities.

Also peculiar was the absence of any of its major investors serving on its board. The company stated that they did this as a matter of practice to make sure minor investors were not always at the mercy of its majority stockholders. Supposedly, it was a way to allow their voices to be heard.

Although this proclamation tested the limits of believability, it was not illegal. Since the company continued to reap huge profits, there were no cries from its stockholders to change it. Thus, the Securities and Exchange Commission had no reason to raise an eyebrow.

It was Wednesday evening when the portly gentleman received the text message. Michael Ranier was at the GCS board of directors meeting, which met once a month in the back room of Giovanni's Ristorante. The setting ensured privacy while at the same time allowing those in attendance to feast on what many considered to be the best tortellini alla panna in the city.

The room was simple in design with dark-colored wood paneling on the walls and red vinyl covered chairs. At its center was a large rectangular table covered in a white linen cloth. Along with plates and silverware were three silver platters near the middle, each adorned with four bottles of Martin Ray's finest cabernet. Those gathered made it look like a throwback to the good ole boy's clubs of the 1930s, not a female or person of color in sight. While these did serve as official meetings, they were hardly formal. Cigars and backslapping were common as waitresses filtered in and out of the room, often complaining of the clouds of smoke they were forced to navigate as well as the occasional pinch on the ass.

Ranier had served as chairman of the board for the last nine years. Standing only about five feet five inches tall with broad shoulders and a body resembling a pear, his joking nature and penchant for the bottle made him seem more like a middle-aged frat boy than the leader of a multibillion-dollar company. Although, one could hardly blame the man for his frivolity. The latest projected quarterly earnings would put any individual in such a mood.

Yet that demeanor soon changed from joy to one of deep concern upon receiving the text message. It was from the only man he answered to. It simply read, "We need to talk. We have a problem."

Immediately gulping down the rest of his glass of wine, Ranier forced a smile, made an excuse, and hustled out of the restaurant. *What the hell could be the problem? It's going so smoothly.*

The night was warm and humid, causing him to perspire excessively before he could reach his car. Thoughts of the upcoming meeting flew through his head. He went over his mental checklist. Everything seemed to be in order. *What could this be about?* He still had no idea, but what he did know is he would not have been contacted if it wasn't of extreme urgency.

CHAPTER 47

New York, New York

AN EMOTIONALLY ZAPPED Des continued to stare at the photos. He was still in a semi-state of shock and disbelief. What he originally thought might be the ridiculous theories of an unsettled individual now appeared to have tremendous credibility.

For years, he had always viewed conspiracy theorists as loons, people who had lost touch with reality, and in most cases, for good reason. Their beliefs stretched the premise of conceivable possibility. He agreed with many experts that most conspiracies were born out of a need to make sense of the world around us.

In one documentary he had seen, a psychologist broached the subject as it pertained to the assassination of President Kennedy and the many conspiracy theories that were still bantered about over sixty years later. He explained why many of us need these theories, stating, "The Holocaust, in retrospect, makes sense to us. It was the worst crime committed by the worst criminals. The scales were balanced. But when we look at the JFK assassination, it's hard for us to believe that someone as insignificant as Lee Harvey Oswald could kill a man as significant as President Kennedy. We can't believe the world is that random. The scales are unbalanced. A conspiracy theory balances out those scales nicely."

Des never wanted to fall victim to this kind of thinking. But he could no longer discount what was before him. As he continued to stare at the grotesque images, his inner turmoil began to reach new points of unrest.

Things were beginning to make sense, which he had never considered before. Being led to historical figures such as Alexander Hamilton and Andrew Jackson was once perplexing. However, Hamilton's desire for a strong centralized government and Andrew Jackson's refusal to follow Supreme Court decisions played more and more into the idea of executive and federal power run amuck. Combining them with the disgraceful miscarriage of justice in the Sacco and Vanzetti trial and the symbolism of those victims, it was becoming apparent that this was the strongest possibility of why these murders were taking place. The killer had it out for the Department of Justice and anyone who supported it.

Des detested violence, having seen enough during his military service to last ten lifetimes. However, in spite of his revulsion to these acts, he was beginning to understand the rage. So much, in fact, he noticed his own feelings of empathy.

In beginning to understand the corruption, the absolute blasphemy to the Constitution the United States justice system had become, he too felt anger. Hundreds of corrupt US attorneys committing an endless array of felonies to get a conviction; FBI agents stealing, destroying, and fabricating evidence; judges who had essentially been castrated and subjugated to mere ceremonial figures had reduced the nation he loved into a massive kangaroo court. How did it come to this? When did the legal system cease being about justice and become nothing more than a large business enterprise? How did the American public get fooled into believing the powers that be, the ones they thought were their protectors, in reality, were engaging in the very criminal activity they swore to defend the citizenry from?

Des was becoming ill. His stomach churned, and his head swirled as this inner conflict grew. *I can't empathize with a killer.* The physical effects he was experiencing were stemming from two questions he did not want answered. How should you feel about a person who does the wrong thing but for the right reason? How do you deal with evil deeds done for a justifiable rage? The more he contemplated the situation, the more he was surprised something like this hadn't happened before.

Des splashed cold water on his face, took a few moments to gather himself, and then left the hotel, hungry and disillusioned. It was the type of disappointment a child felt when they learned there was no Santa Claus.

Walking out into the evening air, he noticed that the humidity had increased. A sticky New York summer had commenced. It was just past 10:00 p.m., but one not from this part of the country would be able to tell. The metropolis was still alive and bustling, keeping intact its reputation as the "the city that never sleeps."

He walked around the corner, having noticed a small pizza joint there earlier. It had tables on a sidewalk patio where he grabbed a chair. The traffic flowed by as the endless rhythm of car horns kept its steady pace. Right above the entrance to the eatery were two small TVs playing an old Laurel and Hardy film. He had seen it many times but still found it a wonderful release for his stress and indulged in the classic humor.

He ordered a Jamaican jerk chicken pizza, something he saw as a delicacy, having never seen it in Georgia. He paired it with a frosty stein of beer. He took a sip, allowing the crisp coolness to slowly trickle down his throat. For a moment, the tension dissipated, allowing him to get lost in the beverage.

He looked across the street, caddy corner to where he was sitting. There was a small coffee shop, which was so indicative of old New York. It wasn't the cookie-cutter model serving the patron fancy overpriced java in sizes with ridiculous names. It didn't offer souvenir cups and the latest mind-numbing CDs to accompany your caffeine habit. There was no cheap furniture to give off a false sense of warmth.

Instead, it was simple in design. Intimate booths, homey barstools, and a brightly lit interior were its only accommodations.

It was filled with customers enjoying simple cups of coffee and a piece of pie. No one was sitting with their face buried in a computer screen or their smartphone, cut off from the world around them. Rather, they were engaged in animated conversation with another human being. It made Des long for a simpler time, one in which face-to-face contact was all that was required. He shook his head and sarcastically laughed to himself at the irony of it all. In a world so interconnected, the people who possessed the best of technology seemed the most isolated and lonely.

He continued to watch as people filed in and out of the quaint coffee shop. Small clusters went back and forth as they crossed the street. Looking at their expressions, he tried to imagine what their evenings had been like. Some were moving toward him and others away.

There were two pretty girls who looked to be in their early twenties, laughing as they gossiped. There was an elderly married couple walking arm and arm. There was a skinny black kid who could not have been much older than eighteen, with a perplexed look on his face. He was wearing a red T-shirt, baggy jeans, and snow-whitecolored tennis shoes. Des noticed he was holding an envelope while staring in his general direction. As their eyes met, he moved toward Des with a look of hope.

"Are you Mr. Cook?" he asked pensively.

"Yes."

"I was asked to give this to you."

He handed Des the envelope. Immediately Des's heart jumped into his throat. The red lettering flashed before him like a warning sign. He leapt up from his chair fast enough to make the kid jerk backward.

"Who gave this to you?"

"Some weird-looking dude in the coffee shop gave me twenty bucks to give it to you."

"Is he still there?"

"I think he just left. He went down there," the kid said, pointing south on 104th Street. "He was wearing a black shirt and a white pinstripe Yankees cap."

Des turned and darted across the boulevard, barely being missed by a cab whose driver swore at him while shaking his fist out his window. The street was dimly lit by pasty-colored streetlamps. There was no foot traffic, creating a hauntingly eerie scene. New York was always chaos; thus, serenity and calm was unnerving.

Des ran further down 104th with only the sound of his feet hitting the ground to accompany him. He scanned the area, desperately trying to penetrate the darkness.

He ran to the next cross street and then the next, still nothing. He turned 180 degrees before he finally caught the silhouette of a strong-looking figure walking east. Des sprinted at the shadow, his panting becoming more and more pronounced. He saw the figure turn left, allowing Des to catch the profile of his ball cap outlined against the light from the lamp above. The silhouette disappeared behind an apartment building. He took what little he had left of his waning strength to push harder in the direction of his target, rushing to reach the corner. Sweaty and out of breath, he looked frantically. But the figure had vanished, like the steam emanating from beneath the manhole cover in front of him.

He walked a few feet north and then repeated the action in the opposite direction, but it was obvious he had failed. Out of frustration, he kicked a trash can at the edge of the sidewalk, causing a dog to bark at the commotion. Placing his back against the side of the building, still panting from the chase, he tried to regain his composure.

It was frightening having someone like this targeting you. It was even more disturbing knowing your anguish was being observed in such close proximity.

Having forgotten he was still holding it, he glanced down at the envelope. On the front, it read "Cook." He was still fatigued, and it required extra effort to break its seam. As he pulled the paper out, he momentarily closed his eyes, mentally preparing himself for the next terrifying chapter. Unfolding it, he was surprised at its contents:

With great frustration, I write you this letter.
I find it disconcerting that you may not be up to the challenge.
Loss is inevitable.
Life is full of failure.
I know you are my enemy.
And this means I cannot relent.
My anger continues to grow.
However, I will not give up on you.
And I am sure you will come to understand.
Tomorrow is another day.
Terror will bring you to comprehension.
Only you can stop it.
Now regroup and let the world know what you find.

There were no clues, no instructions, and no chase. It was encouragement dispensed by a demented soul, and Des could read nothing else into it. But he knew someone who might.

CHAPTER 48

New York, New York

THE MEETING LOCATION was always the same, a parking garage located on the Upper East Side. It was chosen because of an idea hatched from watching the film *All the President's Men.* Bob Woodward, during his Watergate investigation, would meet his infamous informant Deep Throat in a parking garage to get the dirt on the scandal that would rock the Nixon administration. Here, they could talk candidly, out of public view.

It was a little before midnight when Michael Ranier, chairman of the board of General Correction Services, pulled his Mercedes sedan into a parking space on the second level. Ever mindful of prying eyes and ears, he made sure his vehicle would not be seen in close proximity to the designated meeting spot.

Walking to the stairwell, his $1,500 designer shoes echoed throughout the cavernous cement structure. *Why could we not just meet on a park bench?* he thought as he huffed and puffed his way up the steps, moving his sizable frame to the sixth floor. By the time he had reached his stop, his shirt was already drenched, the sticky night doing nothing to alleviate his overheated condition.

Looking to his left, he saw the glow of a cigarette lighter near the corner parking stall, then saw it go out as the acoustics of the garage registered the click of the lighter being closed.

"I thought you were going to quit," said a panting Ranier.

"I was meaning to, but this is not a good week to take on that challenge."

"So what's the problem? Is the main man having second thoughts?"

"No, he's still in line if it comes to that. The bill is locked in committee. I'm trying to get it to his desk. If I can't, it will be up to the next in line."

"Then what's the issue?"

"The issue is you're leaking secrets like a goddamn sieve!"

Ranier was stunned by the accusation. For as much as he maintained a carefree persona, he always prided himself on running a tight ship. "And you think it's me?" he asked defensively.

"No, you wouldn't be that fucking stupid. But the leak must be coming from someone underneath you."

"What do you mean?"

The man handed him emailed copies of a balance sheet and another of a photograph taken two years earlier. "You better find out where the hell this is coming from, or we all go down."

"There's only a couple of other people who would have access to this, but they have as much to lose as we do," answered Ranier.

"Did you hear about Gertig?"

"Just that he was missing."

"They found the son of a bitch's body near the docks on the Upper West Side."

"Do you think it has anything to do with this leak?"

"Doubtful… That guy was in bed with so many thugs that I would think he got onto someone's shit list. Plus, he was on his way to Tokyo on business. He wouldn't have carried this with him. Probably pissed off one of those Mexican cartels… And no one else I know has any idea that we have ties to the company. It has to be coming from somebody else in the know. Just find it!"

With that, he threw his cigarette on the ground and walked away. Ranier stood there for a moment, trying to digest what he had just been told. Then, like a soldier given an order, he did an about-face and headed to the stairwell to make the descent back to his car. The knowledge that any failure to find the source of the leak would result in utter devastation was the heaviest of burdens.

His pace quickened. He knew he was not being watched, but at the same time, he could feel the world's eyes resting their gaze upon him. Reaching his car, he opened the door and squeezed into the front seat. Starting the engine, he immediately blasted the air-conditioning while placing his head against the steering wheel. There would be no rest tonight.

CHAPTER 49

※

East New Jersey

I WILL NOT let them get away with this. I will expose everything. Dr. Gregory Feller had just completed his workout, and it was a monster. Crunches, squats, curls, and lunges left his muscles massive from the rush of blood, as well as exhausted. It was a satisfying feeling. The sensation of impurities leaving his body could be felt with every drop of sweat falling from his skin.

He walked to his full-length mirror and removed his shirt. It had taken a long time, but the transformation was complete. The change had to be drastic. He could not be satisfied with simply quitting his job. He needed a complete break from his past, a move from who he was to what he had become. It was an alternate being. A persona opposite of the soul that once possessed him.

For years, he had always been the one waiting in the wings. Despite his talents, despite his success, it was always someone else who had control. It was always someone else who had their finger on the trigger.

Not this time... He allowed the persona to take over. *I'm in control. I'm manning the wheel. I will show them their mistake, and then it will all come crashing down around them. They are in the chase, but they will soon discover the true nature of the situation. They will witness my talent.*

As the change took place, a slight grin edged the corners of his mouth. The hours he spent examining every detail was soon going to produce the fruits of his intricate design. Soon they will have their revelation, and then he would immerse himself in the joy of their mistake. They would see what he had become.

It was driving to a conclusion. No matter what happened to him, the goal would be attained. His survival was not necessary for that to be accomplished. Shortly, it would reach the final event. With its culmination, those who betrayed him would pay the heaviest of prices.

He took a few moments to admire his chiseled abdomen. Running his fingers over the area, he remembered the once-embarrassing bulging midsection. It was now hard and ridged with each muscle leading to a *V* as it moved further toward his pubic region. The arms, the legs—they too were sculpted to perfection.

He had done it. It was flawless. They would never figure out the plan. *What idiots! They're going the wrong way. They're looking in the wrong direction. They have created the killer, but they will never find one.* He was so close, just a little bit more time and he would finally end it.

CHAPTER 50

New York, New York

HE DID NOT receive a return text for almost an hour.

"Sorry about the delayed response. What's up?"

"Something just happened. Can I see you now?" he sent back.

"Of course. Are you okay?"

"Yes, well… I'm not sure."

The next text he received was her address near Chelsea. It took him about ten minutes before he could flag down a cab. But the drive there was a relatively short one as traffic was not as intense.

Her apartment building was utilitarian in design, matching Amanda's work persona. It was kept up very nicely, and its lobby was more modern than its exterior would lead one to believe.

When he arrived at her place, Amanda opened the door to a noticeably disheveled and nervous Des. His expression was one of worry, and he was panting as if he just finished a ten-mile run.

"You got another message, didn't you?" she said as she tied her robe.

He nodded in confirmation. "I think something big is about to happen."

"What did he tell you?" she asked as she invited him in.

"He didn't tell me anything. He had a kid give me this while I was eating at a pizza joint," he said, handing her the envelope.

She looked at him intently, immediately recognizing the significance. "He was watching you. Did you see him?"

"I tried to catch him, but the only thing I saw was his shadow."

Amanda pulled out the letter but then stopped herself before reading it. "Forgive me, you look exhausted. I sometimes forget that I only profile the killers. I'm not threatened by them. This must be horrible for you."

Des gave a slight smile of appreciation but then quickly displayed a look of dismay. Amanda put her hand on his shoulder, guiding him to her family room couch.

"I'll put some coffee on. Do you want cream and sugar?" she asked as she headed for the kitchen.

"Thanks, that would be good."

After returning, she sat in the chair across from him and began to read the letter. Des could tell she was studying each syllable carefully.

"He's not making any demands or leaving any clues or instructions."

"I know, it seems like he just wants to taunt me some more," he said frustratedly.

"But that's not like him. He doesn't fit the profile of the type to just taunt without a purpose. He's too sophisticated for that. There has to be something here."

"Well, I read it several times on the way over, and I couldn't make any sense of it."

"I'll be right back."

Amanda left again and then came back with a cup of coffee in each hand. Handing one to Des, she said, "I'll take another look at it in a second. By the way, we've found another victim, but there's no definitive proof that it's the same perp."

"Who?"

"James Gertig."

Des recognized the name. "Isn't that the bank president who went missing the other day?"

"Yeah, why?"

"I read about it in the paper this morning. Was there a note or something left at the crime scene?"

"No, but the body was displayed in a very unusual way."

"How so?"

"He was seated and dressed only in a loincloth. He had a book glued to his left hand, and he was wearing something resembling a tool belt with a hilt on his right side."

Without the revelation he had earlier, it would have sailed right by him. But Amanda's description was spot on for the other symbol opposite the DOJ's Spirit of Justice.

"What was the book he had in his hand?"

"It was a biography on Galileo."

Des recognized the significance of that as well. He placed his coffee cup on the table, leaned back into the couch, and bowed his head.

"What? What is it?" Amanda asked.

"I think I know what this is about. I think I know what drives him."

Amanda leaned forward. "Yes."

"He's protesting the federal justice system. He has a hatred of it."

At first, she paused with an expression of disbelief. "You're kidding… right?"

"No, I'm not. Look how the bodies have been presented. The first three victims were female, nude from the waist up and blindfolded. The two plates exactly mimic the scales the Spirit of Justice holds. Even the chains binding their wrists was part of the picture."

"Yes, that's true, but Gertig is male."

Des just looked at her until she had her own epiphany.

"Oh my god! The Majesty of Law. How could I have missed that?"

The Majesty of Law is the male form accompanying the female Spirit of Justice. He is depicted in the seated position, holding a book in his left hand while his right rests on a sword fixed to a hilt on the right hip. He represents the rule of law standing watch over his mistress, Justice.

"When did you figure this out?" she asked, shaking her head.

"I had my suspicions tonight. But they were confirmed just now when you told me about Gertig. Especially when you mentioned the book."

"The biography on Galileo?"

"He's the most famous unjustifiably imprisoned man who ever lived."

Galileo is generally considered one of the greatest scientists in history. His theories on the solar system and planetary movements were revolutionary. But the famous astronomer's theories, while true and ahead of their time, proved too controversial for the justice department of the Catholic Church. He was arrested, put on trial, and imprisoned for suggesting the earth was not the center of the universe.

"So, he's protesting the federal courts," she said, making the same mistake Des did earlier.

"I think it may be more than that."

"What do you mean?"

"Look at the victim's backgrounds—an assistant US attorney, a retired federal probation officer, and now a—"

"President of a bank which was indicted for funding criminal organizations and terrorists and who never served a day in jail. But what about the second victim… the seamstress?"

"There must be something in her background we overlooked." Des wanted to tell her everything but was weary of doing so. The explicit warning to keep how he obtained his insight to himself was still fresh in his mind. Yet the guilt of leaving Amanda handicapped by withholding his knowledge ate at him.

"It still does not explain one thing," she said.

"What's that?"

"The soot in the plates."

"I have no ideas on that one. Maybe he's ritualistic like you initially thought."

"Maybe, but something's amiss. With the killers I've tracked before, their ritualism was often only symbolic to them. This one seems like he's making an effort to be symbolic for us. I think we need to keep an open mind."

She stood up, walked to the window, and looked out at the city lights. "You know, I've done so many cases, but I'm beginning to fear something that I've never feared before."

"And that is?"

"That this one is smarter than me."

The monotone way Amanda said those words sent shivers down his spine. She was considered the best of the brightest. If he was smarter than her, what chance did they have to stop him? What chance did he have to survive?

Amanda turned and looked down at the letter once more. Taking another sip of coffee, she suddenly stopped and started coughing violently.

"Are you okay?" Des said, standing up.

Still coughing, she motioned for him to come over to her. Des, having already been put through the emotional wringer, became alarmed.

Seeing his concern, she said, "I'm okay, I'm okay… but look."

He stared at the letter once more but could see no difference.

"Look again," she commanded.

Des took the paper and stared at the message. Still, he could see nothing. He began to read each line slowly again:

With great frustration, I write you this letter.
I find it disconcerting that you may not be up to the challenge.
Loss is inevitable.
Life is full of failure.
I know you are my enemy.
And this means I cannot relent.
My anger continues to grow.
However, I will not give up on you.
And I am sure you will come to understand.
Tomorrow is another day.
Terror will bring you to comprehension.
Only you can stop it.
Now regroup and let the world know what you find.

Des had a completely puzzled expression.

"The first letters, don't you see it? Look!"

She grabbed a pencil off the table and the letter, made some markings, and handed it back to him. "Look!"

> With great frustration, I write you this letter.
> I find it disconcerting that you may not be up to the challenge.
> Loss is inevitable.
> Life is full of failure.
> I know you are my enemy.
> And this means I cannot relent.
> My anger continues to grow.
> However, I will not give up on you.
> And I am sure you will come to understand.
> Tomorrow is another day.
> Terror will bring you to comprehension.
> Only you can stop it.
> Now regroup and let the world know what you find.

Des felt lightheaded, like he was on the verge of passing out. He had finally reached the point where he was not thinking about William Hatton every minute of every day. But once again, the monster had reappeared. This could be no accident. The killer knew his greatest horror. Wobbly, he walked back to the couch and sat in a motion resembling more of a fall.

"Are you okay?" Amanda asked sympathetically.

"I don't know… I don't know why I've been chosen for this. I feel responsible and at the same time helpless."

She sat down next to him. "I know what you mean. You never get over the injustice of it all."

"I'll be all right," he responded unconvincingly. He tried to reach over for his cup of coffee, but his hand was trembling so much he fumbled for it like an infant trying to grasp his first object.

Noticing his struggle, she said, "Are you sure you're okay?"

"Yeah… I'm fine… I don't know. When I was in the Army, we knew who we were fighting. We understood the objective. Here, I'm chasing a ghost who haunts me by killing others and then calls me 'The Enemy.' I'm nobody."

"I guess I'm in a different position. I just try to analyze them. I've never been their focus."

"I'm sorry. I don't mean to unload this on you."

Amanda reached over and gently squeezed his arm. Her auburn hair fell daintily across her cheek. Her almond-shaped eyes were both intense and tender. Her scent swirled around him as her knee gently touched his. She then leaned in to kiss him. Their lips touched as she pulled him toward her with tremendous force.

It was warm and soft, her tongue touching his with enticing skill. Her hand ran up his thigh as she let out a slight gasp of pleasure.

Des was torn, his heart confused. He longed for feminine comfort and was captivated by this woman before him. His thoughts were already fixated on what it would be like to touch her skin, to taste her body, and to feel the incredible warmth as he penetrated her. But he was pensive as well.

She continued to kiss him while taking his hand and placing it on her breast. She slid her hand between his legs as she felt his hot breath against her neck. Amanda reached underneath his shirt, running her fingertips over his abdomen.

Yet his inner conflict was too great. *I want... I can't... I can't do this.* Slowly he pulled away, looking ashamed.

"What's wrong?" she asked.

"I'm sorry... believe me, I want to. But I'm with someone else."

A look of hurt encompassed her face, which was followed by tension with a hint of anger. Then it dissolved into an expression of embarrassment. There was a pause and silence seeming to last an eternity.

"I'm sorry," she said. "It's my fault. You must think I'm an idiot."

"No, not at all. You're beautiful and brilliant, and God knows how attracted I am to you."

Amanda stood up and walked back to the window. "She's a very lucky girl."

"No, I'm the one who's lucky."

She turned and gave Des a conciliatory smile. "I guess this is one of the pitfalls of my job. I spend so much time analyzing psychos I misread people. I forget people have lives and regular interactions away from the criminal elements of society… that others are normal," she lamented.

Des, recognizing her self-deprecation, protested, "What are you talking about? You are normal."

She let out a slight scoffing chuckle and then turned away again. "Do you ever think there'll be a time when someone can look at me and see beyond my degrees… beyond my profession?"

Des stood up, moved in behind her, and placed his hand on her shoulder. "Well, what I see is an extraordinarily accomplished and beautiful woman that any man would be incredibly fortunate to have in his life."

She reached back over her shoulder and touched his hand in recognition of his sincerity.

"I better go. We have a lot of stuff to work on, and I won't be worth a damn if I don't' get some rest. Thank you for seeing me tonight," he said.

Des turned and walked to the door. Reaching for the knob, he paused and looked back. She was still standing on the other side of the room, facing the window, her blue robe sloping down her torso and the curvature of her hips. He wanted to say more, but the only words that left his mouth were "good night" before exiting.

Amanda shut her eyes at the sound of the door closing. A heat rushed up her spine as the flush of embarrassment and frustration welled up inside her. She had failed to get his attention. She was outdone by a woman who she theorized was not her equal, not as worthy.

She took a few steps toward the door, wanting to go after him. Then stopped, kissed her palm, and placed it against the portal. She knew better. She could not allow these feelings to cloud her judgment. She needed to unwind. Tomorrow would be sure to have more challenges. A shower would do nicely.

CHAPTER 51

Location unknown

WITH THE OLD persona temporarily extinguished, the new one of predator was enraptured by pure focus. The next phase was about to begin. Today would be the day in which a scene unlike any other would be discovered. The Enemy wouldn't need any use of deductive reasoning to figure out obscure clues. All they would need was to see the rage.

Every piece of information leading to the final phase had already been provided. The first four presentations, if deciphered properly, would hand The Enemy the final target.

The message left by this latest brutality was straightforward and served as a reminder of what they were dealing with. The game had been played fairly. There was no need for regret that Desmond Cook had still not figured it out. The fault was his. He had failed at putting it all together. Eventually, The Enemy would come to the conclusion that he had left out one piece of the puzzle, and it was the only piece that truly mattered.

CHAPTER 52

New York, New York

DES ARRIVED AT the FBI offices that morning, only to be greeted by the somber looks of Keller's and Amanda's faces. Seeing their dark mood, he asked, "What's wrong?"

Keller pointed at his desk. As Des looked down at the oak fixture, one of the most gruesome things he had ever laid eyes upon came into view.

The photographs looked more like stills taken from some horror film. A man who appeared to be in his late forties or early fifties and a woman in her late thirties were slaughtered in what was obviously a deliberate mutilation and desecration of their bodies. The ghastly wounds went far beyond what it would take to induce death.

They were laid on the ground next to each other and stripped nude. There were puncture marks covering them from head to toe, especially to their necks, far different from the clean lacerations on the previous victims.

The male had his penis cut off and had large vertical cuts to his face and abdomen. The female had her breasts removed, and some type of bloody mass had been shoved into her mouth.

"Jesus…!" Des exclaimed. "Who did this?"

"Who do you think?" Keller responded.

"But this doesn't look like the others. How do you know?"

"Because this was left at the scene," he said, handing Des a piece of paper.

He didn't need confirmation. There was no doubt now. The note was the simplest thus far:

Desmond Cook—
It's all in the presentation.
Your knowledge of history should be your guide.
It marks the position of the target.
You have the answers.

"Was this all that was left?" Des asked, looking over at Amanda.

"No, if you look in the corner of the photos, you'll see a mound of soot, but no plates."

There was no pattern, no meticulous display, nothing that would suggest the killer meant to convey any type of message. It was a bloodbath, pure rage, plain and simple.

"What's that in her mouth?" Des inquired, pointing to the woman in the picture.

"According to the report, that's the male victim's penis," answered Keller. "You're right though, these aren't like the others. It's like he had a personal vendetta with these two. I'm sending Amanda to California to investigate."

"California?"

"The victims were guards who worked at the federal prison in Lompoc, California. They went missing a couple of days ago. They were found on a small farm about two miles from the prison," Amanda answered.

"Amanda is going to the prison to conduct some interviews," added Keller.

"Whom are you going to talk to?" asked Des.

"I'm going to interview some staff and prisoners to see if anyone might have had a motive to do this. These murders were very personal. There's a possibility someone there might have some vital information."

"When will you be leaving?"

"In about two hours."

"Is it typical for a serial killer to change the way they do things like this?" Des asked.

"Not really," Keller interjected. "Most are pretty consistent, which makes this one more disturbing."

"How so?"

"It's almost like he knows how we investigate. He recognizes what patterns we look for. He's actually conscious of it. Most serial killers don't break patterns. Their drive for consistency overshadows their need to throw us off the scent… but not this one."

"But we're not out of hope," Amanda broke in. "I think our killer knew these two personally. It has an air of revenge to it."

"He never gave us a chance on these victims. There were no taunts or clever clues for us to follow," Keller said. "He never attempted to contact you."

"Same with Gertig," Des replied.

"Yes, same as Gertig."

Des looked at the pictures again and shook his head in disbelief. He had seen carnage before, but it was always through the impersonal lens of war. There were no political or religious objectives here. This was killing in a manner that was as personal as it gets.

CHAPTER 53

Lompoc, California

IT WAS GREEN richness everywhere when Amanda looked out her car window as she made her way to the prison. Gently rolling hills were marked off by fenced pastures of grazing cows and fields of various crops. Small houses and farm equipment also dotted the area of this small community.

The town of Lompoc is nestled in the hills behind the coastline, just north of the city of Santa Barbara. Its tranquil setting, mild temperatures, and gentle ocean breezes make it an ideal agricultural location. While many products are produced there, it is mostly known for its number one export—flowers. Visitors will often see green pastures interrupted as the valley will turn into a showcase of rich yellows, passionate reds, and soft pinks and whites, stretching across the terrain in a virtual kaleidoscope of colors.

However, behind all the candy for the eyes that the beautiful floras create are concealed items that are much less peaceful. A large swath of the land is federally owned and provides a key installation for the United States Military's Vandenberg Air Force Base, which sits across from the center of town. Fighter jets, cargo planes, and satellite rocket and missile launches are common sights and sounds in the skies above, interrupting the peaceful scene below.

Sitting to the east of the highly active base, one could find the federal government's other town industry, the correctional institutions. Although the name sounds humane, everyone in the area is aware of the massive oppressive prison complex lying on its borders.

Divided into three levels, Lompoc holds a camp for minimum-security inmates, who are considered such low risk that there are no fences on its perimeter; a low-security prison, which houses inmates in barracks and consists mainly of nonviolent offenders; and a medium-security facility, which resembles their more traditional state counterparts. Yet it is all well concealed, hidden from prying eyes and the very people who pay for its operation. In a way, it is a microcosm of the system, doing a fine job of keeping from the public the reality of what makes up its parts.

As Amanda drew closer, the correctional institution came into view. Chain-link fencing stretched in all directions. It was capped by intimidating razor wire meant to cut to pieces anyone who attempts to breach its apex.

To the right was the cement block structure of the medium-security facility. It was a lifeless facade, as desolate looking as the absence of foliage surrounding it. Rising above it were a group of towers that one might see at an airport, casting shadows over the grounds like giant birds of prey. To its east was the low-security facility, which was her destination. Although this particular prison was supposed to house mainly nonviolent offenders, by its outer appearance, one could hardly tell. The same razor wire surrounded it, as well as a series of three fences encasing its front.

Amanda pulled into the parking lot and took a deep breath. While she had done interviews many times before, she was never quite comfortable with them. She much preferred to be engrossed in pages of evidence, trying to grasp at the motives, habits, and personalities of the offenders she chased.

She exited her car and entered the front building. Behind the desk in the lobby was an officer dressed in the sanctioned uniform—a light-blue shirt with his name embroidered on the front and an

American flag on the sleeve, black pants, and a black belt, which held a hook with dozens of keys that clanked together with every movement.

Amanda took out her FBI identification badge and flashed it at the officer. "Hello, I'm Agent Hertzel. I'm here to see Officer Weber and Officer Callaghan."

"Just a moment please," the officer replied.

After seeing him pick up the phone to notify his superior, she could tell by his expression that her reception would be an icy one.

"They're sending over an officer to escort you. He should be here in a few moments. You can have a seat over there," he said, pointing to a small group of chairs.

It was uncomfortably silent as the guard went back to working on his computer, only occasionally looking up to give her a suspicious glance. Amanda felt very unwelcome. The environment almost had the feeling of walking into a mine field. Even though their agencies both fell under the Department of Justice, there was no friendliness or sense of cooperation.

It took about ten minutes before a gangly young kid, who looked like he should still be in high school, rather than working in a federal prison, approached her. "Agent Hertzel, I'm here to escort you to your meeting. My name is David."

"Thank you," Amanda answered as she gathered her belongings and joined the young officer.

They proceeded through a couple of locked doors into a small area surrounded by two chain-link fences. To their left was an open area, which had an athletic field laced with holes that had been burrowed by the hundreds of squirrels residing there. To the right was a very small encased area marking the visitors' location.

"How long have you been working here?" Amanda asked her young escort, trying to engage him in conversation.

"Let's see," he said, looking up. "I was hired in the first week of November and then went through training and started here in the second week of December."

"That's only five weeks of training," she said a little shocked.

"Yeah… not too bad… huh?"

"What made you want to do this type of job?"

"Where else can I eventually make $70,000 a year with just a GED degree?"

He unlocked a second gate, allowing her to pass before resecuring it. As they turned the corner, they were hit by a pungent odor that was as sickening as it was strong.

"Oh my god! What is that awful smell?"

"Oh, that happens a lot. The sewage line running out of this place always gets clogged and overflows. Make sure you don't step in that water," he said, pointing to the river of raw sewage as they approached.

The smell was enough to gag a maggot. Amanda did everything she could to avoid the disgusting sight, trying to step over the debris and fecal matter floating by.

"Before I take you to the office, I have to check something in one of the units. It will only take a moment," he said.

They entered a courtyard about thirty yards across and fifty yards long. It was surrounded on three sides by very stark concrete structures. It was crowded with inmates wearing their khaki-colored shirt and pants uniforms. Some were sitting at tables playing cards; others were huddled under a small canopy that held TVs. The smell of cooking fish wafted through the area as the chow hall reheated its food, only adding to the nauseating combinations of aromas.

They turned to the right heading toward a building marked as Unit A. As she looked up at its facade, the piles of bird feces that had built up over the years clung to the windowsills in mounds nearly a foot high. Some of it was so prevalent that the windows were completely covered with the encrusted matter, allowing for almost no passage of light. White stains ran down the side of the building, covering plants at its base with a white film thick enough to where one could barely see the greenery peeking in beneath it.

The guard, noticing the look of revulsion on Amanda's face, attempted to explain. "Sorry, the place is not more cleaned up. When we have planned visits or inspections, it's in a lot better shape. But you came on such short notice."

"So, this is how it normally is?" Amanda questioned. The guard just shrugged his shoulders in a kind of an "oh well" manner.

As they entered the building, the smell of fish and raw sewage was replaced by body odor. The floors were caked with dirt and grime as they moved into the stairwell, which was equally as filthy.

The guard led her to the second floor, where she was immediately hit by the smell of urine. To her left, there was a door propped open with a paperback book. Prisoners walked back and forth through the portal in a constant flow.

"Please wait here. I'll be right back," the guard said, disappearing through the door. Out of curiosity, she moved closer to the open portal to see what lay behind it. She was shocked at what greeted her eyes. Row after row of steel-plated bunk beds, no more than three and a half feet apart from one another on either side, covered the room with such density that if viewed from above, one would hardly see the floor. The space, clearly made to hold no more than forty to fifty inmates, easily had twice that number. To add to the congestion, each inmate had a locker to hold their belongings, making the entrance between the bed and storage area about a foot and a half across.

There were bars on the windows, and most of the clasps to be able to open them to allow for ventilation had been welded shut. Hanging from the bars were pieces of laundry struggling to dry, while at the same time increasing the stifling humidity and foul odor. An inmate passed her through the doorway holding a mop that he took to the adjacent bathroom to wipe its urine-stained floors. Refuse poured out of an overflowing trash can with dozens of flies hovering above it, making Amanda wince.

When the guard returned, he escorted her past the open bathroom, providing her a clear view of the four toilets meant to serve the massive population of that one floor. Toilet paper was strewn across the mildew-covered ground, and the smell of decaying food left its interior as she spotted inmates cleaning dishes and bowls in the same sink they shaved, brushed their teeth, and washed their faces in.

Amanda could feel her gut stirring while she did everything she could to avoid throwing up. As they moved down the hallway, they passed an office where another guard sat completely oblivious to the squalor around him. Before turning down another stairwell, the door across from it swung open as an inmate exited, revealing a second prisoner housing area identical in size and congestion. How so many inmates were packed into the obviously too small facility was particularly troubling to her.

"How many people does this facility hold?" she asked.

"Officially or unofficially?" the guard responded.

"Both, I guess."

"Officially we have about 1,100, unofficially, about twice that."

"Why the two figures?"

"I don't know. I guess they don't want the public to get wind of it."

They continued their descent until two more levels had passed before entering a twenty-by-twenty-foot space crowded with over a dozen inmates.

"What are they here for?" she asked.

"Oh… they're waiting to see their case managers."

"Does that take long?"

"Well, once they put in a request, it usually takes four to six."

"Days?"

"Months," he replied.

"Why so long?"

The guard just shrugged. "What does it matter? Where are they going to go?" he replied with a grin of someone who had finally obtained a power they had never previously possessed. "You'll meet with Ms. Callaghan shortly. Just have a seat in here."

The young guard opened the door to a small office that was neat, but very sterile looking. The furniture was obviously inexpensive, but modern. A black lacquered desk with sharp cut lines was in the left back corner of the room. Two black leather chairs were placed across from the desk, trying to take up as little space as possible in the limited confines. No decorations of any kind adorned the walls, perfectly matching the impersonal demeanor of the facility itself.

Amanda sat uneasily, trying to digest what she had just seen. Emotions flooded her—sadness, frustration, and anger, but mostly a feeling of shame that this existed in her country.

"Hello, Dr. Hertzel," a curt female voice said behind her.

Amanda turned around to face a woman in her fifties. She had a pale complexion and gray hair styled in a way resembling a little boy. Her eyes were like charcoal, and her thin pursed lips gave her a dour expression.

"Hello, Ms. Callaghan," Amanda answered, extending her hand. "I'm sorry to have to meet you under these circumstances, and I'm sorry for your staff's loss."

"Yes, me too," she said, sitting behind her desk. "What can I do for you?"

"Our office has been investigating a series of murders by this individual, and I'm trying to find out why he would target two of your guards."

"And you think one of our inmates is connected in some way?"

"Current or former, yes. It's one of the several possibilities we're looking into. Were there any particular inmates, former or current, who had filed complaints about these two guards?"

"Dr. Hertzel, this is a prison. Most inmates have gripes against the guards. So, if you're suggesting they had it coming—"

"Ms. Callaghan, I'm not suggesting that at all. I'm trying to get a profile on a serial killer and to find the motives of what's driving him. So… there were complaints filed?"

"Yes," Callaghan answered defensively.

"Were the complaints severe enough to motivate someone to kill?"

"Dr. Hertzel, this is a low-security prison. Over 85 percent of the population is here for nonviolent crimes, and the ones that have committed violent offenses have worked their way down from higher-security facilities over a period of years."

"Well, let me ask you this way. What kind of correctional officers were Officer Shara and Philes? What were they like?"

"They showed up on time and did their jobs," she answered evasively.

"Had they ever been reprimanded or disciplined for any issues relating to prisoner treatment?"

"Dr. Hertzel, I don't know what you're getting at, but I don't like where this is going. They were the victims, not the perpetrators."

"Ms. Callaghan, this individual has already killed six people. I need to know how he's choosing his victims. The other victims were killed in a relatively quick and simple manner. But Officers Shara and Philes were slaughtered in the most brutal of ways, including Officer Philes having his penis cut off and shoved into Officer Shara's mouth. The killer treated them with considerable savagery and hatred. We believe he might have known them. I don't think you want to see other members of your staff suffer the same fate."

Ms. Callaghan nodded in a conciliatory manner. "Officer Philes was not well liked by the prisoners. He had to be reprimanded on several occasions for getting too physical during searches. Let's say… he had issues."

"What kind of issues?"

"General stuff, really—pushing prisoners against walls, taking things that were not contraband… verbally assaulting prisoners… things like that. He seemed to be on a power trip most of the time."

"What was his background?"

Ms. Callaghan went on to paint a less-than-flattering picture. She presented him as a small-minded man with a limited attention span and a major inferiority complex.

His employment file held his academic and work records. He was not much of a student and seemed to bounce around from job to job until he landed one with the Bureau of Prisons as a guard. Callaghan described him as an individual who longed for recognition, who longed to be someone important, but had a disdain for hard work, keeping him from reaching those goals.

Philes had two marriages, both ending in nasty divorces in which his wives left him for greener pastures, with Callaghan even stating that both of his exes wanted someone who had "potential." What he lacked in motivation and intellectual capacity, he attempted to make up with an abundance of testosterone and an ever-increasing waistline. Chasing women was what he spent most of his free time doing, both at play and at work. He had been released from two previous jobs due to claims of sexual harassment filed by his fellow female employees.

With his limited skills, meager looks, and a major chip on his shoulder, his options were at the shallowest end of an already shallow pool. The Bureau of Prisons offered good-paying jobs with limited required skills. For Philes, it fit perfectly.

Outside the prison environment, he was a microbe, a bottom dweller, the lowest on the food chain. As a prison guard, he could indulge in his fantasy of a world that asked "How high?" when he demanded them to jump.

Yet his methods were sloppy and dangerous. However, like most of this branch of federal legal system, he, along with his colleagues, saw little to concern themselves with. Most incidents were brushed under the rug; this included one where he shoved an elderly prisoner so hard against a wall during a search he broke his nose and wrist. And another, during an inmate disturbance, where he shot without cause numerous prisoners with rubber bullets, as well as about half of the facility's windows.

The report on Officer Shara was no more flattering. Although she was not as physical with inmates, she seemed to take great pleasure in being verbally abusive, often screaming obscenities at prisoners for no apparent reason. She also made it a habit of blaming prisoners for her mistakes.

"She was always looking to cover her ass," said Callaghan. One incident reported happened immediately prior to an inspection. "She dismissed the inmates from cleanup duty too early and then blamed them for leaving when she realized she screwed up. She tried to give them all shots, all thirty-five of them."

"Shots?" Amanda questioned.

"It's a disciplinary measure we use for breaking rules. It takes away good time toward an earlier release."

"So, it adds time to their sentence."

"Yes. Prisoners can earn a small amount of time off their sentence for good behavior, 15 percent at most. A shot will take that away."

"And it's left up to the guard's discretion to take that away?"

"Yes."

Amanda was stunned. The kid who escorted her in looked barely old enough to tie his own shoes, let alone mature enough to be entrusted with such a decision.

"I noticed there were a couple of other incidents in one of the units where Philes and Shara worked together," Amanda said, looking at their files.

Ms. Callaghan leaned back in her chair and gave Amanda a begrudging look. "Which ones are you referring to?"

"Well, there's one that says a Mr. Jameson, who was seventy-nine years old at the time, slipped and fell, but both Shara and Philes failed to get him medical care even though several prisoners said he had been crying out in pain for hours and requested help."

"The officers thought he was faking it."

"Was that before or after he soiled himself? Because it says here that he was in so much pain he couldn't get up to use the restroom on account he had broken his hip in two places."

Ms. Callaghan did not respond, instead, glaring at her inquisitor.

"Ms. Callaghan, I would like to talk to some of the inmates who were interviewed about the circumstances surrounding some of these incidents."

"I don't think that will be necessary. They're convicted felons. What could they tell you that you can trust as being accurate?"

"Just because they've been convicted of a crime does not disqualify them or their opinions. It will help me identify their frame of mind and if anyone may have been angered enough to take action on their own."

Ms. Callaghan barely nodded her head in the affirmative. She then hesitantly picked up the phone to notify her superior. *This could get ugly.*

"I have one last question," Amanda stated. "If Officers Shara and Philes had so many incidents and complaints, how come they were allowed to continue to work here?"

"You've obviously never dealt with the Prison Guard Union."

CHAPTER 54

Washington, DC

ROBERT CANTWELL SAT in his office in the nation's capital. He had taken the red-eye back, then took a short rest and a quick shower, before returning to work.

After checking with his secretary for the day's schedule, he went to his workspace to tie off some loose ends on other projects. However, his mind was still racing. There was so much out of his control, and this latest wrinkle was proving to be the most worrisome.

While finishing off a letter to the governor of Texas concerning issues at the border, he was continually distracted. He found himself working on the same sentence for ten minutes. His train of thought was repeatedly interrupted by constant glances at his email.

But he had to get back on track, as he had a fairly full schedule for the day: a quick briefing with the president, another meeting with the state attorney general of Arizona, followed by what he considered his most important appointment, a meeting with Senator Wayman.

The two men had a cordial relationship, but both knew they would soon be locked in battle for the presidency. Wayman would be running on the platform of cutting unnecessary domestic budget spending. Like many politicians, he believed some vital services could be provided to the public if some frivolous and illogical expenditures could be curtailed.

He examined the budget for what he believed were financial drains on society. At the top of his list were federal justice system costs, which had been spiraling out of control. Since the 1980s, the country had seen an explosion in the federal prison population from just below thirty thousand when Reagan was in office, to nearly a quarter of a million today. An increase of over 800 percent, with no signs of slowing down.

Yet most politicians were too scared to take a stand against what everyone knew was unsustainable. The current budget for the system was $100 billion a year and nearly a trillion over the previous decade, and this did not even include other Department of Justice expenses.

However, those running for office were weary of being labeled "soft on crime," choosing instead to steer clear of the issue altogether. That, coupled with the over a quarter of a billion dollars spent by private companies a year on lobbyist and campaign donations for longer sentences, more prisons, and more limitations on defendant and prisoner rights, kept the system intact and growing.

In order to feed this beast, monies had to be taken from other domestic programs, such as job training, student loans, and medical research. With its ever-increasing appetite, even more would have to be cut to maintain the growing business of incarceration.

It was when $30 billion had to be taken from a meal program for hungry and disadvantaged children, one of Senator Wayman's most cherished, that he started looking for ways to save it. After exhaustive research, he came to the conclusion that one of the biggest drains on the budget was the federal legal system, particularly its Bureau of Prisons and US Attorney's Office. He took notice that small-time, first-time offenders, which in state courts would get probation, were serving ridiculous sentences of ten and twenty years for the exact same offense. One case he used as a prime example was a man serving seventeen years for selling $500 worth of marijuana. This was despite the fact he had no previous record and that marijuana sales in several states had become legal. He could not understand why there were virtually no programs offered to lessen a prisoner's sentence, as was common practice in almost all state prison sentences. Everything, from his point of view, was directed to be as punitive as possible, with no regard for costs or justice.

In a powerful speech before Congress, Wayman railed against the ridiculous waste and the callous way in which the federal legal system threw away lives over a first-time mistake or infraction. He showed in an array of charts and graphs that America had more people in federal custody than its counterparts in China, Russia, Eastern and Western Europe combined. "How can we pretend to be the moral leader of the free world?" he cried. He urged his fellow members of Congress to, "Find the courage to reach beyond the false appearances and do what was right and moral by embracing my reforms."

He finished his oratory with a dramatic and spine-chilling prophecy. "If we do not act. If we do not correct this injustice, this affront to what our founders had envisioned, then your grandchildren and my grandchildren will know an America where one out of ten of their fellow citizens will be locked in a federal prison before the close of the century. Do we want an America where one transgression, where one mistake in judgment drains all hope of redemption? Have we become so conditioned to throw away lives with the false argument that it protects society, when all evidence clearly demonstrates it accomplishes the opposite? We look to our history and have assigned the great leaders with monikers which have echoed through time. Washington was the 'Father.' Lincoln was the 'Great Emancipator.' The question we must now ask ourselves is, what will our label be? Do we wish to be remembered as the 'Great Incarcerators'?"

The speech was hailed as one of the finest by any senator in the last fifty years and made Wayman's popularity and career skyrocket. His newfound prominence shot him to the forefront of his party's potential nominees for president. It was also this sudden rise in the senator's prestige that was now causing Attorney General Robert Cantwell headaches.

With his impassioned plea, Wayman had made his proposed bill to reform the system the centerpiece of his résumé and for his run for president. The highly touted piece of legislation was being used to keep his ascension in the polls at a constant into the election. It's effectiveness in doing so was becoming evident as his popularity was beginning to rival Cantwell's. This threatened not only Cantwell's own bid for the highest office in the land but also his entire plan to have the legislation killed.

Until recently, Wayman was planning to send the bill to Congress, where it would most likely pass with little opposition. However, while the president was noncommittal publicly, privately he was against the legislation and would veto the bill once it hit his desk. When Wayman became armed with this knowledge, he decided to withhold the bill from a congressional vote until after the president's final term was completed.

This put Cantwell in extreme jeopardy and in the nearly impossible position of trying to convince Wayman to release the bill to a vote immediately, under the false pretense that he supported it and could get the president to endorse it. Cantwell knew and intended that the bill would never be signed into law. But at the same time, he had to convince his future rival that he was 100 percent behind the popular legislation. If he failed in his efforts, he would face Wayman in the election campaign with no ability to control the outcome of the proposed bill. If that happened, it could lead to disaster.

In addition, the problem was now being exacerbated by this latest development. If Wayman stuck by his guns, and refused to release the bill to a vote, it would also become the most talked-about policy during the presidential campaign, and that would inevitably lead to a vetting. If Cantwell's connections and involvement were found out, it would ruin everyone. If what he had received in his email a day earlier was any indication, this secret would not remain one for long.

As he exited his office and mumbled a few last instructions to his secretary, the attorney general felt like he was preparing for an appointment to plead for his life. With events going the way they were, it may come to that.

CHAPTER 55

Lompoc, California

AMANDA WAITED ANXIOUSLY for Ms. Callaghan's superior, Officer Kyle Weber, to bring one of the assigned inmates to interview. It was one of three she needed to conduct that day.

After about fifteen minutes, a tall wiry man with dirty-blond hair, a heavily pockmarked face, a '70s porn mustache, and a suit that looked like it had been borrowed from the set of Miami Vice entered the room. The bright purple shirt he was wearing seemed to be doing battle for attention with his equally gaudy tie.

Standing next to him was a very nervous and frail-looking old man who was so thin it appeared as if his frame could barely carry the wrinkled prisoner uniform that hung on him like a paper bag.

"This is inmate Nielson. He will be happy to answer your questions," Officer Weber said in a daunting tone as he eyed his prisoner.

Mr. Nielson sat down in the leather chair across from Amanda. Weber stood directly behind him like a vulture hovering above a dying animal, waiting to pick at its carcass.

"How are you, Mr. Nielson? I'm Amanda Hertzel. I'm a psychologist and profiler for the FBI."

"Nice to meet you," he answered in a crackling voice riddled with nerves.

The elderly man was visibly frightened; his repeated glances at Weber and Callaghan displayed his discomfort. Amanda, realizing the atmosphere would be unproductive, turned toward the officers. "Mr. Weber… Ms. Callaghan, could you please excuse us? I think it would be better if I spoke with Mr. Nielson alone."

Weber gave Amanda a look of disdain while still pausing at the request. A few more moments of uncomfortable silence passed before she spoke again. "Thank you both for your assistance today, but I'm really short on time."

Weber nodded to Callaghan in a gesture confirming they should go. Callaghan exited first, followed by Weber, who gave one more intimidating glare at the old man before closing the door behind him.

"I could tell you were uncomfortable," Amanda said with a reassuring smile.

"Yes, ma'am."

"So, Mr. Nielson, how long have you been here?"

He hesitated for a second, still unsure of the situation. "Well… let me see. I came in when I was fifty-two. I'm sixty-eight years old now, so I guess it's been sixteen years," he answered, looking up at the ceiling.

"May I ask you what you're here for?"

"I was convicted of fraud."

"Fraud?"

"Yes, I was accused of stealing money from investors in a business I was involved in."

"How much more time do you have left?"

"Oh… I guess it would be about six more years with the good time I've accumulated."

"That's got to be tough on you."

"And my family… at least what's left of it," he added.

Amanda looked at the man with a sense of empathy. He did not look like a hardened criminal or some type of menace to society. In fact, he reminded her of her own kindly grandfather.

"I'm here to investigate what happened to the two guards… I'm sure you've heard."

"Yeah, I heard. It doesn't surprise me."

"Why do you say that?"

The old man peered over his shoulder once more and then turned and bowed his head. The silence was deafening.

"Mr. Nielson, no one will have access to what you tell me. You're not in any kind of trouble."

He just shook his head in a way that said, "How naive are you?" "Ma'am, with all due respect, nothing said here will stay confidential. Just by the fact that you requested my presence puts me in a very vulnerable position."

"Have you been threatened?"

Mr. Nielson remained mute, simply staring into Amanda's eyes. It was all the confirmation she needed, and it didn't take much to figure out by whom.

"What was Correctional Officer Philes like with the inmates?"

He fidgeted in his seat for a moment, placing his hand on his forehead then removing it and putting both hands on his knees as he hunched over. Amanda did not repeat herself, allowing him to regain his composure and sort things out in his mind. Then he took a deep breath and mumbled something that she could not make out.

"I'm sorry, Mr. Nielson. I didn't understand what you said."

Looking down once more, he answered, "I said, never lose the meaning."

She gave him a perplexed look. Noticing this, he repeated the phrase, "Never lose the meaning... It was something that I always told my children."

"Never lose the meaning of what?"

"Integrity... I always told them that no matter what happens in life, always be honest, and always be sincere... and that withholding the truth is a form of insincerity. It's my definition... my meaning of integrity."

Amanda smiled softly. "I think that's the best definition I've ever heard of that word."

"What good does it do if I don't put it into practice? If I don't practice what I preach?" He took another deep breath. "It's all for nothing if I start turning back now. So, you want to know about Officer Philes?"

"Yes."

"The honest truth is that I've never known a more heartless individual. The only blessing was that he was too stupid to gain more power."

"Was he physically abusive?"

"All of the time. But he seemed to get his biggest kicks out of provoking us."

"How would he do that?"

"He would yell at you… try to embarrass you in front of the other inmates. He would always say things like, 'You deserve to be here.' He would read through your private letters for no reason and then make derogatory comments about what was in them."

"Were there any inmates who you heard make comments about him?"

"Oh hell, all the time… tons of them."

"Did you ever hear anyone threaten him or say they wanted to harm him?"

"I never heard anyone threaten him to his face… although there were plenty of guys who wanted a piece of him. Most of it was just idle threats… things prisoners would say to each other to pump up their rep. None of it was serious."

"I see… nothing that stuck out in your mind?"

"No… not really. Although I did see Philes get into an unusual conversation… but it wasn't with a prisoner."

"Staff member?"

"No, I don't know who it was. He was dressed in civilian's clothes."

"When did this happen?"

"Just recently… like a few days before they found him dead."

"Were they arguing?"

"You know, I'm not sure… It was kind of hard to tell if they were going at it. You could see them talking on the other side of the fence line. They weren't inside the prison. They only talked for a few moments and then Philes walked away and kind of waved his hand… like you know… in a 'go away' motion," he said, mimicking the movement.

"What did he look like?"

"He looked like he was in his midfifties… gray hair on the side of his head. The one thing I do remember is that he was in really good shape. Kind of looked like a weightlifter."

"But you never saw him go into the prison?"

"No… why?"

"Well, the prison would keep records of visitors."

"Oh… I see."

"What about Shara?"

"Oh, she was a real piece of work," he said, rolling his eyes. "We called her the 'daily double.'"

"How did she get that name?"

"For two reasons really. One reason was that she seemed to have two personalities… both bad… but one was worse than the other."

"And the other reason?"

"She had this pronounced double chin, which was kind of weird because she wasn't fat. We used to joke that she had to settle for a job here because she failed as a Pakistani porn star," he said with a slight chuckle. "I'm sorry, I shouldn't have said that."

"It's okay," Amanda responded, trying not to laugh. "Was she abusive like Philes?"

"Verbally, yes… nasty woman… cursed like a sailor. I could swear that woman had to pee standing up."

"Mr. Nielson, I want to ask you about another incident… a man who had a heart attack in the barracks you were in."

His expression suddenly changed from intensity to one of sadness. She could immediately tell she had struck a nerve.

"You must be talking about Peter… That was a horrible night."

"Did you know him well?"

"He was in the bunk across from mine. He was a really good guy… pretty quiet most of the time… but he helped me a lot. I'd only been here a year when it happened."

"Were Officers Philes and Shara working your area that night?"

He nodded in confirmation.

"Can you recall that evening?"

"Yes," he said hesitantly. "Peter told me he wasn't feeling well after chow. He said he felt dizzy and his chest hurt. I told him that I would go with him to see Ms. Than—the wicked witch of the east."

"Ms. Than?"

"She was the medical staffer who worked that night. What a bitch! Always got offended if you called her 'nurse.' She wanted to be called 'doctor.' Ha! What a joke! She most likely got her degree through one of those Filipino online classes. If she was a doctor, then I'm the starting quarterback for the Dallas Cowboys."

"What happened when you got there?"

"She did what all the medical staff does here—nothing! She didn't want to be bothered. Peter kept telling her something was wrong. I remember him saying he was short of breath… that his chest hurt, and he had pain running down his arm."

"Classic signs of a heart attack."

"Yeah, you would think she'd try and do something and call an ambulance."

"She didn't, did she?"

"No," he said, shaking his head. "She just told him nothing was wrong and to drink some water and sleep it off on his bunk. The bitch just wanted to go home… didn't want to have to work late."

"Didn't he protest?" Amanda said, feeling anger building inside her.

"Yeah, he did… but you're not in control. They are. The medical care for inmates is a joke here. It's even written into their health code that it's defined as 'experimentation.' We're not people to them. All they do is pass out medication, and they even get that wrong a lot of the time," he paused for a moment, his lower lip beginning to quiver. "I'm… I'm sorry."

"It's okay. You have a right to be upset."

"It's unbelievable what they do to us… Do you know before I transferred here from the main detention center in Los Angeles what the doctor there told me?"

Amanda just slightly shook her head.

"I was being given my physical, and I asked the doctor what makes an obviously educated man want to work in that kind of an environment. He told me he was paying off his student loans, but the prisons still have problems getting doctors. When I asked him what they did if they couldn't get them... he told me they hire veterinarians."

Amanda's mouth dropped open. *That can't be true, can it? But he has no reason to lie.* "That's terrible."

"I'm sorry, you want to hear more about Peter... I got off track."

"Take your time."

"I took him back to his bunk. About an hour later, he was almost in tears with the pain. I went over to Philes and Shara to tell them I thought Peter needed a doctor... that he needed to go to the hospital. I got them to come take a look at him. Peter was already as pale as a ghost. They told me he would be fine and not to waste their time. Hell, you could even hear them laughing as they walked away. All night I could hear him moaning. All night!" he cried, burying his head in his hands. "I kept talking to him... I told him to just try and relax and I would get him to the hospital in the morning. I sat in a chair next to him most of the night. I fell asleep there," he said, his face turning red, fighting against the emotion. "When I woke up the next morning, I reached over to wake Peter... but... but he was already dead."

Amanda was as flooded with emotions as the man sitting in front of her. But she had to maintain her professionalism. "Did you report what happened?"

"Yes, I reported it to Weber. I told him everything I've told you. But he just kept repeating the same thing. He kept telling me that they took Peter to the hospital and they did all they could for him. All they could—ha! He was already dead! For God's sake, rigor mortis had already set in. They did nothing more than load a corpse onto that gurney. But... no one ever dies on the compound."

"No one ever dies on the compound?"

"It's an old running joke here. They don't have anybody on the compound who is legally able to declare someone dead. So whenever someone dies at a federal prison, they're never reported as having died on the inside, but are shipped to a hospital and then declared dead there. It's the Feds' way of escaping responsibility and cooking the books. There've been dozens of deaths since I've been here. One was even a guy who committed suicide by nearly decapitating himself. But their ledger, when it comes to deaths on the compound, will always read zero."

Amanda was stunned, enraged and embarrassed. She too was a "Fed." She did not want to conceive of such a system in her country.

"Did anything happen to Than, Philes, or Shara?"

"What do you think?" he answered rhetorically. "Nothing ever happens… Like the inmates say, the staff is always right."

Amanda tried to collect her thoughts. She inhaled in an effort to regroup before resuming. "Do you think someone close to Peter, perhaps a family member, would want revenge?"

"Wouldn't you?"

Amanda just nodded. "Mr. Nielson, you said you were here for fraud. How much money did they claim you gained from your crime?"

"Thirty-four thousand."

"And they gave you twenty-two years for that?" she asked shocked.

"They first offered me five."

"Why didn't you take it?"

Mr. Nielson gradually stood up on his feeble legs and stared directly into Amanda's eyes. "Integrity, Dr. Hertzel. I wasn't going to plead guilty to something I didn't do."

"Well, if you were innocent, your attorney should have been able to prove that."

He smiled. "You would think so, but all the computer files at my home and office were confiscated by the FBI. It took them nearly four years before they charged me, and all the evidence on those computers, which would have proven my innocence, just magically vanished. When I asked about it, they said there were no files on any of the computers that were relevant to my case. My whole goddamn business was on those computers!"

"So, when you refused to plea, they tacked on seventeen more years?"

"Dr. Hertzel, I don't have money. I don't have property, and I don't have my wonderful wife… God rest her soul. But I do have integrity, and what kind of example would I be setting for my children if I took that deal? Good luck with your investigation." He then politely shook her hand and walked out the door.

The two following interviews provided little additional information with the only valuable piece being that one of the inmates heard Philes tell the man he encountered outside of the prison, "You're crazy."

Amanda gathered her notes and placed them in her briefcase. When she opened the office door, Weber was standing there waiting.

"I trust the inmates were cooperative," he said.

"Yes, they were all helpful."

"Well, I hope you find the son of a bitch."

"Me too."

"I called an officer to escort you out. He'll meet you at the top of the stairwell."

"Thank you," Amanda said as she turned to walk up the stairs. But before she could proceed, a clamp came down on her elbow, halting her. It was Weber's hand.

"You know, Dr. Hertzel, we're all on the same team. I hope you understand that. We need to support one another," he said in an effort to intimidate.

"We may both work for the government, Mr. Weber, but we're not even on the same page, let alone the same team," she answered in disgust.

With that remark, she pulled her arm from his grasp and stormed up the stairs. The guard met her a few moments later and escorted her out the gate of the prison. When she got back to her car, she calmly opened the door, placed her briefcase on the passenger seat, and sat behind the wheel. It took a few seconds, but when she began to cry, the tears came down in rivers.

CHAPTER 56

Savannah, Georgia

IT WAS MORNING as Madison sat in the kitchen, her eyes fixated on the decorative vase sitting on the table. It held a collection of yellow and white flowers that Kelly had picked the previous day. Yet in actuality, Madison didn't see it. It was just an object her eyes had glued on to while her mind was somewhere else.

No contact, not a word from Des, and it had been such a long time. What did this all mean? He was supposed to be coming to Savannah in just a few weeks. They were going to spend the remainder of the summer together. She had even entertained the idea of them moving in together. *Did he sense that? Was I moving too fast? Did he find someone else?*

Kelly entered the room and looked at the clock. "God, it's only seven fifteen. How long have you been up?"

"Oh… I don't know… for a little while, I guess."

Kelly noticed Madison's red eyes and the bags hanging beneath them. Her hair was tied in a ponytail, and she was wearing the same T-shirt as the day before. When Kelly looked down, she saw Madison hadn't touched her coffee but continued to stir it incessantly. No steam emanated from its surface, having dissipated all of its heat.

"Honey, you can't keep doing this to yourself," Kelly said.

"I was pushing him too hard. I should have taken it slower."

"You did no such thing."

"It's like my marriage."

"Madison, stop it! Your ex was nothing more than a first-class prick who never knew how good he had it."

"I know we've only been together a year, but I thought I knew him better."

"You're jumping to conclusions again."

It was at that moment the beep of her phone could be heard, indicating a text message had come in. She grabbed it as if it was the last life preserver left on a sinking ship. Madison didn't recognize the number, but she knew who was its sender. It read, "I'm okay… talk soon… Braves."

The Atlanta Braves was Des's favorite sports team. Yet the message conveyed little else, only adding to her anguish. Madison handed the phone to a bewildered Kelly and put her head down onto the table.

CHAPTER 57

— ✦ —

New York, New York

HE KNEW HE had failed to adhere to the FBI's protocol. He kept the message as brief and innocuous as possible, still heeding both Agent Keller's and the killer's warning about contact. Des had only broken it once before, just prior to departing for New York. But earlier, during the morning, he felt he needed to give her some kind or reassurance, no matter how vague. *What must she be thinking?*

Amanda was supposed to be returning from California in a few hours. She had called him earlier, wanting to meet him at her office. She told him she had a detailed profile of the killer ready to go as there might have been a potential sighting of him by the federal prison in Lompoc a couple of days prior to the murder of the two prison guards.

Des anxiously awaited her return. He had been going over scenarios in his head about the context of the killer's last note.

"It's all in the presentation. Your knowledge of history should be your guide. It marks the position of the target. You have the answers."

However, he could not find anything of significance. He knew the killer always combined his savagery with his knowledge of Des's history background. So far, Des's abilities had led to the discovery of several key components through those talents. This was not by accident. The killer was too smart, too meticulous for that to be just coincidence.

All that he had discovered thus far, he was meant to. The Spirit of Justice, the Majesty of Law, the grave of Alexander Hamilton, and the town of the Sacco and Vanzetti trial—all led to the same conclusion: a hatred of the federal government, and in particular, its justice system.

However, there were still mysteries that seemingly were beyond his reach, namely, the meaning of the soot. With the first three murders, the soot was placed neatly into the brass plates. But with the murder of the prison guards, the soot was found, but no brass plates were left to hold it, and in Gertig's case, none was left at all.

Maybe Amanda was right about the possibility of it being a ritual, a way to purify oneself of evil deeds. Yet if that were the case, why was it absent from the Gertig crime scene?

The other puzzle was that Gertig did not seem to be related to the legal system in any way other than the fact that he had beaten the Feds, which one would think the killer would approve. Every other victim had some direct connection to the system, as was confirmed by his mystery informant. More was added to the puzzle by the fact Gertig's body was the only one not found in a rural area. But whether this held any significance or if it was happenstance was impossible to say.

Des hovered over the photographs for hours, but it proved to be a fruitless endeavor. Hopefully, when Amanda returned, the information she attained on her trip would shed some new light and break the stalemate in his own investigation.

Evening began to descend on the city, and Des finally gave up trying to find any more clues. He left the hotel to grab something to eat before heading over to Amanda's office.

As the cab made its way to the FBI building, his thoughts were no longer on the killer. The lights of the city were now just streaks of color. The sounds had muddled together into a sort of white noise. He was, for the moment, not in New York, no longer in the twisted thoughts of a murderer's mind. He was with Madison.

He was pressed against her body, her brown eyes gazing so deeply into his, reaching parts of him he thought no one could touch. He wondered whether he'd ever see them again.

"Sir… sir! We're here," said the driver.

Des was startled out of his dreamlike state to find he had arrived at his destination. He nodded in acknowledgment, handed the driver his fare, and begrudgingly walked toward the building. He was saddened that the reality had pulled him away from his momentary bliss.

CHAPTER 58

New York, New York

BREATHE... BREATHE. THE final task is nearing. Breathe... breathe. Let him take over. Let him infiltrate your being. Breathe... breathe. It's almost here.

Dr. Gregory Feller had been waiting for this moment since the day he stormed out of the FBI offices. It was the spark which had ignited the inferno. From that point going forward, his whole life would be dedicated to a sole purpose, to invite the world to see his true self, his true talent.

Casing the structure, he repeatedly ran his hand over his bicep, enjoying the sensation of this perfection he created. Without even recognizing the action, his palm was soon moving over his torso, the hard ridges pushing through his shirt, sending torrents of confidence, feeding the transformation.

It was coming to a head. Preparations had been made. Every last detail was attended to. The confrontation was coming. Those who had devastated him would now reap the consequences of the catastrophe they had invited. The senses were heightened, the body honed to its most ideal state, the mind conditioned to conceal its true intent.

All that was left was to implement the final phase. The beauty was in the design. Regardless of the outcome, there was no way

220

to fail. His survival was not necessary, only the aftermath. Either direction would lead to victory; no matter his fate, the result was guaranteed one way or another.

I no longer recognize the being of my past. I am reborn. I have risen. I am the Phoenix. Nothing exists but my true purpose. Nothing exists but the goal. It's time. Breathe… breathe.

CHAPTER 59

⚜

New York, New York

WHEN DES ENTERED Amanda's office, she was sitting at her desk with the manila folder labeled "Legal Killer" opened in front of her. Its contents stretched to all corners of her workspace.

Her expression was a mix of exhaustion and concern. To her right, the photos were laid out in neatly assigned piles, and in the center were documents filled with all the evidentiary information that had been collected thus far. Closest of all to her was a steaming cup of coffee, black as the night, with not even a hint of dilution from any other substance.

"You've got to be exhausted," Des stated.

"I'll be all right. It's just all this flying back and forth that has gotten to me a little bit. Do you want some coffee?"

"No, thanks, I'm good. Tell me, what did you find out in California?"

"That prison is a goddamn nightmare. It should be condemned."

"That bad… huh?"

"Worse, but it does lend credence to your theory about this being an attack on the federal legal system."

"How so?"

"Those two guards were far worse than any of the inmates they have locked up there—abusive, arrogant. They seemed to take a certain sick pleasure in other people's misery."

"They sound like real assholes."

"That's an understatement," she said before taking another sip of coffee.

"May I take another look at those photos?"

Amanda nodded in a "go ahead" fashion.

Des started sifting through them, staring at every detail they offered. The first three victims, women, laid out to look like the Spirit of Justice. *It's all in the presentation. Your knowledge of history should be your guide. It marks the position of the target. You have the answers.* He contemplated those words over and over again. Thoughts of the fourth victim, James Gertig, his body displayed to look like the Majesty of Law, now swam through his head. Then there were the two guards who were mutilated in the most brutal of ways, with only a pile of soot to accompany them.

In Des's mind, there was no question his motives were to harm the legal system. Yet where and who was going to be the recipient of the killer's next crime? What definition of the word *position* was the murderer using? *Could it mean a location? Maybe it's a type of job? It's vague.*

A location was hard enough, but narrowing it down to a single job was nearly impossible. There were literally thousands of positions making up the federal legal leviathan. The individuals who had been targeted worked in various capacities or had connections to the system in a plethora of ways, but not to each other. None of them were particularly important to the system as a whole. They were just small cogs in a massive wheel that would hardly miss their presence.

"What are you thinking?" Amanda asked, noticing his concentration.

"There's something that still bothers me."

"The soot?"

"Yes, the soot."

"I know I was not 100 percent certain, but I believe this is just a purification ritual."

"You're probably right, but there's still something that doesn't fit."

"That is?"

"There was no soot found at the Gertig crime scene."

"I can see how that would be confusing, but you're forgetting one important thing. Gertig's body was left inside a major city. There's a good chance our killer realized he couldn't go through that process without drawing attention. All the other victims were found on small farms… rural areas… away from the general population."

Des nodded in affirmation. It made sense. Setting a fire near a busy dock could be problematic if you're trying not to be noticed.

"There are a couple of items though that I was able to put together that I think will give us a profile," she said.

"What items?"

"Well, first and foremost were the condition of the bodies of these two," she said, pointing to a picture of the mangled guards. "I believe the killer knew these two. The first four murders were straight killings—clean… no wasted time. These two were completely mutilated… almost in a manner to cause as much humiliation and pain as possible. The others were much more precise… unemotional… unconnected."

"How does that contribute to the profile?"

"Because both of these guards had been in the system for a while, which, to me, suggests the individual we're looking for is more mature. He had a history with them… He's not a kid. That history certainly caused rage. You add into it that what the two inmates witnessed on the fence perimeter… a man in his fifties, in an uncomfortable conversation with one of the victims just a couple of days before his death, I think gives us a good indication."

"I agree that's pretty convincing evidence, and I'm not trying to step into your territory… but doesn't that description fit a lot of people?"

"Yes, but there's more. The road the prisoners saw that suspect is on federal property."

"I don't follow you."

"Most of the roads surrounding that facility can only be accessed if you have federal credentials. Civilian visitors are not allowed. They have to take a different route, or they'll be stopped by the authorities. So, whoever this individual was, he had to have some official government or law enforcement identification to be where he was spotted."

"What else did they say about what he looked like? Was he in some kind of uniform?"

"That's just it. He was in civilian clothes—jeans and a T-shirt. He was definitely not a guard or someone who was making an official visit to the prison. But he's someone who must have quite a bit of knowledge on how the system works."

"I remember Agent Keller saying this person seems to know how you investigate these types of crimes… Are you thinking he was once an agent?"

"Yes, or possibly still one."

"But I still don't understand what this has to do with me. Why does he consider me the enemy?"

"Well, the only way he would know of your existence in such a prominent way was your involvement in Arlington."

"You think he might have worked the Arlington case?"

"It's a possibility."

"So, we're looking for a middle-aged man who once worked for or is still working for the FBI, and in particular, the Arlington case, who holds a massive grudge against the system."

Amanda nodded. "Yes."

"These inmates who saw this man… they couldn't make out any more of his features?"

"They told me he appeared to be in his fifties. He had gray hair on the side of his head and that he was built like…" Amanda stopped and immediately turned and stared blankly at the wall.

"What? What is it?" Des inquired.

She shook her head. "Nothing… I had a thought for a moment, but I realized it was ridiculous."

"You were saying that he was built like?"

"Like an average-size man."

"That's not going to be easy to track. There must be many men in the bureau that fit that description."

"Yes, but not many who worked the Arlington case. I think we've narrowed it down. I'm going to talk to Keller first thing tomorrow so we can start heading in this direction." Amanda looked at the clock on the wall. "It's getting late. I'm pretty much fried."

"I can imagine with all the traveling. You need to get some rest."

Amanda took one more sip of coffee before standing up and gathering her things. It had been an emotional evening, and they were both drained. But for the first time, they both felt they were close. They now had a direction to go in.

Although they were encouraged, it was also unnerving. This individual was obviously very bright. That, coupled with a law enforcement background, made him particularly elusive and dangerous. He seemed to know every move and every pattern of thought they had utilized.

Amanda was particularly troubled. She had hesitated in giving Des all she knew. She didn't want to believe it, but her suspicions were now coming to a very frightening conclusion. *How is this possible?* But the more she thought about it, the more it made sense. He had the knowledge. He had the experience, and he sure as hell had the motivation. But she needed to deal with this herself. If her thinking was correct, she, better than anyone, could solve this problem.

As they entered the elevator, both of them were in their own worlds. While Amanda was contemplating this unexpected possibility, Des was dealing with the emotions of his own disillusionment.

He was a student of history. He loved and believed in his country's institutions, especially when it came to the concept of law and justice. It was the bedrock of the nation's founding. The Declaration of Independence, which gave its birth, eloquently stated like no other document the concept of human rights. It was followed by the Constitution, which was predicated on the idea that America would not make the mistakes its European parents had committed. It would not fall victim to the injustice and inhumanity that had plagued the Western world for a millennium.

But what he had seen and learned in the last week flew in the face of those enlightened ideals of America's founders. They were in direct denial of the country's past. The current federal legal system treated those magnificent concepts as a relic, refusing to use the principles that were supposed to be the genesis of the New World. Instead, they had been returned to their puritanical beginnings, ruled by superstitions, hysteria, and political motives… in which the very existence of the United States would become a memory as the people reverted to a medieval past. The nation was teetering on a facade where the wisdom and morality of the founding fathers were used only as a cover, a clever ruse to hide the fact that justice was now a profit center.

They exited the building into the balmy night, walking together, speaking in barely audible whispers.

"Sometimes I wonder if this thing is ever going to end," Des said.

"It will, it always does."

CHAPTER 60

AMANDA COULD FEEL the pressure building. It was pushing against her skull, making her feel like a balloon slowly being inflated. *How did Feller do it? How could I have missed the warnings?*

As they headed to the parking garage, for a moment, the city did not seem to be spitting out its torrent of noise. The illumination of the metropolis was presented in front of them like a silent movie, only displaying the blacks, whites, and grays of a classic film.

When they reached the structure, Des began to follow Amanda up the stairwell. As he placed his foot on the first step, she reached back and gently touched his arm.

"You don't need to walk me to my car," she said.

"It's getting kind of late. I don't think it's a good idea to go walking into a dark parking structure alone at this time."

"Why, Desmond Cook," Amanda responded, putting on her best Southern accent. "Are you worried about li'l ole me?"

"Well… yeah," he said, smiling at her teasing.

"That's sweet, but I'm sure I'll be all right. Besides, I'm FBI. We're always packing," she said, patting her purse.

"Okay… okay, point taken. I guess it's just the Southern chivalry in me."

"Good night, Des, I'll see you tomorrow." She then proceeded up the stairs.

He just shook his head and grinned. Turning toward the street, he walked a little ways more before looking behind him once again to see her ascending the flights.

Amanda reached the fifth floor, still smiling over their last exchange. Picking her keys out of her purse, she pressed the button, initiating the beep and releasing the lock on her vehicle.

All she wanted now was a glass of wine and a hot shower before retiring for the evening. Yet when she reached her car, the epiphany struck like a lightning bolt. A release of euphoria encompassed her. She needed to—

"Hello, Amanda."

Startled, she jerked around quickly. "Dr. Feller, oh my god, you frightened me," she said, clutching her purse to her chest.

"Well, that's a surprise coming from someone like you," Feller replied with a sarcastic grin.

"What are you doing here?"

"I think you know," he said, moving in closer, his muscular frame being backlit by the garage lights. "You got very close. I have to congratulate you on that."

"Close to what?"

"Oh, come on, Amanda. You know what I'm talking about," Feller said. His eyes grew larger with anticipation, his face expressing the satisfaction of finding his target so off guard.

Des had just about reached the street when his phone rang. *Jesus, Madison, why are you calling me?* "Madison, I told you not to call on my phone."

"Des, I'm worried. You've never kept secrets from me before. Where are you? I want to know what's going on."

He knew he could not protect her anymore from where he was; he had to tell her. There was a moment of silence before he answered. "I'm in New York."

"New York? What are you doing there?"

"I'm mixed up in something, but I don't know how I'm quite involved."

Amanda took a step back as Feller approached. She could see all the emotions he was experiencing as they were etched on his face.

"For a long time, I've been waiting for you to fuck up," Feller said. "I just never thought it would be like this. You've always been so meticulous… so attentive to detail, but you hesitated too long. That was a very costly mistake."

"You don't need to do this," Amanda stated. "It doesn't have to be this way."

"Don't do that, Amanda. I'm not some freshman psychology student. We know there's still one thing left to do on the list."

Des paced as he tried to calm Madison in the wake of her fear.

"I'm so scared," Madison said with a slight crackle in her voice. "This can't happen to us again. Please come home!"

"Honey, I can't let more people die on my account," Des pleaded.

"Who says this has anything to do with you? It's obvious that this guy's crazy."

Des didn't know what else to say as he searched for any words to soothe her. He felt helpless. She was only a short plane ride away, but Madison's voice sounded so distant, like she was on another continent.

"You need to be safe here with me," she said. "Or I need to come up there."

"Madison, I don't want you in danger too. I almost lost you once."

"As I did you," she said sternly.

Des inhaled deeply. The air felt heavy, the humidity only adding to the tension. He tried to gather himself. He knew she was right. This is the woman who watched him nearly lose his life at the end of William Hatton's gun. By the time he reached the hospital, he was on death's door. It must have been unimaginably difficult for her.

He closed his eyes and pictured her beautiful face. He missed the graceful lines of her body, the color of her skin, which was the warmest of browns, and the feelings he experienced when he was near her. But what he wanted now was her touch. He ached to feel her skin against his body, her breasts pressed against his torso, her hands cascading down his back, her soft lips touching his, and the sheer ecstasy of being inside her.

As Des turned once more, his pacing was suddenly interrupted by a thought. He realized he had yet to see Amanda's car leaving the structure.

"Des… Des!" Madison spoke in an ever increasingly worried tone.

"I'm here… I just…"

It echoed like thunder emanating from the garage in two distinct bursts. It was the unmistakable sound of gunshots.

"Des, what was that?" Madison cried. "Des… Des!"

He sprinted to the parking garage, trying to reach the stairwell as quickly as he could. "Amanda…! Amanda! Are you okay?" he shouted frantically while bounding up the flights.

Passing each floor, his fear increased. It felt like his gut was about to implode. What would he find? Was there someone lying in wait? Would he be gunned down? Third floor… fourth floor… fifth. He swung the door open. It slammed against the iron railing, sending out a bang nearly as deafening as the gunshot.

"Amanda!"

There was no one lying in wait, no bullet tearing through his flesh, and no screams of pain. All he could see was the shadow of a woman standing as rigid as a statue. All he could hear was her panting.

Des moved slowly toward her. She turned, jerking her gun up, pointing it directly at him.

"Amanda, it's me… Des," he said, with his hands up in the air. "It's me. You're okay… you're safe now."

She gradually brought her arm down, removing the gun from its threatening position. She then looked at the body of Dr. Feller. He was lying on his stomach with his face turned to the left. His legs were extended. His hands were to his sides, showing no indication he tried to break his fall. He was dead before he hit the ground.

Amanda shivered violently and then ran to the ledge of the garage and vomited over the side of the structure. When she lifted her head, Des could see she was in anguish. She dropped the gun and began to fall to her knees. Des grabbed her before she hit the pavement, just as she began to whimper.

"It's okay… You're okay… It's over," he said as she sobbed in his arms while embracing him tightly.

He looked down at the body. A pool of blood had gathered around its edges while a small stream of red fluid began to trickle in their direction.

Feller's face displayed a ghostly pale. A look of surprise was frozen on his profile as his eyes continued to stare at them. It was the look of a mission left unaccomplished. His massive arms were still taut and powerful looking, making him appear as if he were about to force himself up at any moment, but there was only stillness.

Des remained with Amanda until the police arrived and then drove her home as she seemed to be in a state of shock. As he accompanied her to her apartment door, she assured him she was all right.

Before entering, she gave him a hug and touched his face. "I really wish you could come in with me tonight," she said. "I want you here, but I know that wouldn't be a good idea… Thank you."

"If you need anything at all, don't hesitate to call me."

She smiled at him once more before closing the door behind her. Des stood quietly for a moment. He felt a sadness for her, but at the same time, he felt relieved.

CHAPTER 61

East New Jersey

DES COULD NOT help but be impressed by the grandeur of Dr. Feller's home. It was located in New Jersey, by the eastern border of the state, about a forty-five-minute drive from New York City.

He and Amanda arrived that morning to sort out what Feller might have had in his future plans. As they walked through the entry hall, gloved FBI agents were huddled in various corners of the adjacent living room, collecting evidence. A parade of more agents passed them with boxes in their hands as they shuffled by before exiting.

As Des looked around, he noticed that if Feller was one thing, he was meticulous. Nothing in this home was out of place. Everything was so precisely located that it looked like one of those model homes real estate agents use to entice buyers. There was not a speck of dust anywhere as the polished furnishings glistened in the sunlight streaming in through the windows.

The kitchen was like an altar to organization. Every cupboard was categorized, every plate stacked neatly upon the other. Spices were alphabetized; glasses were arranged not only by size but also by maker. Even the dish towels looked like they had been sent to the cleaners to be pressed.

"Is this common with serial killers?" asked Des.

"A lot of killers are obsessive-compulsive. That's why their crimes are so regimented," Amanda answered. "It's a way of reinforcing the reasons why they're killing in the first place."

They left the kitchen and proceeded down the hallway to the bedrooms. No pictures hung on its walls, making it as sterile as the kitchen.

The first room they encountered was set up like a gym, stocked with the latest workout equipment. There was a treadmill, which had more computerized measuring devices than a NASA control center, a collection of weights of every size, weight benches adorned in red leather, and nautilus machines filling the space. Across from the workout area were red mats laid out on the floor, strategically placed by the south wall, which was completely covered in full-length mirrors.

Des could almost hear Feller grunting as he powered the weights up and down, his rage increasing with every plate he added to the bar. He could visualize him throwing the mass to the floor as he finished another set, then immersing himself in the pleasure of the blood rushing to fill his muscles with enriching fuel. Finally, this machine, this killer, would walk to the mirrors to examine the display, searching for any imperfections requiring further sculpting.

"Dr. Hertzel, could you come here and take a look at this?" one of the agents called from down the hallway. Following the voice, Amanda and Des entered a massive bathroom.

"Jesus, this is bigger than my apartment!" Des exclaimed as he looked around him. "I never thought of a bathroom as being elegant before."

It was brick red in color, with three sinks on its north side, a walk-in closet for towels and bathrobes, and a computerized toilet from Japan, complete with a heated seat and a jet sprayer and dryer to clean the occupant's undercarriage. However, its most impressive structure was the shower, which ran the complete length of the west wall. There were six spigots allowing the bather to be drenched from every conceivable angle.

"Dr. Hertzel, do you know what this is?" the young agent asked, handing her a small bottle.

Amanda eyed the container. "It's Dianabol, an anabolic steroid. It's used mainly by body builders. I would be careful when you're going through those cabinets. This drug is administered through a hypodermic needle."

"Well, that definitely explains his size," said Des.

"It could also explain his rage. A lot of steroids cause tremendous changes in an individual's personality. They often become more aggressive," Amanda replied.

The two of them left the bathroom and continued down the hallway until they entered Feller's bedroom. It had a cavernous feel brought on by the sparse furnishings. At its center was a king-size bed covered with a deep-brown duvet cover, which looked as if it had never been slept in.

The wood floor was stained a golden brown, which reflected the light coming in from a sliding glass door leading to the backyard patio. Adjoining the bedroom was another walk-in closet with racks of clothes that were every bit as organized as the kitchen cabinets. Suits were hung in descending color patterns from dark to light. Dozens of shoes were on racks placed in order of designer. Even his undergarments were sorted according to color. When they exited the closet, another young agent was standing outside it.

"We didn't touch anything," he said, pointing to a door on the other side of the room. "We thought you should look at it first."

They approached the entry cautiously, almost afraid to see what was on the other side of the barrier. Des, noticing Amanda's trepidation, asked, "Are you okay?"

She only nodded, her muteness making the tension rise. As they entered, their silence was greeted with a sight justifying their lack of words.

The room itself was plain, with only a desk and chair that looked to be manufactured at one of those trendy furniture shops. On the desk was a small laptop computer. The walls were painted white, and the floor was polished black marble.

The east and south walls were unadorned, not a single decoration to break up their plainness. But that barrenness was starkly contrasted by what was attached to its north and west walls. It was vibrant, angry, and at the same time, brilliant. However, more than anything, it was pervaded by frustration.

The north wall presented the entire case that had made Amanda a star and cost him his promotion. Every article, photograph, and evidence description of the case of the kidnapped teenage girls was intricately arranged. It included terse notes he had written to himself about his failure to see the signs. They were attached to photos and other clue descriptions.

To the right of that display were more pictures and magazine articles about Amanda. There was one from *Newsweek* with her on the cover, the words "Case Cracker" emblazoned on it; another from *Time* magazine, which read, "The FBI's Rising Star"; and still another from *People*, which featured stories of survivors expressing their gratitude to this "amazing young profiler." Just below those were more sticky-notes reading, "I know what you are!" and "fraud." Amanda turned away in the face of the hatred.

"I think this clearly shows motivation. He was obviously trying to punish you for taking what he believed was his," Des said, looking at the wall.

When they turned to the west wall, any doubts they still harbored were obliterated. Every story, every lead and photograph of crime scene areas was there. Even a photograph of Des was hung with a red question mark over it. Next to that was a huge map of the United States with red circles indicating all the locations of where the bodies were found.

"Des, look at this," Amanda said.

She had opened the drawer of Feller's desk. Inside were airline ticket receipts for return trips from California, Louisiana, and Massachusetts, every place a murder had occurred.

She shook her head. "It's so hard to believe. I worked side by side with the man for three years."

Des, reflecting on his experience of a year ago, could comprehend her bewilderment. "I understand… Sometimes the people you least suspect are capable of doing the most horrific things. But there's still one thing that bothers me."

"Still the soot?"

"No, it's not that… he said the presentation would mark the target."

"Yes, I believe that target was me."

"But we didn't find anything in his presentations that would indicate it was you."

"Des, you're dealing with a person bordering on what would be diagnosed as psychosis. What he thought was being presented in his own mind may not make any sense to a sane individual. This whole presentation convinces me that I was the target and that the soot was for purification. I mean, look at this place. It's a freakin' monument to obsessive-compulsive disorder. Feller was the textbook definition of it. Plus, if you combine that mental illness with psychosis and then add mood-altering steroids to the mix, you have a pretty lethal cocktail."

"You're right. I just like a clean ending. I guess that's my disorder," he responded.

Amanda then walked over and placed her hand on his shoulder. "Besides, if there was a different target, he's no longer around to see it through."

"So it's over?"

"Yes, it's over."

Des took a deep breath. Having experienced what he did last year at Arlington, it was difficult to not hold on to the suspicion. He had witnessed firsthand what could be left behind and the damage it could cause. He understood when the obsessed departed this earth that not everything necessarily departed with them. But in this case, he would go with the expert's opinion. He still had no idea why Feller had taunted him. But if Amanda thought it was over, he had little problem letting it go.

CHAPTER 62

Washington, DC

FOR THE FIRST time in months he was able to relax. It seemed like an eternity since anything had gone as planned. Now finally, everything was falling into place.

US Attorney General Robert Cantwell sat in one of Washington's finest eateries, enjoying a medium rare filet mignon, fresh green beans, a baked potato with all the fixings, along with an ice-cold beer. It was a celebratory meal, and with good reason.

In a stunning turn of events, he had convinced his soon-to-be presidential race rival, Senator Andrew Wayman, to restart the process of getting his federal justice reform bill turned into law. The act he put on was Oscar-worthy, convincing the senator that the president was having a change of heart and would sign it.

"The budget is out of control right now," Cantwell told him. "The president is desperate to find any way to trim it down. He has to make a compromise with the House to get his agenda passed. The iron is hot, it's time to strike!"

It was a brilliant show of political trickery. He knew the president had no such plans. He recognized full well that the bill would be dead as soon as it hit the president's desk.

But by convincing Wayman otherwise, two things were accomplished. He would escape any culpability for killing a popular piece of legislation, instead, being seen as a supporter of the bill. He could also distance himself from a president who was experiencing rapidly declining poll numbers. All this, while putting his darkest incendiary secrets back into the closet where they belonged.

If this was not enough, two more pieces of great news came in as well. Jason Ranier had done a thorough search and cleaned house of anyone whom he had even the slightest suspicion of being the source of the leak. Then while reading the morning paper, it was reported that the FBI had found and killed the suspect who they believed had committed a string of murders, including the CEO of Trans International Bank, James Gertig. Thus, eliminating the remote possibility of the former bank president being the source of the divulged information.

With Ranier's cleansing and the killing of Gertig's murderer, all possible cracks had been filled. No more constant reports from Ranier would be required, and the anxiety-inducing emails had stopped. Everything was safe. Nothing would be interrupted.

Tomorrow would be a wonderful day, the most monumental of his life. He would be leaving for the Big Apple in a few hours to address the New York Chamber of Commerce. Dignitaries, important businessmen from all over the East Coast, top law enforcement officials, and even celebrities from the entertainment world would be there. The speech would be delivered at the famous Lincoln Center. It could not be more ideal. The city that adored him would welcome him home with open arms, and he would reward them with a major announcement.

CHAPTER 63

New York, New York

"DES! OH MY god! I'm so glad you called. Are you okay? Baby, please tell me you're okay?"

The sound of her voice was the most soothing of tonics, and this was the happiest of phone calls. It was the one he had been waiting to place to Madison since this whole nightmare began.

"It's over. They got him," he answered.

"Thank God! Thank God you're safe! When will you be coming home?"

"I leave tomorrow night, and yes, I'll be with you in just a few weeks as planned."

A squeal of delight came through his phone so loudly it sounded like it was coming from a megaphone. They spoke for only a couple minutes more before he finished the call, telling her, "I'll see you very soon."

When Madison hung up, she looked over at Kelly, who was standing next to her. "I guess you'll be losing a roommate."

"It's over?" Kelly asked.

Madison just smiled before sitting down at the kitchen table, placing her head upon it and letting all the emotion go.

CHAPTER 64

New York, New York

AGENT KELLER DID not have time to sit back and enjoy this latest successful end to a serial killer case. Instead, he was assigned double duty.

With the attorney general coming to town the next day, his office was inundated with security issues dealing with all the VIPs who would be in attendance.

The job was a massive one, requiring the coordination of several different law enforcement agencies as well as many other city departments. If that wasn't enough, he was personally requested by Robert Cantwell to join him on stage as he wished to honor the agent and his department for their latest success in stopping this most brutal of murderers.

Although he appreciated the recognition, Keller much preferred to be hands-on during an event like this one. It made him feel more confident that the job was being done right. However, he knew he would have to relinquish control as he could not turn down such a request.

Not wanting to hog the spotlight, Keller asked Amanda to be in attendance so she could also be recognized. Keller invited Des as well, but he politely declined. He had had enough of being the center of attention, and the fact that Keller was not his boss, he had the luxury of doing so.

Keller did not press him. He understood his civilian aide was done, saying "Good for you," after Des chose to rest and then go home. Keller was not only impressed but envious as well.

CHAPTER 65

New York, New York

IT WAS AFTERNOON the next day, and from what seemed like divine providence, the relentless humidity had broken. The weather resembled more a beautiful spring day rather than the oppressively hot and exhausting ones of a typical summer.

For the first time since arriving in New York, Des was going to take in a few of the sights in the city without an albatross hanging around his neck. He did so with a lightness of step that comes with the relief of the lifting of such a burden. He took pleasure in the silence of his phone, not having to deal with his heart jumping into his throat every time it rang. He slowed at his leisure as he walked, admiring the architecture of the buildings, the fountains of Central Park, and the smells of the various food vendors on every corner, peddling their delicacies.

It was exactly what he needed. Nothing brought him more pleasure than to immerse himself in such a historic setting. He loved going to a new place and purposefully getting lost, forcing himself to examine every detail to find his way back. Most people would find this as something that would only induce stress. Des saw it as a priceless adventure.

He was determined to enjoy his last few hours of being in New York. He didn't want to leave it with his only memories being that of terror and heartache. His only regret was he would only be able to touch such a small part of it. He knew one could spend a lifetime there and never see it all. But he lamented he had only seen the smallest of slivers.

He didn't even have this whole day, as Amanda had called him earlier to ask if he would like to join her for a celebratory lunch, stating that their whole time with each other had been wrapped around such horrible circumstances, that it would be a shame for it to end in such a depressing state.

So Des returned to his hotel, cleaned up, and prepared to meet Amanda at two o'clock. She said she wouldn't have time later due to her required attendance at the attorney general's speech that evening, something she dreaded going to.

Des caught a cab and headed to her apartment. She had suggested her favorite Italian restaurant, a tiny place located among the brownstones in Greenwich Village. He loved Italian food. But at this point, any type of nourishment sounded perfect, as long as it was accompanied by vast quantities of wine. A nice merlot would be preferable.

As he exited the cab and entered her apartment complex, he felt contentment. There was to be no more letters in blood-red ink, no more cold computer voice ordering him on frantic tasks throughout the country, and no more death. It was over, and he was going to allow himself to relish in the moment.

He reached her front door and gave a gentle knock. He could hear footsteps and the television in the background.

"Coming," he heard her say as the steps drew closer.

When she opened the door, Amanda was in her bathrobe and a little out of breath. "I'm sorry, I'm not ready yet… I got tied up at the office. Come in… please."

"Do you want to do this another time?" he asked.

"Oh, don't be silly. I'm just going to hop into the shower. I'll be really quick, I promise. Have a seat and watch TV," she said, gesturing toward the family room.

Amanda hustled down the hallway to the bathroom, while Des sat down on the sofa in the front of the television. Within moments, he could hear her singing as she bathed, causing him to grin at her unfettered demeanor. He had not seen her like this before. Gone was the studious, methodical, and professional persona she used at her job. In its place was a jovial girl just looking to enjoy one of the most exciting cities on earth.

Des leaned back on the couch and stared at the screen. He smiled in playful disbelief as he noticed she had been watching a reality show about women in Beverly Hills. It was such a break from the identity he had known over the past week. It was good to see this side of her.

However, he was not interested in sitting through that drudgery. He located the controller and started flipping through the channels, but nothing garnered his interest.

He saw a light below the TV, indicating the DVD player was on. With Amanda still in the shower, he saw his opportunity. *I wonder what kind of movies she watches.* He pressed Play on the controller and could hear the hum of the spinning disc.

What came on the screen though was not a movie. Instead, the picture displayed some sort of small platform, with a podium at its center. In the backdrop was a blue curtain, which appeared to be covering two statues, as you could only see their bases. To the right of the podium was an American flag, and pasted to its front was the seal for the Department of Justice. The video looked slightly dated, maybe fifteen to twenty years old, definitely not current.

A moment later strode in a smiling distinguished man in a dark suit. He looked like the picture of confidence as he began to speak. Then graphics appeared, identifying him as US Attorney General John Ashcroft, the one who served under George W. Bush.

"Good morning, and thank you for being here," he started. The press conference began as most do, general and nonspecific in nature. But as he continued to speak, it became evident this was not your typical Department of Justice briefing. Ashcroft's words immediately turned to the need to get tougher on crime and how mandatory minimum sentencing was needed to ensure criminals were adequately punished.

Des leaned forward. Something was askew, and it began to stimulate his brain. Yet he could not identify it. But there was something of familiarity, and then, he realized what it was. Initially he had thought this speech was taking place at the White House, but soon he realized his error. It was taking place in the Department of Justice's Grand Hall. The covered statues were that of the Spirit of Justice and the Majesty of Law. Their concealment was purposeful, meant to convey the message that federal law enforcement would not recognize due process. Justice was no longer blind.

Des stood up and moved closer to the television. He sensed he had discovered something of importance. It was too coincidental. They had been able to decipher all the clues but one, the soot.

With Feller dead, the need to delve deeper into that clue was deemed of little importance. Amanda had written it off as a purification ritual common to serial killers.

Your knowledge of history should be your guide. The words of the cold computer voice still rang in his ears.

He became mesmerized at what he was watching. He reached a clarity. This was the press conference that announced to the world that the very principles that had served as the basis of the nation for nearly two hundred and fifty years, were now being tossed onto the scrapheap of history. They were being replaced by a philosophy and practices contradicting those of its founding fathers.

Your knowledge of history should be your guide.

Images of the murder scenes bounced in his mind. Symbol after symbol they displayed were at the center of each picture. *What was he trying to tell me?*

It's all in the presentation. It marks the position of the target. You have the answers.

Des looked down, trying to contemplate its meaning. *There's something left.* He kept picturing the mounds of soot found at the sites, struggling to look beyond its ritualistic implications. To this point, they had not viewed it in any other context.

But it didn't make sense. Feller had always used the presentation as being symbolic of what he wanted to say. Everything else at the murder scenes was utilized for such a purpose. So why would he display something so prominently which was not?

Symbolic… symbolic. It grabbed hold like a vice around his brain. They had ignored it—the location. They had always assumed it was part of the cover—an out-of-the-way place to discreetly dispose of the bodies. They never saw the location as part of the message.

Your knowledge of history should be your guide.

Five of the six murder victims were found on farms. The only one who was not, Gertig, no soot was left to accompany the body. It wasn't arbitrary. Feller was trying to communicate something. The soot and the location of a small farm were conveying a message.

Your knowledge of history should be your guide. It's all in the presentation. It marks the position of the target. You have the answers.

The soot was not ritualistic; it was symbolic of a word… the word *ash*. Des swallowed hard because he knew the other symbolic context of the location. In colonial days, a small farm was referred to as a "croft"… "Ash" and "croft"—Ashcroft!

It marks the position of the target.

The position wasn't a location, but a job. The position of attorney general!

Yet how was this possible? How could have Amanda come across such an obscure twenty-year-old press conference? She would be too young to remember it. Was she doing her own research? Had something triggered an idea in her head?

It still wasn't possible. Amanda was amazing at profiling devious minds, but by her own admission, historical questions and contexts were not her strong suit.

There's no way she could have figured this out… unless. The realization felt like a sledgehammer to the chest as he could hardly breathe. His heart was racing. The adrenaline pumping through him was so intense he cracked the DVD controller in his hand. He didn't want to believe it. He desperately tried to push the thought out of his mind, but the terrible wave of truth was crashing over him.

It was then he heard the footsteps behind him. His body became tense. His feet felt like they were rooted to the ground. Nausea took over. A heat flashed through him in jolts like a beating pulse. His chest knotted. His knees nearly buckled beneath him. But he did not turn around.

"Feller wasn't there to kill you. He was there to confront you. The prisoners who saw him in California… saw him warning that guard. Those maps we saw in his home… they weren't of him plotting his murders… but tracking yours. He was conducting his own investigation," Des said with the dismay of betrayal in his voice.

"I never wanted to kill Feller… but I guarantee you he took pleasure in what he discovered," Amanda replied. "He was never part of the plan, but he left me no choice. Obviously, I couldn't let him continue."

There was no remorse in her voice. The jovial girl he had encountered mere moments ago had reverted back to the determined professional. Yet now, she had more than a strong hint of coldness.

"Why… why did you do this?" he asked.

She moved closer to him, easing in like a cat. "I could tell you, but you'll be no different," she answered softly.

"All those people… why did they deserve this treatment?"

"Turn around."

He didn't want to. He had no desire to see the woman he had admired, that he had affection for, in this new light.

"Turn around, god dammit!"

He slowly turned and faced her. Des was in awe. She was completely nude with a body that manifested raw power. Her frame was muscular and toned, not an ounce of fat. Her form looked like it had been chiseled from marble. Every anatomical detail was highlighted to such a degree that she could have been used as an anatomy chart. She glistened from the water, which had yet to dry on her skin, and she was completely shaven clean, ensuring no impediment would disrupt the beautiful lines of her artwork. The only visible blemish was a slight redness from what appeared to be a fresh tattoo above her left breast.

In her right hand she held a gun, which looked like it had a silencer on the end of its barrel. It was not yet held in a threatening position, but only a split second would be required to change her stance.

"Don't you look at me like I'm some kind of fucking monster!" she said sternly.

"How can you justify what you've done? You're supposed to stop murders, not commit them."

Des's face held a tinge of sadness, but most of all, a sense of loss. Nothing was as it should be. The world of justice had been turned into a freakish universe, where everything contradicted any pattern of logic or sanity.

"Don't you judge me! Don't you dare fucking judge me! You have no idea what I've been through," she stated emphatically.

"What you've been through had nothing to do with those people."

"They had everything to do with it… and don't stand there like some innocent child. I know all about you, Desmond Cook. You've killed before. Even the innocent. Remember what you did in Afghanistan?"

"I killed in war," he answered defensively.

"This is war! I kill because they have to feel the pain their system has caused me and millions of others. Anyone who has participated in that system on any level is guilty."

"I don't understand. What did they do?"

"They destroyed my family!" she cried. Every vein in her neck bulged to the surface. Her face, once serene and beautiful, was now red with rage and indignation. "My father was a good man… a decent man. After my mother died, he struggled to keep us afloat… to keep food on the table and a roof over our heads. He wasn't a murderer or part of a drug cartel. He was a poor man desperately trying to care for his children. The Feds busted him for moonshine and a few marijuana plants… and they gave him fifteen years—fifteen fucking years! Like he was some kind of monster. If he had been busted by the state, he would have gotten probation… a slap on the wrist at most. My brother and I were split up… our mother was gone. They left us with nothing."

Des paused for a moment. "Where did he serve his time?" he asked softly.

"He was first sent to Texas and then California."

"Lompoc?"

She nodded. "We couldn't even see him."

"That's why you killed those guards."

"They treated my father like he wasn't human. Philes and Shara taunted him and made his life miserable. They killed him!"

"They killed him?" he asked with nerves on end.

"My father was having chest pains. He went to the quack on medical duty that night complaining of that, shortness of breath and radiating pain down his arm—classic symptoms of a heart attack. The fat bitch didn't feel like staying late. All she did was tell him he was fine and to drink some water and sleep it off. My father suffered in horrible pain all night… He begged Philes and that cunt Shara to get him help. They ignored him. He was dead the next morning!"

Tears were streaming down her face. The gun she held was now shaking with anger. Des empathized with her emotion. It was the same rage he felt on that fateful day in Afghanistan.

"How can they treat their fellow citizens that way?" she exclaimed. "It's not about punishment. It's about profit. Ha! And the stupid fucking public thinks they're being protected… What idiots! They're being duped by everyone… The entire Department of Justice, the FBI, the US Attorney's Office—all of them."

The room fell nearly silent, the only sound being that of Amanda's sniffling. The tension in her body was so great that every muscle in her frame was taut, exposing all the hard ridges in her naked display.

Her expression had shifted from anger to hurt and disappointment. It was disappointment in the way her colleagues conducted themselves, disappointment in the government she worked for and disappointment in her country. "When did the land of the free become the world's prison ward?" she sobbed.

Des, too, felt a deep sorrow. He hated what she had done and was overwhelmed that one such as this, so beautiful, so courageous, so intelligent, could be capable of such ugliness. As he stared into her eyes, looking at the tears trickling down her face and dampening her breast, he tried to delve into her mind. They had essentially switched roles, as she was now the one looking for answers, while he was left trying to psychoanalyze her.

"Amanda, I understand everything you're saying. What they did was horrible," he said in a clumsy attempt to show compassion.

"Don't patronize me, Des! You forget whom you're talking to," she said, her anger quickly returning.

"I'm not trying to do that. But there's one thing I don't understand. Why me? Why did you set this all up to torture me?"

"Because you're The Enemy. You stopped him from accomplishing his goal."

Des scanned her face but saw nothing. Then his eye was drawn to the tattoo just above her nipple. It was simple in design, dark black and red in color that stood out against her fair skin. The top of the tattoo consisted of two beautiful calligraphed letters, *W* and *H*. Below, in bold red with black outline it read "Martyr."

His heart sank into his stomach as he felt a chill flow through his body. "William Hatton? This is about William Hatton? He was a murderer!"

"He was a soldier! He had the courage to give his life for a larger cause. I know all about him, Des. I worked the case... remember? He saw an America where the Constitution was treated as a sacred document... where the laws were meant to protect its citizens... not exploit them. He was attempting to take out that bastard president for not doing his job... What's his job, Des? Tell me! What's his job?"

At first, Des hesitated. "To preserve, protect, and defend the Constitution," he answered dejectedly, remembering the Presidential Oath of Office.

"He's the one who is supposed to enforce the law. Instead, he let it be hijacked by reactionary politicians and profit-hungry business. He doesn't care his failures rest on the suffering of others. He doesn't care that the last time we took people's freedom for profit, it was called slavery. We both know damn well it has nothing to do with punishment. You stole the opportunity from William to end it!"

"But he killed thirty-seven innocent people!"

"Yes, he did. But because of you and your sense of self-righteous bullshit, the president lived. You ensured it was business as usual. You ensured thousands of more deaths and millions of more good people, like my father and their families, will suffer. But it's not over. I still have one thing left to do."

"Amanda, you've made your point. No one else has to die. You got rid of whom you needed to."

"No, not everyone. You know there's still one more." She stood for a second collecting her thoughts. Her body now glowed with a flushness brought on by the emotion. "Do you know why I got my tattoo here?" she asked, pointing to her left breast. "It's where William made his last mark on you. Just above the heart."

She raised her arm, bringing the barrel of the gun in direct line with him. He knew what was coming next, but he had nowhere to go. She had him cornered and was still too far away to grab before she could get off a shot.

"Still," she said. "You need to see it."

The gun fired, not with the pop typical of such a weapon, but with the muffled sound of an air rifle. The stinging sensation was different from the bullet he was struck with at Arlington a year earlier. It didn't hollow him out. It wasn't the same shattering pain that nearly tore him apart. It was localized in the abdomen, which soon turned numb. He looked down to see where he had been injured, but his vision blurred. He tried to move toward her, yet his limbs did not cooperate and he crumpled to the floor at her feet. Des's last sensation was of Amanda kissing his forehead; his last thought was of Madison.

CHAPTER 66

∽᎒꧂∾

New York, New York

IT TASTED LIKE sand and itched on his face. He had not felt like this since he first awoke in that Washington hospital room last year.

Des was lying on his side with spittle running down his lip, which connected to the area rug he now lay upon. His head was pounding, feeling like the worst hangover he had ever experienced. He moved his hand to his face in an effort to quell the tremendous discomfort. However, as soon as he carried out this motion, a sharp pain in his abdomen interrupted the action.

It was a tranquilizer dart, its sharp point still imbedded in his midsection where it found its mark. He reached down and pulled it out, but it took a few more moments for him to gain his bearings and for his eyes to focus. Once he reacquired some cognitive skills, he was able to ascertain his location. Then the memory flooded in. *The attorney general… he's the final target!*

He raised himself listlessly, still attempting to shake out the cobwebs. He stumbled through Amanda's apartment, desperately searching for his phone. He had Agent Keller's direct line stored in it. He had to warn him. He clumsily moved into the kitchen. He eyed the counters, but his phone was nowhere to be seen. He opened up various drawers, yet to no avail. *She probably destroyed it. Maybe Agent Keller's number is somewhere else.*

He moved down the hallway toward her bedroom, bumping into walls as the drug still coursed through his system. Passing the bathroom, he looked to his left to see a closed door. He pulled on the handle. It would not release. He threw himself into the barrier, trying to break through, but still, it did not give in. Placing his back against the adjacent wall, he kicked the portal with every ounce of strength he could muster. On the third kick, a loud crack sounded as the wood broke free of its clasp.

Des flung himself through the doorway and was greeted by a sight even more eerie than the one he encountered at Feller's home. On the back wall were a collection of photographs showing a man who appeared to be in his late forties or early fifties. There was another of that same man in a younger state. He was sitting on the front porch of a house in a chair swing with an attractive brunette at his side. There were two children, a little girl and a baby, sitting on their laps. The photo was a happy one of a family enjoying a leisurely day. Even though the faces of the children were very young, the distinctive auburn-colored hair of the little girl gave away that it was Amanda.

Next to that picture were two obituary columns. One talked about the tragic death of Shelly Hertzel, who was killed in a violent car accident. Des could tell it was old, the yellow tinge of the newspaper showing its age. A slightly less dated obituary was next to it. It had no cause of death or detailed information. It simply read, "Peter Hertzel, loving father and husband, passed away on April 19th. He is mourned by his daughter Amanda and son Cal. He will be laid to rest at Brother's Methodist Cemetery on Friday."

Des turned and looked at the adjoining wall. It was not organized or meticulously arranged, as was so typical of her personality. Instead, it was a collage of emotion, mainly anger and frustration. There were articles about the president and his rejection of federal justice reform. Attached were more columns about various politicians who supported mandatory minimum sentencing guidelines. To the left of those were a collection of photographs of the destroyed fields of

Arlington National Cemetery. Scribbled beneath the pictures, in the same red ink she had used to terrorize him, was the word *Betrayed*.

Des had seen the pictures and videos of the terrible scene many times. But he had no recollection of the explosion and still had a difficult time contemplating how more people, including the president, had not lost their lives. It was surreal looking, as if it never took place. However, it did, and his role in the episode obviously fueled her rage.

On the closet door were photographs of each of the murder victims prior to their death with various documents pasted alongside of them. There was the young assistant US attorney with a case file attached and a prominently displayed internet article announcing her success in getting an eighteen-year-old twenty years for selling fifteen thousand dollars' worth of marijuana. There was the seamstress, who apparently sat on a grand jury who indicted a mother of three for tax evasion, ending in a seven-year sentence. The total amount of her owed taxes, eighteen thousand dollars. Then there was the probation officer, whose picture was plastered next to an item called a presentencing report, recommending a twenty-two-year sentence for a defendant named Peter Hertzel.

Des noticed the door ajar. He gingerly opened it. His nerves immediately went on end. On its inside were two life-sized pictures. One was William Hatton. A halo was painted above his head. Next to it was a picture of Des with a sniper's crosshairs drawn over his face. At his feet on the closet floor was a pinstriped Yankees cap and a false beard. It's what she wore during the night he gave her chase. The feelings of horror and deflation combined in him, forming a sour stew, tearing holes in his gut.

He moved over to her desk, fumbling through the clutter, hoping to find a book, a notepad, anything with Keller's number. Papers fell to the floor like rain, until in frustration, he pushed everything to the ground. It exposed a small desk clock.

Oh Jesus! It's 6:32 p.m. The attorney general's speech begins at 7:00!

There was no time left. Even if he could call Keller, it would most likely go to voice mail. If he was in close proximity to the attorney general, he might be in harm's way too!

He had to get to the Lincoln Center. It was about a mile and a half away. He darted out of the room, his unsteadiness still hindering him as he slammed into the hallway wall. Deciding not to waste precious seconds on the elevator, he lunged for the front door and down the stairwell.

Exiting the building in a mad rush, nearly knocking over an old lady walking her Yorkshire terrier, he looked for the familiar street. He remembered when traveling on it to get to Amanda's place, seeing the Lincoln Center on the way.

Locating it just to his left, Des sprinted toward the street sign and then dashed north. He knew several minutes had already elapsed. It wouldn't be much longer before the final target met his end.

CHAPTER 67

New York, New York

ROBERT CANTWELL WAS excited about his future. The latest poll numbers about who the public would want as their future president were just released that afternoon. It showed the US attorney general had a 67 percent approval rating and that 44 percent of the electorate would cast their vote for him if the election were held today. His nearest rival, Senator Wayman, would garner only a paltry 29 percent despite his recent rise in popularity. Other considerations for the office were left to pick up the crumbs. It seemed as if the path had been cleared for him to reach his dream without the fear or pressure of his dark secrets coming to light.

Tonight was the night that would make it official, and he could do so with the joy and excitement that should accompany such an announcement. Returning to the town where he got his start, he knew it would be a wonderful piece of theater, and what better place to perform than the Lincoln Center.

Cantwell had arrived in New York in the early afternoon to a rock star reception. Everyone who was anyone was there. The mayor, the governor, Broadway stars, CEOs, and other business dignitaries, not to mention dozens of television stations, were all in attendance. Everyone wanted to be a part of the worst-kept secret in politics.

After this evening's speech, the week's activities would only increase. He had a scheduled appearance on the *Today Show*, lunch with the heads of three of the city's largest investment firms, and even a quick cameo on *Saturday Night Live*. Then it would be dinner with the governor, before being whisked back to Washington to perform his duties while gearing up for his campaign.

Agent Keller, on the other hand, arrived at the Lincoln Center with a much more modest entourage. His immediate superior, Charles Lort, was there, as well as a few people from local law enforcement agencies who had assisted in the investigation. Amanda would be arriving shortly to join Keller on stage when he would be called up to receive his honor by the man of the hour himself, Robert Cantwell.

As he approached the building's magnificent all-glass facade, it was a little difficult for Keller not to feel like he was at a Hollywood premiere. Red carpet lined the pathway leading to the entrance. Paparazzi were cordoned off from guests by a red velvet rope. Flashes from their cameras burst brightly with every movement of those making their way into the building. The media was in an absolute frenzy to witness the prestigious list of invitees as they clamored to see who would most likely be a part of the next president's inner circle.

Keller, however, was not comfortable. He was a law enforcement officer, not a movie star. As he headed to the entrance, he could not help but worry as he looked to make sure every piece of security was in its proper place.

The officer presence along the velvet rope seemed strong but not overbearing, with a Secret Service agent about every ten yards. At the entrance, guests had their wrist ID scanned before they moved through the metal detector. All purses were inspected, and even though it was cumbersome, no one seemed to be too annoyed with the process, even having a good laugh when the underwire in one of the female guests' bra set off the metal detector.

Keller, just after he passed through the entrance, felt a tap on his shoulder. "Amanda, wow, you look beautiful!"

"Thanks, Zack, you look pretty dapper yourself."

"I'll never get used to wearing suits. I much prefer my sweater and jeans."

"Oh, come on, Zack… It's nice to play dress-up every once and in a while. Plus, there are a lot of good-looking ladies here tonight. It's important to dress to impress," she said, playfully elbowing him.

Keller rolled his eyes. "Believe me, these women are here to ogle Cantwell. They're not interested in a fat middle-aged lawman."

Just at that moment, a bell tone sounded in the lobby, signifying it was time for the crowd to start going into the theater. Keller would have a seat alongside the rest of the VIPs on the dais, while Amanda would be called up from the audience when the time came.

It was 6:45 p.m., Cantwell was scheduled to speak at seven. However, rarely did these things start on time. Nonetheless, Keller was told Cantwell would recognize him and his staff about thirty minutes in. Keller wouldn't be required to speak much, which was fine with him as he felt he was lousy in front of crowds. At least until the designated time, he could try and relax.

CHAPTER 68

❦

New York, New York

IN THE ARMY, it was one of his least favorite activities. Running was a part of their daily regimen, and he knew it was the best way to get fit. Yet he enjoyed other forms of exertion much more to replace it. Playing racquetball and trips to the batting cages were his most preferred substitutes.

However, after William Hatton inflicted the gunshot wound upon him, those physical fitness endeavors had to be placed on the shelf. Now Des wished he had at least chosen to put in a few miles of running a week as he huffed and puffed his way toward the Lincoln Center at as steady a pace as he could maintain.

Every few moments a cab would pass by, causing him to entertain the idea of hailing one. But he realized that would be fool's choice, as the cab would most likely get bogged down in the infamous New York City traffic. It would only cause more time to elapse.

Des continued down Tenth Street. Sweat poured from his brow, and his shirt was becoming drenched. He passed a bank with an electronic display flashing the temperature and time. Still a little fuzzy from the tranquilizer, he prayed his eyes were playing tricks on him when he saw it was 6:51 p.m. He thought he might be getting close as some familiar landmarks came into view. But with only nine minutes to deadline, his fear had ratcheted up to severe levels.

He passed by Forty-Second Street and through the Theater District. As Fifty-Fourth Street approached, he noticed the increase in commotion as cars and people made their way into Columbus Circle. Fordham University appeared to his right, and then it finally came into view, the Lincoln Center for the Performing Arts.

Its massive complex includes three separate structures. One's for the New York Philharmonic, one for the Metropolitan Opera, and the final one for the New York City Ballet. At the center of the complex is a huge plaza encased on three sides by the buildings and garnished with pavement decorated with concentric circular designs leading to a beautiful fountain.

The buildings on the north and south sides are rectangular in shape with straight columns running from the ground to the base of the roofs. Intricate lighting makes their grayish-white exteriors glow. The sole building on the west side, the Metropolitan Opera House, however, is its most eye catching. Only six columns mark its entrance, which is arched toward the apex of the building. Glass windows from its foundation to its top allow its interior light to project outward, providing the visitor with a view of every floor from its exterior. Breathtaking murals adorning its third-level walls exude beautiful reds, blues, and yellows onto the plaza, while elegant chandelier lighting illuminated its center.

Des ran up the stairs and through the plaza, not really sure which building he was supposed to enter. That question was quickly answered when he spotted the red carpet leading directly into the Opera House. Yet the relief in finding the correct building was soon broken by the realization that he had no way to access it.

Security was everywhere on the border of the red carpet, along with three guards manning the front entrance. Inside, he could see more security pacing the bottom floors, looking for any suspicious activity. They each wore wires running up the base of their necks, eventually curling into an earpiece, providing them instant communication. *How the hell do I get in?*

Des asked a passerby for the time; it was 6:58! He sprinted up to the red carpet, pushing his way through the press stuffed along its edges. Reaching between two photographers, he tugged at the sleeve of one of the security guards, who immediately pulled his arm away.

"Hey, what the hell do you think you're doing?" the guard shouted sternly at him.

"Sir, you have to get the attorney general out of there. He's in danger," Des said, panting.

The guard took one look at the sweaty, disheveled man before him and was not impressed. *Great, another fucking wacko I have to deal with.* "Sir, this is a restricted area. If you do not have credentials, you'll have to leave."

"You don't understand, the killer is inside. He's being targeted!"

"Sir, we have everything under control. Now, please leave this area."

"But you don't—"

"Sir, if you do not leave right now, I'll be forced to place you under arrest. Now get the hell out of here!"

Des could not let that happen. He stepped back. He did not know what else to do. He placed both hands on his head and turned a full 360 degrees, trying in vain to come up with another way. Panic started to settle in as every assessment resulted in a dead end.

He faced the structure and peered into the interior. *I could try and break the glass, but what the hell would that do? They would just tackle me once I got inside.*

It was then he saw her. The beautiful auburn hair stuck out from the crowd milling about the lobby. It bounced gracefully as she moved west. The black dress she wore clung to her form, hugging every curve and accentuating every movement. He struggled to visually follow her path. The only thing he caught was a quick glimpse of her calm face as she ducked into the ladies' room.

CHAPTER 69

New York, New York

THE MAYOR OF New York strode to the microphone to the applause of the packed house filling the theater. Smiling and giving proper acknowledgment to the crowd, he prepared himself to speak.

Agent Keller sat on the stage to the mayor's left, with the rest of the honorees, behind a table draped in red linen cloth. The only thing in front of him were his notes, a small glass, and a silver water pitcher. Even though he tried to appear at ease, anyone who knew him would recognize he was about as comfortable as a sheep in a lion's den. He looked out at the mass of people staring in his general direction and immediately noticed one seat was unoccupied. It was the one being used by Amanda.

As long as she's back by the time I speak, he thought.

"Good evening, ladies and gentlemen," said the mayor. "Welcome, and thank you for joining us for what promises to be a very informative and exciting evening. As I'm sure you're all aware, New York has provided the country with some of its most important and influential leaders. Many have gone on to shape our nation into what it is today, the greatest nation on the face of the earth."

Amanda could hear the hum of the microphone in the ladies' room and knew the final introduction would be soon as the roar of applause came through loud and clear. Just as she had expected, she was the restroom's only occupant. She calmly walked over to the third stall on the right and entered it. Looking at the tile behind the toilet, she smiled. It hadn't been disturbed. It was ready to be initiated.

However, first things first. She undid her dress and efficiently pulled it off to reveal a pair of black Lycra bicycle shorts and a black sports bra. Reaching into her purse, she pulled out a wet cloth and quickly wiped away her red lipstick along with most of her makeup.

Satisfied she now looked more like a woman on her way to the gym than on her way to a gala, she moved to the next step. Reaching behind the toilet, she pulled on the twelve-by-twelve piece of white tile until it gave way. There lay a pair of running shoes, a digital recorder, and a speaker that she had left in the morning during the security inspection. Her FBI credentials and guest of honor status allowed her free reign in the center prior to the evening's activities. It gave her ample opportunity to get everything in place.

She put on the shoes, took out the rest of the contents, and then placed the tile back into its previous position. She could hear the crowd applaud once more. Amanda closed her eyes and let the moment sink in. In just a few minutes, she would bring the system to its knees.

Exiting the stall, she placed the digital recorder on the sink countertop, hooked it up to the speaker, turned the volume to full power, and pressed Play. Then she calmly left the restroom and walked toward the front doors. As she exited the building, the guard gave her a look, letting her know what an oddity she appeared in such a setting.

Not missing a beat, she turned and said, "I always hated these things. I'd rather work out. I'll be at Nico's Bar if you want to join me for a drink later." She then gave him a seductive wink and breezily strolled through the plaza. The guard smiled and watched the shapely woman walk in the direction of the fountain. After a few more steps, Amanda turned to catch him gawking and then continued on her path with the satisfaction of knowing it was only moments away.

CHAPTER 70

DES HAD MOVED to all corners of the plaza, looking for any other possible ways to enter the building. He dashed back and forth, but his actions were as useless as a hamster on a spinning wheel.

Left without options, he began to move back to the red carpet. Slowly, he once again tucked in behind the mass of photographers. He knew it was past 7:00 p.m., and whatever was going to happen would happen soon. *I gotta do something!*

His nerves were shredded and his heart was beating so rapidly he could feel its force extending to his fingertips. The near hysteria inside him expanded as the feeling of helplessness was nearly overwhelming. It was like watching a kitten wander onto a freeway and he was on the overpass looking down.

Inside the theater, Keller was beginning to wonder where Amanda could be. *The guest of honor is about to be introduced!*

Then the mayor said, "And now, Ladies and Gentlemen, please, will you join me in welcoming home one or our city's favorite sons, US Attorney General Robert Cantwell."

The audience erupted into applause as the handsome man stood up and waved to the crowd. His smile was luminous, and already he looked to have the aura of the next leader of the free world.

Des could hear the roar seeping out from the theater, bouncing off the walls of the lobby and into the plaza. *Maybe I can make a run for it.* He looked up and down the red carpet for an opening—still nothing.

Suddenly, over the background of the crowd, a loud shriek of a woman screaming could clearly be heard. Des looked to his right and could see the agents in the interior grab their ears almost simultaneously. Then, like animals chasing prey, they all ran to the west end of the lobby. Another agent burst through the theater doors in pursuit of his colleagues. Des looked at the entrance and noticed two of the security guards had left their posts, while the one who did remain was clearly distracted.

Inside the theater, Robert Cantwell warmly embraced the mayor and gave another wave to the crowd before he approached the podium. He then checked the teleprompters to make sure his speech was ready and proceeded to speak.

"Good evening, it's great to be back home."

The crowd, once again, roared their approval.

Des knew something was happening. *It's gotta be now!* He pushed between two photographers with all his force, knocking them both to the ground, while sending their cameras smashing to the cement pavement. He leapt over the velvet rope, dodging one of the agents manning its perimeter, who reached out in vain to grab him. The agent called out to the security at the entrance for assistance as Des sprinted as fast as he could toward the doors.

"Grab him!" the agent yelled.

The officer at the entrance turned around just in time to see a crazed man barreling down on him. He tried to reach into his holster for his gun, but it was too late. Des drove into him with all his leverage, sending the agent flailing backward, while causing excruciating pain to pierce his previously injured left shoulder. Both men landed with a definitive thud onto the tile floor.

The guard was clearly dazed when Des looked back, only to see a myriad of flashes as photographers tried to capture this chaos. As the bright lights continued to spark, he could see the silhouette of the guard he had evaded at the rope furiously running at him. Des got up and dashed to the theater entrance.

"We have a breach! We have a breach!" yelled the agent into his communication wire.

Realizing they had been duped, the agents burst out of the ladies' room in time to see Des grab for the door handle.

"He's there!" yelled the pursuing agent. Des flung open the door as one of the agents discharged his weapon. The bullet struck the door with such power it was shoved right back into him.

"Keller! Keller! Cantwell is the target! Cantwell is the target!" Des screamed.

The agent drove into Des's back, slamming him into the ground.

"Cantwell is the target!" he cried out again.

Keller had stood up, recognizing the face of the intruder immediately. Then he looked over at Cantwell. "Oh shit!" He sprinted at the clearly confused attorney general as the crowd had now stood to see the disturbance. Keller launched himself into Cantwell like a defensive back making a tackle, sending both of them several feet into the air before landing hard onto the stage. Instinctively, Keller covered the attorney general's body with his own when a massive explosion ripped through the very spot where Cantwell had just stood, sending a bright-yellow fireball up to the ceiling. Pieces of the splintered podium sprayed the audience.

The screams that followed were even more deafening than the explosion. Then on cue, a white cloud of choking smoke began to fill the room. It was tear gas.

Mass panic ensued as people poured out of their seats. The agent who was restraining Des was knocked off him in the mad rush. Women were crying, and men pushed and shoved as the terrified crowd pummeled each other trying to reach the exit.

Des tried to stand up but was knocked to the ground again by the human tsunami crashing into him. He strained to get to his feet, but he had become part of the flooring as he was stepped on a dozen times. One women's high heel dug into the very spot of his shoulder wound, causing him to howl in pain.

He pulled and clawed at a seat, trying to get upright as bodies pulverized him with every effort. Finally, he managed to get to his feet, but the power of the hysterical mass pushed him back out the theater doors and into a heap on the lobby floor.

Security was in a state of utter confusion as they could find no way to stop the rush. Their guns were drawn, but they had no idea of who their target was.

Des lay flat on his stomach, tossed to the side like a piece of driftwood pushed onto the shore. He looked out toward the plaza, but the tinted glass made it hard to see outside.

Then he saw the figure standing by the fountain, outlined against its light. Although he could not see her face, he knew it was Amanda. Her powerful frame was unmistakable. She stood there in a proud pose, undoubtedly brimming with the results of her handiwork.

Des looked to his left. The chaos had not died down as hundreds of people were trying to get through the small doorway. Others had fallen in the main thoroughfare, only to be trampled on by those behind them. There was no way to get out. *She can't continue!*

He glanced behind him and saw a large decorative waste basket with an ashtray crowning its top. Des pulled himself up, went over, and lifted it. Even though it did not appear as such, it was extremely heavy. He grunted, struggling to raise it to shoulder height, and then turned and ran at top momentum at one of the front glass panels. As he released the load, he yelled with a combination of pent-up anger and the deep pain from his wound. The basket smashed into the glass, causing chards to plummet like rain. The sound of the wall disintegrating before him only added to the pandemonium.

Des jumped through the new opening with a tunnel vision focusing solely on the figure by the fountain. However, crossing the threshold, a large chunk of glass released its hold on the frame and came down on him, gashing his head. He immediately fell to the ground as the warm blood poured over his forehead and face.

Looking up again, he saw Amanda turn and run. Des ignored his injury and vaulted after her in mad pursuit.

People from the theater began to spill into the plaza, creating a scene that looked like something out of a disaster film. Men and women bellowed in pain. Their faces were beet red and their eyes and noses dripped fluid onto the finery they wore. It was loud and confusing as photographers and journalists mixed in with the chaos, trying to cover the bewildering event.

As Des ran past the fountain, he was nearly bowled over by a line of police officers scurrying in the opposite direction. When he reached the base of the stairs, he spied the area to see if he could locate Amanda. Out of the corner of his eye, her auburn hair, once again, gave her away.

She had turned south on Tenth Avenue. Des dashed after his target. He followed her, but his vision was constantly blurred by the blood continuing to ooze out of the cut and then seep into his eyes. Yet he was not under any circumstance going to let himself lose sight of her.

However, the blood and consistent coughing brought on by inhaling the acidic gas was not his only impediment. Now, the very streets he trod upon created a variable obstacle course. It seemed like everyone in New York was going the opposite direction. He felt like a salmon swimming upstream as he was constantly forced to dart left or right while at the same time trying to keep Amanda in view. He passed Forty-Second Street and proceeded through the Garment District. But every time he made up ground, he would get stalled or bumped nearly to a stop.

He tried to increase his pace. However, he was also starting to attract unwanted attention as people began to stare at this blood-stained individual tearing down the sidewalks and streets. As he hit Thirty-Sixth Street, he smashed into the cart of a hot dog vendor who was wheeling his business to another location, sending Des cascading to the ground.

Ignoring the screams of its operator, Des rose and continued his chase, but he had lost sight of her. He ran further down Tenth, intermittently adding a jump to his run to gain a better view over the crowds. He passed Thirty-Fifth and was approaching Thirty-Fourth. *Damn it! She couldn't have gotten that far ahead of me.* He turned left and then right, and that's when he saw her bounding west on Thirty-Fourth.

Where the hell is she going? he thought as he dug deeper into his last reserve of strength. He was practically gasping for air by the time he passed West Coast Highway, and then he had a realization. At that moment, he understood he had an advantage. She had not once looked behind her. *She doesn't know she's being chased.*

While in the Army, he had been involved in several reconnaissance missions. He had been taught, as well as experienced, that the best way of finding out the enemy's intentions was not to let on they were being watched. *Back off, Des.*

He slowed his pace. There was really no place for her to go. She would soon run into the natural barrier of the Hudson River. The only way she could get away is… *She has a boat! She's going to the docks!*

Amanda had stopped running, confident in the infallibility of her plan. Des astutely tucked behind a building, knowing the instinct was always to look behind once they ceased their movement.

She did exactly that. Seeing the desolate sidewalk behind her, she now strolled casually in the direction of the river. Des began to move in closer to her, cutting the distance between them by nearly half. He was only about twenty-five yards behind. Putting to use all his tracking skills he learned during his service, he managed to follow without alerting her when the docks came into view. Even though he was within striking distance, he still had to exercise extreme caution, not knowing if she was armed.

As she passed the workers who lined the warehouses by the river's edge, they immediately took notice of the pretty woman now among them as a flurry of catcalls came her way. While running down 10th Street, she appeared to be a fitness fanatic getting in her workout. Now that she was off the beaten path, the beautiful girl with the knockout figure looked very out of place in her tight-fitting fitness gear.

Amanda paid her new admirers no heed as she walked with a determined gait to one of the mooring docks jutting out into the river. Des maintained his cover behind a storage container only yards away.

As he peered around the corner, he tried to make out what she was doing. However, the fading light of dusk was making it difficult. He continued to spy patiently, witnessing her releasing the ropes holding a boat to the dock, then climbing aboard when she completed the task. The boat was of medium size, certainly one capable of making a long excursion. *They will never look for her here.*

Des rubbed his forearm over his brow, covering it in blood. He stared at the boat once more, knowing in moments, he would have to make his move.

A few more anxious seconds passed before he heard the engine come to life. He had to time it just right. There was no question in his mind that if she wasn't carrying a gun on her, she most certainly had one on the boat. He could not afford another confrontation like the one he had earlier.

The boat started to slowly ease out of its slip, but still he waited. He needed for it to be turned around, or he would be seen. As it gradually began to edge west and face the river's main thoroughfare, he knew it was time to go.

CHAPTER 71

DES JUMPED OUT from behind the container and sprinted for the dock. He passed by slip after slip, almost becoming a blur as the distance between him and the craft dissipated. It was only a few more strides before he realized the boat was accelerating faster than he had anticipated. He drove harder but was beginning to fear he would not make it. As he reached the end of the dock, it became apparent he would fail to reach its deck when he leapt.

For a moment, everything seemed to move in slow motion, like he was suspended in midair. It was like time had purposefully slowed down to exacerbate the futility of the effort. He reached out his right hand just when Amanda had kicked it into another gear. His hand grasped the metal railing lining the deck as the rest of his body slammed into the hull and immersed into the waters.

Amanda looked back at the stern when she heard the bump but saw nothing. She gazed at the dock, and it was just how she had left it. She turned the other direction and increased her speed, anxious to get away from Manhattan.

The water still had not been warmed by the upswing in heat during the previous weeks, its chill spraying and bouncing Des from side to side as he desperately clung to the railing. The noise of the motor was deafening, and the exhaust that it belched, suffocating.

He tried to swing and grab the railing with his other hand, but every time he attempted, the boat would bump up, sending him backward. He was quickly becoming fatigued. His strength and ability to hold on was waning.

He lurched up once again but could only grasp the railing briefly before his hand slipped from the metal surface. His right hand now began to lose its hold. Two of his fingers lost their grip, causing his body to flail toward the motor. He regained his hold just in time to keep himself from being cut to ribbons by its blades.

Des knew he had only one good attempt left before he would find himself alone in the middle of the Hudson. He threw himself with one last surge that required all his effort. He barely managed to get his left palm onto the railing, but when it touched, he clamped down around it.

He pulled himself upward, trying his best to absorb the searing pain in his shoulder, which was so intense he felt like he was going to pass out. Managing to hook his left foot onto the wood surface just below the metal grating, he heaved his body upward. Des felt heavy, the water seeming to add a thousand pounds to his frame. Yet he was able to crest the top and then slowly lower himself onto the deck.

Strangely the motor, which was his nemesis while he was in the water, was his ally now that he was out of it. The noise it generated had left Amanda completely unaware of his presence. He could see her through the glass of its cabin, still at the helm.

Nonetheless, he proceeded with extreme caution. However, he was encountering another dilemma. What was he going to do once he confronted her? As he took three steps forward, he noticed her purse on a chair just outside the cabin.

"Besides, I'm FBI, we're always packing," he remembered her saying the night she was confronted by Feller. Opening her purse, those words proved prophetic as he found the weapon exactly where she said she kept it.

Grabbing the gun, he took a deep breath and carefully walked around the cabin. He had held weapons many times in his life, but since that horrible day in Afghanistan, they now only gave him feelings of revulsion. "Shut it down, Amanda. It's over."

She swung around like a spinning top, only to be greeted by a dripping wet Des pointing her own gun at her. Amanda's reaction, though, was different from what he expected. Her face became red with defiance as pure anger emanated from her glare. "Are you going to shoot me, Des? Can you kill me with what you've learned? You know what they've done. You know what they continue to do. Do you think I deserve to be punished?"

"What you've done can't be justified."

"Justified! Justified! How many millions have been robbed of their lives using that word as the excuse? How many children have been made to grow up without mothers and fathers because of this charade of a legal system? Don't talk to me about justified!"

"You have to—"

"I have to what… Des? Turn myself in? That's not going to happen."

"I can't just let you leave," he said in a wavering voice.

He knew he was going to have to make a decision. He knew he was going to be forced to make a terrible choice.

"You're going to have to kill me, Des," she said without fear or remorse. "Believe me, at this point, you would be doing me a favor."

It was still impossible for him to conceive that this beautiful, brilliant woman before him could have killed over and over again, in cold blood. But she did not relent from her position, either physically or intellectually.

He looked over her shoulder and could see the Statue of Liberty in the background, drenched in light. Her green magnificence standing watch over the city. Yet to Des, it was now a symbol defying the very institutions she represented. This was not the "land of the free" as he had known it. The beautiful sculpture had been rebuked by the very government who was supposed to protect her meaning.

Amanda stood as rigid as the great monument behind her. The only movement was her auburn mane blowing in the wind coming off the water.

"I'm so sorry this happened to you, Amanda. God knows, I agree with your anger. There has to be another way."

"No… no, there's not. The system thrives on the public's ignorance of it… preying on their unfounded fears and prejudices. As long as there's money to be made, they won't stop. The machine will continue as always."

The rage she held just moments ago was gone. It had turned to numbness. She had exhausted her well of feelings. She had nothing left to express. Her war was over.

"Go ahead, Des… You can end this nightmare… end it for both of us."

"I'm not a murderer."

"Whether you shoot me or try to take me in, the result will be the same… and at this point… I welcome it."

Des cocked the gun and took aim. He felt like throwing up. His legs were about to collapse, and the chill from the wind, as well as his frayed nerves, was making him shake.

The crack of the shot echoed off the hull of the boat. Seagulls squawked as it reverberated into the air. Then there was only the sound of the blowing wind and the water lapping against the hull of the boat.

He looked into the city. The lights of the endless sea of skyscrapers were beginning to increase in brightness as the sun finally dipped below the horizon. It left an orange-pinkish glow in its wake, moving into the deep purples of the oncoming night.

It had to be the result. It was the only choice he really had. He walked over to the side of the boat and placed his hands on the railing. His shoulders sagged underneath the weight of the consequences of his action. There could be no other way.

CHAPTER 72

New York, New York

THE PHONE RANG four times before Keller picked it up. Looking at the screen, he felt furious and relieved at the same time.

"Amanda, where the hell are you? It's chaos here!"

"Agent Keller… it's Des."

"Des? Where are you? What happened here tonight? Where's Amanda?"

"It was Amanda."

"What the hell are you talking about…? Where are you?" he asked demandingly.

"Amanda is your killer."

"Des, I'm in no mood for any goddamn jokes!"

"I'm not joking. Check for yourself. It's over. I'll meet you tomorrow morning at seven at your office to explain."

"Where are you? Where is she?"

"Just be there." Des clicked off the phone and then turned to look at the Statue of Liberty once more.

"I knew you couldn't do it. Not after what happened in Afghanistan," Amanda stated with a look bordering on cockiness.

"What now?"

She inhaled deeply. "I disappear… forever."

"What am I supposed to tell them?"

She paused for a moment, staring out at the city. A look of serenity encompassed her face. Taking another deep breath, she turned to him. "I wish we could have met under different circumstances… I would have liked that."

"But I thought I was 'The 'Enemy'?"

"You still are… Those were the different circumstances I was referring to. Oh well… I guess for now, just tell them I was lost at sea."

Then she smiled, dropped something onto the deck, and dove over the side. The spray from her splash misted onto the deck and upon his face.

He watched her for a few moments, until she was consumed by the darkness, crushed between the deep purple sky and the black waters of the Hudson.

He had seen too much death. He knew the anguish of taking a life and could not bear that feeling again. His emotions swung between relief and disgust. It was the lifting of a burden as well as the bitterness in the knowledge he had let a terror remain in the world.

After his service in the Army, he swore he would never kill again. It turned out to be his only reprieve. He had held true to those principles. Otherwise, his conscience would be inconsolable.

He despised what she had done but also felt shame that he had true empathy for her actions. He did prevent an evil, but in doing so, allowed another to continue unabated. His actions ensured this would be the result.

CHAPTER 73

Savannah, Georgia

MADISON HAD RETURNED to her apartment filled with joy. She was also feeling quite foolish. All her conjecture, all her insecurities had surfaced while staying at Kelly's, and it proved how she needed to change her approach.

In any case, though, it was good to be home. She loved Kelly like a sister, but she could not replace the satisfaction of having things where they should be.

It was a little after 9:00 p.m. and she was involved in one of her favorite activities, eating a piece of key lime pie, sipping tea while curled up on the couch with a good book. This was the respite she needed. *Perfect… just me time.*

It was then that her phone rang right in the middle of savoring another bite of the sweet-tart dessert. *Oh my god, Kelly… what could it be now?* "Hey, what's up?"

"Are you watching TV?" Kelly asked.

"No, why?"

"Turn on channel four."

"Kelly, I just want to read."

"No, you don't understand. Turn it on now!"

"Okay, but this better be worth it."

Madison grabbed the controller, turned on the TV, and flipped to channel four.

"Good evening," a newscaster said. "Tonight, there's a major story brewing in New York as terror has hit Manhattan again. We join our correspondent, Steve Kent, in New York. Steven, what do you have for us?"

"David, it has been chaos here in Manhattan after what took place this evening in the heart of New York. It was supposed to be one of the biggest nights in US Attorney General Robert Cantwell's life, and it turned out to be, but for entirely different reasons."

The picture moved away from the reporter and was replaced by a video taken inside a massive theater with a podium set on the stage.

Madison looked at the television confusedly, "Kelly, what am I looking at?"

"Just keep watching."

The reporter continued. "It was to be a big homecoming party for the attorney general as he returned to New York. The popular figure is expected to be one of the leading candidates in the next presidential election, and many thought he would be declaring his candidacy at this evening's event, held at the Lincoln Center. However, just after being introduced, an intruder got past security and forcibly entered the theater… reportedly yelling, and I quote, 'Cantwell is the target.'"

Madison watched as she saw the picture scan the audience and then suddenly jerk back to catch the briefest glimpse of a young man just before he was driven to the ground. "Oh my god," she said, covering her mouth.

"At that very moment," the reporter said. "Cantwell was tackled by one of the honorees on the stage when an explosive device detonated inside the podium. It has also been reported that tear gas was deployed in the attack. Early released statements say that Cantwell was not hurt, but dozens of injuries were reported, which occurred in the rush of the crowd trying to exit the theater. So far, we have not been able to identify the intruder, and his whereabouts are currently unknown. We will continue to make information available as it comes in."

"Was that Des? Madison… Madison?"

She was too shocked to answer and could barely move enough to sit back down on the couch.

"Madison, are you there?"

"Yes," she said softly. "It was him."

"I'll be over in a few minutes."

CHAPTER 74

New York, New York

DES WAS SO mystified by what he had just experienced he hadn't even looked down to see what Amanda had dropped before diving into the river. Peering at the deck, he saw the small silver object reflect what was left of the remaining light. It was a computer thumb drive.

I bet she has it on board somewhere. He wandered back inside the cabin and saw it sitting on a small table. Amanda's laptop computer was already on. He inserted the thumb drive and waited for it to indicate that it was ready to be accessed.

When the message appeared, he opened it and then clicked on the only folder there; it was labeled "GCS." A series of additional files appeared. One was labeled "General Correction Services," another "US Atty Gen," and still another labeled "Trans Int Bank."

Clicking on the file labeled "US Atty Gen," he could not believe what met his eyes. It showed a list titled "Presidential Donors," with the names of hundreds of people who had already given financial contributions to a campaign that Robert Cantwell had yet to announce he was even involved in. Each name had a monetary amount next to it. But what was curious was that they were all for either $25,000 or $50,000 donations. No other amounts were listed. Yet even stranger was each amount seemed to come from the same four account numbers from the same bank, Trans International.

There were literally hundreds of millions of dollars represented. *How is it possible that all these people are using the same accounts?*

When he clicked on the file "Trans Int Bank," the full financial details of where those accounts led to were before him. Des was in shock. Each one of those accounts were directly linked to General Correction Services or one of its subsidiaries. Though, what was even more peculiar was the same names appearing on the "Donor List" were also listed on those accounts but were accompanied by letters in parentheses. They were either (RC), (JG), (AS), or (MR). Also displayed was a spreadsheet that showed massive amounts of money being dispersed to a group representing a "who's who" of Washington. Prestigious congressmen, department heads, and dignitaries, both foreign and domestic, were all there with those same letters in parentheses and bank account numbers attached to them.

It was confusing to look at. Why would all these people who were supposed to be giving money to a potential presidential campaign be willing to have that money redistributed to people who were at best only associated with Cantwell and at worst political adversaries?

He got his answer in the last file he opened. There he found what those letters next to the donor names meant. They stood for Robert Cantwell (RC), James Gertig (JG), Adam Slayborne (AS), and Michael Ranier (MR). They represented the US attorney general, the former CEO of Trans International Bank, and the CEO and chairman of the board of General Correction Services.

It was apparent the money being distributed was for payoffs to oppose or favor any legislation that was beneficial for GCS and its subsidiaries. There was even a category showing payments to congressmen to oppose the Wayman bill with funds directly funneled from accounts tied to Robert Cantwell.

Next to disbursements was a projected profit spreadsheet showing how much would be made if the Wayman bill was defeated and adversely how much would be lost if it passed. It was a staggering amount, well over $200 billion over a ten-year period. The bill's passage would devastate the corporation.

However, the final nail in the coffin came on the next page Des examined. It was the stock distribution, of which 75 percent was owned by a mere ten individuals. Four of them were Cantwell, Gertig, Slayborne, and Ranier. Much of the stock had been transferred and placed under the names on the donor list. People had been paid for the use of their names in order to open accounts that would hide who were the true owners, how much profit was received, and where any payoffs or campaign donations came from.

Cantwell was not only running for president because he wanted to; he was also doing it to ensure the profits of GCS, as well as its main stockholders, including himself. By setting up this system, it guaranteed a massive influx of cash into his campaign, which could never be traced to him or any of his cohorts.

Senator Wayman's bill was an extreme threat to those monies, as well as GCS. When Wayman first made the decision to withhold the bill due to his fears that the president would veto it, it put Cantwell and his partners in a very precarious position. They had failed to stop support for the bill with their bribes, which meant the only way to kill it was for Cantwell to win the election. The presidency had become their only insurance policy to protect their shady business deals. It also explained why Cantwell, who was normally very aggressive, gave such a lackluster performance in the prosecution of Trans International Bank during its legal proceedings. He needed them to remain solvent in order to maintain his own business interest.

Des did not want to look at the screen anymore. It had become too much for him to take in. He stood up and walked out of the cabin with his hands clasped behind his head.

Des knew he had released a killer on society. Amanda was not an indiscriminate plague, but nonetheless, his principles had set free a potential terror. She had not been random in her violence, and her anger was well justified. Still, he could find no penance for his decision, no way to atone for that sin.

However, there was one more option he possessed. The disgust at what Amanda had done was still fresh, but the impetus motivating her to act was every bit as vile.

The system he once believed in was a fraud, a bait and switch scheme that covered its reality. It was meant to dispense justice but had become an affront to the very name branded on its identifying seal. The United States Federal Justice system's main purpose had ceased being to prosecute crimes but to perpetrate them. It destroyed lives and livelihoods using its name as the purpose in doing so. The Department of Justice's corruption was sealed from the most junior of prison guards to the most senior of US attorneys, FBI agents, and government officials. Their crimes made them resemble more of a mafia than that of a noble public profession. It would have been easy to dismiss if it were just a few individuals. But the fact was, it infected everyone and was sanctioned by those who claimed the most moral of high grounds.

Amanda's frustration stemmed from the fact there was no individual… no entity to hold those who were charged with upholding the law accountable for breaking the very trust the public had extended to them. It was a system designed to preach responsibility and accountability from the altars of justice but accepted none itself. It took the form of US attorneys, unrestrained by a self-granted immunization from obeying the law, whose performance was not judged by a set of values or even competent performance, but through getting convictions with no heed paid to how they were being attained. It was FBI agents who cooperated in the destruction of evidence and used overwhelming power to subjugate the citizens they investigate. It was Bureau of Prison officials and employees, who abused and exploited the inmates they housed, and judges who had essentially been castrated by having their ability to make decisions stripped from them. All these combined to turn the federal justice system into the world's largest kangaroo court. This win-at-all-cost philosophy adopted by the DOJ and its entities had made fools and liars of everyone and hypocrites to the very values America supposedly held most dear.

However, what was most sickening to Des was the privatization of what was supposed to be a societal responsibility. The effects of which were beyond devastating. It created a wall for the general population, a buffer zone in which they were protected from their own ills and then later anesthetized to the temptations that such a system would cause. As long as the public couldn't view what was going on, as long as they obeyed the command to not look on the other side of the curtain, the companies could profit. They could hide the misery they created behind the facade of being the public's benefactor.

As Des looked across the water, he thought back to his days in the service and all the terrible things he had heard and witnessed. He remembered some of the veterans of the Gulf War describing the abominable conditions for many people in Middle Eastern countries.

This was especially true for females. Abused girls forced into marriage before they reached their teens. Women being kept from education, property ownership, and voting rights and all the rest of the trappings of a medieval society were on display. Des was sickened by how we ignored it. As long as they kept the oil flowing, as long as we could keep our gas tanks filled, we were willing to look the other way.

Because it was always "over there." It was the excuse that would pass as plausible deniability. It was their culture, their rules, their people… their problem. However, now he could not escape the parallels with what he now saw in the federal justice system. The American public, which he was a part, was guilty of allowing their power to be taken from them. In return for that surrender, they didn't have to see or feel the pain of a societal problem now being exploited for profit. All they had to do was not ask any questions and pick up the tab. The public was and continued to be compliant in ignoring their principles, while the worst of them made piles of money off the business of incarceration.

It was no longer about right or wrong but net profit and loss. The shame of the system was only slightly relieved by the fact that most were ignorant of its existence.

Des now knew what to do. He possessed the salve that could alleviate some of the pain. He would expose it. He would expose it all.

CHAPTER 75

HE HADN'T RETURNED to the hotel. There was no need. That, in addition to his fear the police or the FBI or both would be waiting for him kept him away. Instead, he hung his clothes to dry, cleaned himself off using a deck hose, and tried his best to pilot the boat back to the area from which it launched. With the night well settled in, he had trouble locating it and settled for a dock about a mile away, eventually pulling up to a slip and paying a guy fifty dollars to do it for him. By the time that whole process had ended, it was about 5:00 a.m.

The docks smelled of mold, fish, and brewing coffee as workers started to file in. There was time before his 7:00 a.m. meeting with Keller, and he was famished. With nothing left to do, he wandered the streets until he found a local diner to get some breakfast. It was good that it was reasonably priced as he had only a sparse amount of cash.

Before he entered the establishment, he purchased a *New York Times* from an outdoor news vendor. As he expected, the previous evening's events were front and center. But only a blurred photograph showing a small part of his face was captured. It stated the FBI had released it as the best photograph of the "unknown" individual that was available.

A smile grew across Des's face. There were many cameras there, which meant there had to be better pictures of him. Plus, Keller could have identified him. *Keller's protecting me. He knows the truth.*

It was the only logical conclusion. If he was in trouble, the FBI would have released mountains of information to the public, including name, photos, physical description, the works. As it stood now, Keller made no public statement other than to say that the individual appeared mentally unstable. It was a clever way to send Des the message, although the "mentally unstable" description he thought a bit harsh. Overall, though, it was satisfying and a relief to know there was at least one person he could trust.

After eggs, coffee, juice, and a bagel with cream cheese, he felt nourished enough to head to Keller's office. It was time to bring this to an end.

CHAPTER 76

New York, New York

DES ENTERED THE lobby of the FBI building with more than a bit of caution. Even though he was relatively certain there would be no problems, the environment made him uneasy, to say the least.

As he passed through the lobby, he saw the emblem of the Department of Justice proudly displayed on the wall. He gave a sarcastic chuckle. *The world's biggest oxymoron.* After passing through security, he got on the elevator and pushed the button for Keller's floor. Even though it took less than sixty seconds, the ride up seemed like hours.

Exiting, he walked down the hallway and entered the waiting room. His secretary stood up with a look of amazement on her face. *He must have told her.*

"Agent Keller is expecting you. Go right in."

Des entered his office. Keller was standing behind his desk, shuffling through a pile of papers. He appeared disheveled and exhausted. Looking up at Des, he said, "You look like hell."

"Funny, I was thinking the same thing about you."

Keller chuckled. "What's that gash you have on your head?"

"It's nothing, I got cut on the glass."

"It looks pretty bad," Keller reached over and paged his secretary. "Sherry, could you please get the doc and tell him I'd like him to take a look at someone, in let's say… a couple of hours."

"Thank you, but I'm sure I'm all right," Des stated.

"I've seen plenty of cuts… trust me, it needs to be looked at."

There was a momentary silence as both men fished for what to say next.

"I'm sorry this happened, Des. I still can't believe it. I guess you never know about someone's inner demons."

"I'm sorry too."

"So, what happened?"

Des told him about the entire episode from beginning to end. He tried to include every detail minus the final part, choosing only to say that she jumped overboard.

"I guess she was lost at sea," Keller said.

"I guess so."

"I'll arrange a search, but I doubt we'll find anything. This must have been a nightmare for you. Is there anything you need?"

"I just want to go home."

Keller moved out from behind his desk and patted Des on the shoulder. "You deserve that. I'll arrange for our boys to fly you home. How does 5:00 p.m. sound?"

"Perfect."

"Good, it's done. I'll take care of your hotel tab and have a check cut to you before you leave to help with some of the other expenses."

"Thank you, Agent Keller."

"No, thank you… and call me Zack, for God's sakes."

Des smiled appreciatively. "Zack, I want to—"

The phone rang and Keller hurriedly picked it up. "Oh, that's great! Please send him in." Keller had a grin stretching from ear to ear. "I have a surprise for you."

Des was caught a little off guard. *Surprise? I think I've had enough of those.* Surprise turned to shock when Keller's guest walked in. The tall handsome gentleman strode toward them until he was just a couple feet away.

"Des, this is Robert Cantwell. Robert, this is Mr. Desmond Cook."

The distinguished man extended his hand. Des responded in kind but felt disgust at touching the individual who was at the source of such corruption.

"Mr. Cook, it's an honor to meet you. Zack filled me in on the details of last night. I wanted to thank you personally. I guess I wouldn't be standing here if it wasn't for you."

Des was extremely uncomfortable but did not wish to embarrass Keller. "Thank you, but Agent Keller was the one who saved you."

"Well, I'm in debt to you both… and I got to hand it to Zack here. I haven't been tackled that hard since I played wide receiver at Harvard."

Keller laughed at the remark. "We're just glad you're okay."

"I'm sorry this has to be short. I've got a crazy schedule today. Again, thank you both. It was a pleasure, Mr. Cook. Zack, you take care. I'm sure we'll be in contact." Cantwell gave one last handshake and another warm smile before exiting the office.

"You just shook hands with the next president of the United States. Believe me, he won't forget about you. That's one hell of a connection to have," Keller said, beaming.

Des just nodded in agreement.

"I still can't, for the life of me, understand why Amanda would want to kill him," Keller said, shaking his head.

"Well, I think this will help answer that," Des said, reaching into his pocket and handing Keller the thumb drive.

"What's this?"

"Everything."

"Everything?"

"Just make sure you're sitting down when you look at it," Des said, offering his hand.

Keller reached out to accept it. "Do you have to go now?"

"Yeah, I think I've had enough. I'm tired. New York is great, but I've had my fill."

"Understood," Keller replied.

"However, can I make one small request?"

"Name it."

"Could I change my flight plans?"

CHAPTER 77

Savannah, Georgia

HE WASN'T SUPPOSED to be there for another three weeks, but he did not want to wait a second longer. Approaching her apartment door, he felt like breaking into a sprint. She was all he could think about on the flight back.

Tapping on the door, he heard her unmistakable gait, as well as the music of Sade playing in the background. Des waited as she performed her ritual of looking through the peephole. Within seconds, he heard a gasp of shock, followed by the sound of a breaking wine glass.

The door flung open, and the teary eyes of Madison greeted him with relief and joy. She threw herself at Des and squeezed him like she had never embraced him before, her soft lips pressed firmly against his.

"Oh my god! Sweetheart, I've been worried sick. I kept calling and calling, but it always went to voice mail."

Des just held on tight. He did not want to ever release her. It was as if she could not get close enough.

"Oh my god... baby... don't ever do that again," she said, continuing to kiss him. "Are you okay...? Please tell me you're not hurt."

"I'm okay. I'm fine now... It's over. I..."

Madison saw the utter despair and exhaustion carved in the lines of his face. She recognized the look. It was the same one he had in the hospital the previous year when he found out he was unsuccessful in keeping everyone out of harm's way at Arlington National Cemetery.

"Baby, come here," she said, pulling him into her apartment.

"I feel that I could have…"

"Sshh, we don't need to talk about that now," she said, gently pressing her fingers to his mouth. She cradled his face in her hands and kissed him on the forehead. "You're with me now. That's all that matters."

Grabbing his hand, she led him to the bedroom where she kissed him once more and began to unbutton his shirt and then removed her robe.

Placing her cheek onto his, she whispered into his ear, "You're going to make love to me all night. It's not open to negotiation." She smiled, completed disrobing him, and then guided him onto her bed.

Their faces met again as the emotion of the moment took hold and their passions took over. Des felt her fingers trail down his back. It felt like the angels were caressing him.

It was Eden. The room smelled of her skin and her hair of jasmine. He could not contain himself. He ran his lips over her neck and could hear her breathing increase as he moved them over her breast. It was a feeling of ecstasy that he never knew was possible, and when he thought he couldn't feel any more, another swell of desire enveloped him.

She guided him to move southward on her body. He ran his tongue delicately over her stomach, tasting the sweetness of her skin. She continued to press him further down until he rested between her legs. She gasped and arched her hips upward while closing her thighs against his cheeks. The rhythm of her body was in perfect sequence with the pleasure he was giving her. The feeling built and increased a thousandfold. Yet before she climaxed, she pulled him upward and, in a move resembling a wrestling pin down, laid him on his back.

With her hair dangling to the sides of their faces, forming a cocoon around them, she looked into his eyes and said, "Not yet."

Reaching down, she placed him inside her. Her eyes closed as she let out the slightest of sighs. Then she opened them, her pupils wider than he had ever seen, and said, "Now you're home. This will always be your home."

Neither spoke another word for the rest of the night, instead, making love, resting, and then resuming until morning. She finally fell asleep, her face resting on his chest, her left leg draped over his, her pubis pressed against his hip.

Des did not want to sleep. He didn't want this time, this peace to pass. He let himself absorb the moment, his fingers meditatively tracing the curvature of her hip.

A soft orange light began to filter through the window as dawn was just beginning to break through the evening layers. He could see the reflection of the warm sun off the banks of clouds slowly drifting by.

She nuzzled his torso in an attempt to get even closer to him. Then her eyes fluttered open, and the sweetest smile came across her face. Her radiance was breathtaking. She lightly pressed her lips onto his chest and then looked at Des with an expressiveness that made him melt. There was no other way to describe this instant other than perfect.

"What are you thinking?" she asked.

He reached over, using his fingers to brush the curly locks from her face. "I'm thinking of how amazing you are... and how incredibly fortunate I am." Then he paused, allowing his feelings to rise to the surface. "And I was thinking... how... how much I love you."

Madison raised her head, awestruck. A single tear welled up, rolled down her cheek, and dropped upon his chest. She moved her face close to his, but no words came out. Yet there didn't need to be any. Madison always wore her feelings on her sleeve, and they were on full display now.

She softly kissed him. "And you will always have me."

EPILOGUE

Lompoc, California

OFFICER WEBER WAS able to leave a little early from the prison. The day was a typical one, but it was nice to be able to get started on his weekend before the usual quitting time.

The week had been relatively uneventful; however, it ended with a certain satisfaction. The previous evening, they had their random prisoner drug testing. Although, there was nothing random about it.

The guards did their 3:00 a.m. round-ups, pulling tired and disoriented inmates out of bed to get a urine sample. Weber had provided them the list and made sure one name was added before they commenced, Stewart Nielson.

This was his way of exacting revenge. This was his way of showing his superiority. Mr. Nielson had to pay the price for his betrayal.

The older gentleman was pulled from a deep sleep to provide them a sample. He had no history of drug abuse. This was punishment, plain and simple.

Weber knew of Nielson's prostate issues as it had been well documented. He was confident that he would not be able to provide a sample in the mandated two-hour time frame due to his medical condition. But it didn't matter. Per BOP policy, failure to provide a sample was registered as a refusal to comply, regardless of the reason. The result would be a punishment.

As Weber got into his car, the image of the old man shivering as he was taken to solitary confinement was gratifying. However, it pleased him even more that Mr. Nielson would also lose the good time he had accumulated.

Weber pulled out of the parking lot and made the turn onto the lonely road dividing the medium-from the low-security prison. Gray clouds were beginning to flow in from the ocean as the evening winds started to bluster, dropping the temperature while picking up clouds of dust.

It was about a thirty-minute drive home as he passed through the main section of town. For a few moments, he contemplated stopping by a nearby watering hole but opted to just go home.

As he headed toward the highway, he noticed a car with its tailend up on top of an embankment. Its front end was out of view. Standing next to the car was a very attractive woman with blond hair, wearing a tank top and a short skirt that left little to the imagination.

As he drew closer, he noticed her trying to flag down traffic. Giving him her most alluring wave possible, her short skirt edged higher as she jumped up and down in effort to gain his attention.

Weber, though married for fifteen years, knew few faithful days since taking his nuptials. This opportunity seemed to come from heaven. It would be another conquest, another notch on his belt. Pulling off his wedding ring, he eased up to where she was standing.

"Hello, are you okay?" he asked sympathetically.

"Oh, thank you so much for stopping. I swerved to avoid some critter in the road and I got stuck."

"Well, let me take a look," he said, getting out of his car while puffing out his chest. "Maybe I can help."

"Thank you so much. I really appreciate it. The problem seems to be right over here," she replied, directing him down the embankment.

"Does your engine start?"

"It didn't a minute ago. But now that you're here, who knows, it might," she said, winking. "I'll try again. Let me see," she said, opening the driver's side door. "But you know, there's one more thing you can do for me."

Weber's ears immediately perked up. His fantasies took over. Maybe she was going to ask him to give her a ride to her place. He didn't see a ring on her finger. There was no question in his mind that she was interested. He could tell by the way she looked at him. The flirtatious smile, the doe eyes, the way she shamelessly bent over in her short skirt to display just enough to let him know the invitation was there. They were obvious signs.

"What can I do for you?" he responded smugly.

"You can take responsibility."

AUTHOR'S NOTES

ALTHOUGH THIS STORY took me a little over a year to write, the research it required took four years to compile, a task that I found fascinating yet at the same time disheartening and terrifying. However, there was a singular advantage to using the Department of Justice in the manner in which I did.

Oftentimes, creating a group or organization to serve as the controversial backdrop for a story is the most difficult part of the process. It is an intricate undertaking, requiring meticulous attention to the various details and threads that must be carefully woven into a tale. Yet, sadly, the controversial group for this story wrote itself. This is because it actually exists.

I realize it may seem difficult to believe (I know it was for me), but the conduct of the Department of Justice and its various entities described in this book was not exaggerated. The tactics utilized during an investigation and prosecution of a case were taken from real events. In actuality, the difficulty lay in trying to figure out which ones to use as models for the story, as the number of examples were overwhelming. That is to say that the description of the process was not an aberration, but standard operating procedure.

I would like to take this opportunity to express my deepest gratitude and admiration to the people who allowed me to see the hidden underbelly of our federal justice system. The individuals I interviewed had prominent current or prior connections to the system. In speaking to me, they took enormous risks to their careers and even their safety and served as the model for Des's mystery informant. I often say they represented the most important character in the book, the character of conscience. I cannot mention their names for obvious reasons, but their service to this endeavor was beyond measure, and without their willingness to come forward, this book could have never been written.